BREAKING AND ENTERING

Breaking and Entering

A NOVEL

Don Gillmor

BIBLIOASIS
Windsor, Ontario

FIRST EDITION

10 9 8 7 6 5 4 3 2 1

Library and Archives Canada Cataloguing in Publication
Title: Breaking and entering / Don Gillmor.
Names: Gillmor, Don, author.
Identifiers: Canadiana (print) 20220472173 | Canadiana (ebook) 2022047219X | ISBN 9781771965231 (softcover) | ISBN 9781771965248 (EPUB)
Classification: LCC PS8563.I59 B74 2023 | DDC C813/.54—dc23

Edited by Daniel Wells
Copyedited by John Sweet
Cover designed by Michel Vrana
Typeset by Vanessa Stauffer

Published with the generous assistance of the Canada Council for the Arts, which last year invested $153 million to bring the arts to Canadians throughout the country, and the financial support of the Government of Canada. Biblioasis also acknowledges the support of the Ontario Arts Council (OAC), an agency of the Government of Ontario, which last year funded 1,709 individual artists and 1,078 organizations in 204 communities across Ontario, for a total of $52.1 million, and the contribution of the Government of Ontario through the Ontario Book Publishing Tax Credit and Ontario Creates.

PRINTED AND BOUND IN CANADA

But Nature, spent and exhausted,
    takes lovers back
into herself, as if there were not
    enough strength
to create them a second time.

Rainer Maria Rilke, Duino Elegies

The desire to make off with the substance of others is the foremost—the most legitimate—passion nature has bred into us and, without doubt, the most agreeable one.

Donatien Alphonse François, Marquis de Sade

one

prologue

At night, the street regained its innocence. Everything still and stored away. A few lights were on, mostly for security. The people asleep, the air heavy and unmoving. The sound of air-conditioning units—rattling, wheezing, struggling, a symphony. A few cats moving languidly. The line of cars, dark and foreign. There were so few lawns now. Everyone had prairie grass or Japanese maples or ajuga, straw-coloured and dry. Once inside you saw the furniture, the incomplete set of dishes, the big screen. In the basements were discarded toys and the faint smell of mould. The third floors abandoned, impossible to keep cool in this weather. The shoes lined up near the door, always more than anyone could practically use. The keys in a ceramic bowl they'd brought back from Seville or Istanbul. Coats for every kind of weather except what they had right now, lined up on hooks waiting for fall. On the refrigerators, reminders and clever quotes held by magnetic bumblebees. On the calendars, days circled in red. A week of half-read newspapers (who has the time). Inside the cupboards were well-intentioned juicers and panini makers, idle for a year.

You needed to look farther than that. Into the drawers that held vibrating toys, into the hard drives that held plans and bank accounts and fetishes. Into closets containing expensive dresses bought on sale and never worn. Revealing journals and medical histories and old love letters tied quaintly with string.

Finally, you had to look into those sleeping heads. Thoughts of adultery, wayward urges. Unnamed panic—standing naked in front of the school assembly (again). Trying to fly but having some trouble, pursued by something lumbering and dangerous. The fear of poverty, of failure, the future. Afraid for their vulnerable children and their suddenly vulnerable parents. And the pragmatic nagging—did I turn off the stove (you did). And finally, a longing that was impossible to name, an ache that starts in your heart and spreads, waves of something, a heavy feeling that brings tears, a mix of nostalgia (Old Yeller getting it in the puss again) and sadness and unmoored memories floating just out of reach.

Every house held this. But you only took what was valuable. That was the key.

deadish

THERE WAS A WOMAN IN Boston who thought she was dead. Bea had read about it in the morning paper. She had a rare psychiatric disorder—Cotard's Delusion—where she denied her existence. Faced with overwhelming evidence to the contrary—her husband, daughter, her reflection—she remained unconvinced she was alive. Because of the current heat wave, she thought she was in hell. Her husband showed her their wedding pictures, a mortgage statement, a photo of their daughter's communion, and she just shook her head, no.

And standing in the gallery, looking at Warhol's Elvis print for perhaps the thirtieth time, Bea wondered if she had a touch of Cotard's. The gallery was almost deserted. It was still morning, a weekday, just her and the King.

There were four Elvises—two in fading black and white, two in lurid colour—all aiming a six-gun straight at her. He was wearing what looked like lipstick, on the right side of the law. If this version could have seen the bloated, sequined version, wobbly on Quaaludes, singing "Unchained Melody" in his final concert, that smile like a broken boy, what would he have done? Though what would any of us do if faced with their future self?

The few people in the gallery may have been there simply to avoid the heat. It was early May and not yet noon, and it was already oppressive. The air was heavy and dirty, the air of August, an anomaly that was dissected every night on the local weather report.

Bea lingered in the Henry Moore gallery for a bit, his heroic bronzes splayed out, those solid, sensuous women. Moore had been gassed at Cambrai, one of the few survivors of his unit. As a child he had rubbed liniment onto his rheumatic mother's bare back. She remembered these tidbits from a course she used to teach—The Aesthetics of Sexuality and Erotic Art, a class that always drew a crowd.

Bea walked into the bright light of the galleria and sat at the small café and ordered an espresso and wondered if she had spent too much time in this gallery and not enough in others. What happened to the Prado? The Tretyakov in Moscow? The Picasso museum in Barcelona to witness the great beast of twentieth-century art? Trips that were planned, or at least mentioned, or at least imagined. How much of life is regret? There should be an app that gives you a running tally, like the remaining battery life on your phone.

Through the soaring windows she observed the street below. On the sidewalk a bearded man stood rooted, staring up at the sun. If she'd had a sketch pad with her, she might have sketched him. As an art student she'd gone to Florence, and carried her sketch pad everywhere, partly an affectation, hoping people would think: there goes an artist. The city was filled with students, smoking and arguing in cafés as if the future depended on them discovering it.

The man across the street hadn't moved. Bea wondered if this was some kind of performance. In terms of aesthetics, there was a fine line between art student and homeless. The man looked to be in his twenties. Maybe someone was filming it from a vantage Bea couldn't see and this was part of a school project. It wasn't the kind of day where you stared at the sun to feel it on your face, enjoying the first rays of spring. This was already a vengeful sun. Bea watched him unbutton his shirt, his face still staring up.

He slipped out of his shirt and twirled it over his head like a stripper and let it go. It landed on the roof of a parked car. He was partly obscured by the car, but he bent down and Bea guessed that he was taking off his pants. He came up holding them. He twirled them too and let them go and they landed on the patio of a café behind him. Another dip and he came up with his underwear, which he slingshotted into traffic. It landed on the windshield of an SUV and the wipers came on and immediately swept them onto the street.

The man resumed his pose, staring up at the sun, naked, his thin, pasty body shining like a landed trout. People on the sidewalk stopped and crossed the street to avoid him.

His eyes were closed. They remained closed when the police car stopped. Two officers got out, a man and a woman. The man had one hand on his hip, ready to pull something out. The woman had her head bent to one shoulder, talking into a microphone fastened to her uniform. They approached the man, talking to him. The man remained impassive, eyes closed, staring up. The woman cop saw his pants on the patio and put on medical gloves then retrieved them. She held the pants up for him. His eyes didn't open. He didn't talk. The two cops looked at each other. Whadawe got here. They were probably telling him he had to put on his pants or they'd take him in. An EMS van pulled up and two people got out. They put on gloves. They talked to the cops. One of the EMS guys said something to the guy. No response.

Bea sipped her espresso. People had stopped now. It was safe with the police there. Maybe this was part of the art project, to see what would happen after the police arrived and film it. A student short with a title like *Adam Discovers the Police State*.

The sun bleached the street. Approaching noon, high and unyielding, two weeks into a heat wave. The police had sunglasses on. They stood on each side of the man, took an arm, and started to move him toward the police car. Suddenly the man snapped out of his catatonia and thrashed violently. They all fell into a heap on the sidewalk, and Bea couldn't see what was happening, a car blocking her view. She wanted to both know and not know. But she saw people with their phones out, filming. She could probably find it on YouTube in an hour. The EMS pair ran to their truck and rolled out the stretcher and wheeled it up to the man on the sidewalk. They managed to get him onto the stretcher with difficulty. There was blood on his face. It looked like blood. They strapped him in and wheeled him to the truck and trundled him in. The police got in their car. Both vehicles pulled away.

Bea was shaken slightly. Even from this distance, with no real sound, it was disturbing. She looked up and saw the barista was looking at her. It was just the two of them in the vast galleria.

City's full of crazies, he said, shrugging.

You think he's mentally ill?

Standing out there, staring at the sun like that. Take off his clothes. I'd say batshit.

Bea took the last bitter sip of espresso. She looked at her phone.

He might be a sun gazer, the barista said.

A sun gazer.

So it's this ancient practice, Mayans and the Aztecs. We studied it in my anthropology class. There are people who stare at the sun, they believe they can achieve photosynthesis, that they no longer have to eat.

So no one in Florida has to eat.

Yeah, not an airtight theory. There's a guy claims he hasn't eaten in twenty years, gets all the energy he needs from the sun. There was a contest. Guys staring at the sun for, like, days. But it turned out someone slipped the winner a Big Mac, which kind of…

Bea looked at the barista, who was roughly the same age as her son. Early twenties, on the cusp of manhood. It used to be thirteen was the cusp of manhood, but it kept getting pushed up.

Would you like another espresso?

No, I can only have one this late in the morning or I'm up half the night.

He nodded and took out the espresso handle and gave it a sharp crack on the knock box.

I work here three days a week, and you should see some of the shit that happens out there.

Bea nodded, waiting for the shit that happened.

Last week this guy in a Spiderman costume perched on the mailbox for, like, three hours.

Saving humanity.

There is so much random shit in this world.

Random was what life did best, Bea thought. It conferred cancer on the virtuous, drunk drivers on the unsuspecting, it matched noble wives to unfinished men, wickedness to wealth, weakness to power. It dealt from the bottom of the deck, blew up buses, lingered in the shadows with a shiv.

Bea got up and gathered her purse. I hope your day doesn't get any more random, she said as she left.

Outside, the air had a surprising weight. It clung to her.

The street was an underdeveloped photograph, the colours leached. She was already hot. Two Asian women walked by with umbrellas against the sun. A girl rode by on a bicycle with a filter strapped to her face. It had a vampire graphic, fangs, drops of blood. Ahead of her a coyote loped across the street with something in its mouth. Bea walked east in the unwelcome glare.

the gathering

SHE'D BEEN TO THIS DINNER party before. Three couples that had had the same conversations, eaten the same salmon teriyaki left just a minute too long under the broiler.

Wild salmon, Katherine said when she served it. It would be cheaper to fly to the coast and fish for it *myself*.

Bea lingered for a moment on the social geometry that bound them: Roger and Penelope, Katherine and Philip, her and Sanger, the cross-hatching of friendship and habit and cultivated desire; Roger wanted to fuck her. He wanted to fuck everyone. Philip didn't want to fuck anyone, especially his wife. Who knew about Sanger? Bea observed her husband with a critical eye that twenty-three years of marriage had sharpened. Sang was toying with his fork, artfully moving things around. Not a man of appetites. Slim, modishly and cautiously dressed, his movements just short of athletic. He was arguing with Roger.

You need to see it from *his* perspective, Roger said.

Actually I don't, Sang said. I don't need to see it from anyone's perspective but my own.

I think what Roger is trying to say— This was Penelope, always the diplomat.

I don't need a fucking *interpreter*. This isn't the UN. Roger pulled the cigarette package out of his shirt pocket and took one out. For a second, it seemed as if he would light it. When was the last time Bea had seen someone light a cigarette inside a house? It had to have been more than a decade, maybe two decades. Perhaps it had been Bea herself. She'd quit twelve years ago, more or less. Everyone had. Except Roger.

Roger got up awkwardly and scooped up his wineglass and walked stiffly toward the sliding door. A messy, ursine man, slew-footed, overweight, bearded, an enviable mane that was greying so aristocratically she thought he might be dyeing it.

Smoke, he said simply.

Close the door behind you, Katherine said. We don't want the hot air coming in.

Or the smoke, said Penelope.

Bea watched Penelope watching her husband stand outside blowing smoke toward the stars, taking another deep drink of his wine. Penelope used a small scale she'd bought at Williams Sonoma to weigh her food. She was a size four and worried she could balloon to a six if she wasn't vigilant. Dark-haired, controlled, a smile that looked as though it came with a set of instructions—*Lift both corners of your lips in an upward fashion, careful not to create lines at the eyes.*

Roger's taste in pornography was exclusively for amateur eastern European women, middle-aged, a bit zaftig, business-like, kneeling. This was his current taste, at least. A month from now, who knew? It could be Asian teens. Men were unable to remain faithful even to their fantasies.

When Roger came back in, Bea felt the rush of hot air. It was 10:30 p.m. and still oppressive. The air conditioning couldn't actually cool the house down, could only keep it from being unbearable.

Sanger got up to help clear the plates, quickly stacking Penelope's barely touched plate on top of his own. Sanger, with that exotic name. At least, it had been exotic when they met. But Sang wasn't exotic. He was a history professor. Even his name was in the past tense. Sing Sang Sung, Roger had once said, one of his sly put- downs. Sang took the plates into the kitchen, making helpful noises.

Katherine wasn't a brilliant cook. Her meals looked more or less like something from a magazine though were oddly bland. One of the reasons Bea had abandoned Facebook was to avoid Katherine's posts, which were often photographs of her dinners. She was pretty in a finite way, the mother of two sour children. Philip, her husband, was late arriving. He'd been at a conference in Paris and was supposed to be back by seven, and Bea wondered if she'd scheduled the dinner party so that Philip would arrive in the middle of it, evidence of their international lives.

Philip finally arrived at eleven, some business at customs. He looked crumpled and itchy. Katherine walked over and kissed him. It was, Bea noted, an awkward kiss, he aimed for her mouth and she turned her cheek.

Philip came over and kissed Bea. He trailed that airplaney scent, a thrift shop mixed with microwaved chicken. He sat down and poured a glass of wine and droned on about Paris. Ghastly heat, worse than here. Old people dying in their attic apartments...

Bea looked at Sang, who was staring at a spot in the middle of the table. She had looked at his face the last time they'd had sex (how many months ago?) and saw that he immediately changed his expression, as if he was trying for something more appropriate. He stuck with it, like a middle-distance runner who knows he'll finish near the back of the pack. He had stopped going down on her two years ago, and she hadn't decided if she was offended or relieved. The last time he'd done it, she wasn't sure he was there. He was *there,* but it was like a dentist's drill in your frozen tooth: you know it's there, but you don't really feel anything.

Forty-two degrees, Philip said. *Forty-two.* Death Valley. They had to police the public fountains. People jumping in with their clothes on. I can't imagine that water was any cooler than the air.

Roger was swirling wine in his glass, looking at a fixed point somewhere near the fixed point Sang was staring at, both waiting for Philip to put a lid on it. All three men were academics, or at least had been; Roger had left his philosophy job to sell real estate. They had once been garrulous and ambitious and argued theatrically, but their careers were no longer visible, like the outline of the moon on a summer morning, neglected and pale.

In the wake of her second glass of wine (limit of three, and only at dinner parties, and only because it was a necessity, something a doctor might prescribe) she forgave them all. Forgave Philip his intellectual bullying and family money, forgave Katherine her prescribed magazine life, forgave Penelope her clenched, tentative engagement with the world, hiding behind the outgoing bulk of her husband. She forgave Roger his enviable and undeserved ease in the world, and forgave her husband though she wasn't sure what she was forgiving him for.

Which only left herself. She hadn't quite managed that. Not yet. Forgiveness, acceptance. Were these steps on the AA journey?

By eleven thirty, it was much hotter inside the house. It was odd. You'd think it would start getting cooler, but it didn't. That didn't happen until 4 a.m. or so. The heat captured during the day still building inside. It didn't help that everyone had gotten so agitated. The Danish film conversation wasn't going well.

I was a fan of nymphomania until I saw Von Trier's film,

Roger said. It takes the Danes to turn you against something like nymphomania. That's a talent.

Maybe that was the point, Katherine said. Not everyone is a fan of a degrading psychiatric condition.

Don't knock degradation, Roger said. It has its place.

Our entire faculty is built on the concept, Sang said.

Von Trier seems only interested in degradation, Bea said. Tarantino does revenge, Von Trier degradation.

What was the one with the Irish pop star? Penelope said.

Not Irish. Scandinavian. Björk. The pixie.

Right, with what's-his-name.

Is that the one where the son kills himself at the wedding?

The son always kills himself at the wedding in Danish films.

No, it was a *British* actor. They're in everything.

Sir...

They've all been fucking knighted...

Björk doesn't sing, though.

There's a rape scene...

There's *always* a rape scene.

It's the one, you know it...Penelope turned to Roger for help. With what's-her-name, Australian sort of...Nicole Kidman!

She gets raped, I think.

Is that the one with Tom Cruise?

Wrong difficult incomprehensible director.

This was how every discussion on film went, Bea thought. No one could remember titles, actors, directors. *Lost the plot.* They needed the group to piece something together. It was less a discussion than a treasure hunt.

There's a name for his style of filmmaking.

Boring.

Dogma...something something. Dogma 22.

Dogme. Dogme 95.

I think Willem Dafoe was in the one I saw, with that French woman. She makes purses.

Antichrist!

This last was said in unison, as if both Roger and Sang were game show contestants, or accusing one another. And that ended the Danish film conversation.

Bea, have some of the truffled pecorino, Katherine said, quickly filling the void. It's from that cheese thug in the village.

Vicious prices, Philip said.

And they're going *up!* Katherine said. Something about a shortage of motivated truffle pigs in Tuscany.

Thanks, I'm not feeling brilliant, Bea said. A touch of Cotard's.

Katherine nodded and took a small piece for herself.

Things crawled on until after midnight, later than usual. Katherine had been sending subtle signals that it was time to go for almost an hour. Perhaps it was simply the heat. No one wanted to go out and face it. Sang suggested walking a few blocks then flagging a cab rather than calling one. Get some air, he said.

I don't know that you can call it air, Bea said. More like oxygenated soup.

There were kisses at the door, and careful, damp hugs. Bea opened the door. The air had a viscosity, it offered resistance. Sang began to tell their hosts a golfing anecdote. It was one of his most irritating qualities, to start a story at a point when everyone wanted the evening to be over. Bea wanted it to be over, and she could see that both Philip and Katherine did as well. None of them golfed, including Sang. He'd golfed once years ago, on a public course where he sliced a ball that hit a city bus going by. Everyone had heard this story, there was no context to introduce a golf story, and they were all hot and tired. As he wound through the familiar curves, Bea could feel a real anger rising.

Sang, it's late…

He bulled ahead with his pointless story. The air in the house seemed suddenly hotter. Bea leaned on the small table by the door for support while Sang droned on about his six-iron.

They finally left, and walked two blocks to Bloor Street, Sang's forehead already shiny with sweat. They turned east and strolled past cafés and restaurants, the street filled with young people. They would be living in apartments that were too hot to sleep in, waiting for the slightly cooler air, hoping that with enough beer and tequila they could fall asleep at 3 a.m. then wake in the stew of noon with a damp stranger beside them. The madness of the wee hours hovered, the poor decisions, awkward mornings, the exhaustion and regret and smoke that clung to you.

There was an optimum temperature for sex. Over the years their sex life had become seasonal, peaking in the welcome warmth of early summer then falling off a cliff with the cold weather. But this heat wasn't conducive to sex. It was steamy, though not in the Tennessee Williams sense, the barely contained sexuality coming out in Southern innuendo. No, this spoke of apocalypse and survival.

Two people were kissing in the corner of an outdoor café. It looked hot and exhausting. What love.

I never know what to make of Katherine's cooking, Bea said. How do you make salmon taste like paste?

I used to eat paste.

Really? You were one of those kids? There was always something hillbillyish about them.

A new fact after twenty-three years. Bea was almost impressed.

It was the spearmint oil, Sang said. That was what they made it with.

I never understood it.

Sang shrugged. I was curious. Then I got hooked.

They walked for five blocks, until the restaurants petered out. A madwoman approached, wearing layers of dark clothes. Bea looked at her wizened face. She wasn't perspiring. How was that possible? She was dressed for November. Everyone else was in shorts and dying of heat.

Can you be too crazy to perspire? Bea said.

Sang didn't respond, lost in thought.

They turned to flag a cab. A dozen cabs went by, full. She thought about their son, Thomas, in his second year of university, three hundred miles away. She had a panicky few seconds where she couldn't entirely place him, couldn't see his face. It was out of focus. His only form of communication was texting, half of them reading like ransom notes.

When Thomas was little, they used to eat at cheap, cheerful restaurants that served mediocre food ordered from plastic menus and Bea had always thought that when he was older they would go to more interesting places and the ten-year-old Thomas would be eating lumpfish roe ravioli and would grow up to be adventurous and well-rounded and comfortable in the world. Bea worried that at twenty he was none of those things. She worried that he was one of those lost boys /men who played video games, microwaved burritos, and saw the larger world through a lens distorted by relentless and consequenceless online pursuits, the happy deaths of war game victims, the joyless grunts of gangbang enthusiasts.

A battered Buick finally pulled up. The windows were open, not a good sign. They got into the back seat and Sang gave their address as the car lurched forward.

You have air conditioning? Bea asked.

The man—Gaetan Azkenazi according to the photo ID, though he didn't look like the photo—just shrugged.

Can you turn it on, please, Bea said.

Espensive, he said.

Well, let's say it's two dollars for the next nine minutes. I can cover that.

Gaetan stared ahead, accelerating toward the red light then hitting the brakes.

Gaetan, seventeen people have died of heatstroke in this city. And it's *May*. This request isn't out of line.

They idled at the light then lurched forward when it turned green.

Either turn on the fucking air or let us out right here, Bea said, as angry at Sang for not getting involved.

Gaetan flipped on the fan. Bea wasn't even sure the AC was on; it might have just been the fan blowing hot air. There was no point in rolling up the windows. She sat there getting hotter and angrier and when the car finally pulled up to their house, she immediately leapt out and slammed the door.

Bea went straight to the basement, the coolest space in the house, and turned on the TV and clicked to the Weather Channel. She watched a tornado in Kansas move toward a farmhouse, shot on someone's cellphone. It was shaky and the air was filled with dirt. She wondered if the tornado would pick up the whole house, like in *The Wizard of Oz,* but it moved past it without any apparent damage. Then grey, wet video footage, the lens obscured by large drops of water, the crawl beneath saying it was the Philippines, the tropical storm upgraded to a hurricane. There was a shot of clouds moving swiftly, time-lapse, the clouds of the world racing to the next city, dispersing, re-gathering, growing darker, bringing unwanted rain to some flood-prone land, delivered with a force that felt like hatred.

But nature was indifferent; hatred was reserved for people. The hurricanes that were extending the hurricane season, held over like a hit play, the tornadoes and floods, the wildfires that consumed northern California like a cancer, had no personal investment in their destruction. The retired couple in their RV who were hurled off the coastal highway, the two-hundred-year-old redwoods, the eight billion insects and start-up wineries were simply wrong-place-wrong-time.

But the people who rose out of the chaos wouldn't be indifferent, Bea thought. They would be driven by blood and anger and they would find hatred somewhere—in their past, on TV, on a website, in their homes. There was more hatred now. Or maybe there was always the same amount but it had lain dormant for years, like those cicadas that live underground for thirteen years then one spring they emerge in their millions like a plague.

The local weather came on and Bea watched the three-day forecast expand to five days, then seven, then finally the fourteen-day graph, the line heading mercifully down. It would break in six or seven days. Within two weeks the temperature would be at or *below* seasonal averages and we can all be grateful for that, the weather person said, a tough-looking blonde.

When Bea went up to bed, Sang was asleep. Her eyes adjusted to the darkness. She could see the shape of the chair, his clothes casually thrown over it. Their ceiling fan was ancient and noisy and met the air with violence. She stood beneath it and turned her face upward and closed her eyes.

chance of rain

THE MORNING BROKE. HER HUSBAND stirred. The weight of the previous evening settled, the sullen dinner, conversations replayed in terse snippets as Bea examined the ceiling. The stillness of the house was like a museum after hours—something that had held life only hours earlier now inert. The air almost cool before the day's assault.

She got up and dressed quietly and ran errands then drove to the home to visit her mother. It was one of the nice ones, for what it was. Her mother had her own apartment, though the kitchen was merely decorative; she could make tea and toast and that was about it. There was a dining room on the main floor. Two nurses lived on-site. It was bright, airy, unaffordable, difficult to get to, guilt-laden, and had an optimistic name—Galileo Sunrise. They all had optimistic names.

In the lobby a few women sat on a bench waiting to get picked up by dutiful middle-aged children. They were sweet-looking and silent, and Bea suddenly imagined them as teenagers at a dance somewhere, sitting in the postwar glow, waiting for shy boys to ask them to waltz. These women would be going to a nearby restaurant, catching up on grandchildren (all their achievements inflated—who was to know?). The dutiful daughter checking her phone when the mother went to the washroom, sending as many emails as possible before wondering if maybe she should go in there and see if anything had gone wrong.

And so much could go wrong. It was odd that at the age of forty-nine Bea was just beginning to understand that. That life was a long parade of unintended consequences. There was a moment in her thirties when she and her friends all seemed to be moving toward a fixed point. There was a linear quality to everyone's lives; they bought houses, had children, renovated kitchens. But that sense of momentum had vanished. Her world now looked like the birth of the universe, random upheavals, black holes that sucked in the light, a loosely structured chaos that might produce anything.

Bea went up to her mother's apartment and let herself in. Her mother was staring at the blank television screen, as if waiting for a picture. Always petite, she was further diminished now, her fine cheekbones still there, the only thing that prevented her face from collapsing. It was as if they held up her whole existence.

Bea's sister lived in Chicago and so all the care duties fell to Bea. Ariel came to town three or four times a year for a testy three-day war on how their mother should be cared for, and Bea got to feel superior and resentful while Ariel (who was two years older) behaved like the managing director of Mother Inc.

Ariel, her mother said. It could rain.

I'm Beatrice, Mother. Ariel lives five hundred miles away. And it hasn't rained in more than a month. It *threatens* to rain, then doesn't. That's why the city looks like the Kalahari Desert.

The girl on the weather—

The weather girl has been so wrong for so long it's a miracle she has the nerve to show her face on TV.

But if it *does*—

It won't, but if it does, we'll find a café and have a tea.

I don't like tea.

We'll drink gin.

They went down in the elevator and in the lobby Bea signed out one of the wheelchairs. Her mother could walk without it, but it was slow going. Easier to push her. She wheeled her mother outside, and within half a block sweat trickled down her spine. Her T-shirt began to cling. The park was five blocks away and by the time she got there, there were large dark blotches of perspiration.

How is Mrs Wheeler? Bea asked. She thought this was her name. A thin, slightly demented woman whom her mother sometimes ate with.

Alma? A bit bitey. She bit Mr Fetherling. They warned her.

She *bit* someone?

Not hard. Not a *wound*. I felt a drop. Did you feel something?

It's not raining, Mother. Bea looked up. Those clouds hadn't been there an hour ago. Bea wondered what they would do in the park. The Japanese flowering cherry trees had failed to blossom, an ominous sign in what was becoming a season of ominous signs.

We'll go around the path, then maybe stop for tea, Bea said.

I don't like tea.

Bea pushed her mother along the paved path, past geese and children and picnickers. The old-growth trees drooped above, light coming through in impressionist splashes. There were animals in cages along the steep hill, motionless in this heat, mounds of fur languishing in the shade. Bea had come here as a kid, before animal rights.

The light suddenly darkened. Bea looked up at the clouds, a midnight blue. The air changed, cooler, both welcome and menacing. There was a flash of lightning then crashing thunder, the kind that sounds as though it's ten feet away. Bea looked up. It would open up any second.

That was thunder, her mother said helpfully.

Yes.

The café was about two hundred yards away. Bea turned back to head toward it, stepping up her pace. It was suddenly very dark.

I felt something, her mother said.

Bea was almost running now. Others were running, mothers with small children racing for their cars. Another crack of lightning. Bea half expected to see a tree fall across their path. The thunder roared.

Thunder, her mother said.

Then the deluge. They were soaked through in seconds. The rain coming down so hard she couldn't hear what her mother was saying. The landscape was blurred and dark grey, her glasses useless. She picked up her pace, running as fast as she dared, pushing the wheelchair, which rattled over the paving stones. It hit something—a raised stone maybe—and the wheelchair turned violently to the left, tipping, her mother sprawling out onto the path with a small cry. Bea fell over the wheelchair awkwardly and felt something tear and landed hard on the stones. There was a sharp pain in her knee. She brought her hand to her face and tasted grit. It took a moment to orient herself. Her mother was lying on her back, her thin legs spread out, a child's legs, the rain assaulting her face.

Mother.

Bea couldn't tell if there was any sound coming from her. The rain hammered loudly.

Mother, are you all right?

Bea crawled toward her. Her mother was on her back, her face up, her mouth open, rain splashing in, coughing.

Oh god. Mother, here, we have to ... She looked around. Could someone ... There wasn't anyone around them. The rain came down so hard it bounced. When the next crack of lightning came, Bea thought the earth would open up.

Jesus Jesus. Mother. Bea got up, hobbling slightly. There was blood on her knee, her pants torn, the red instantly diluted by the downpour. She got the wheelchair upright then went to her mother.

We need to get out of here. Mother, are you okay? Oh, please be okay.

A soft moan.

She tried to put her mother in the wheelchair, but as she bumped against it, the wheelchair moved backwards and she had her mother's dead weight in her arms, bringing them both down. Her mother cried out in pain. The rain was violent, wrathful.

Are you okay? Where does it hurt?

Her mother didn't say anything. Bea collected the wheelchair again. Her limbs were instantly weary, everything so wet and heavy. She looked around. She couldn't see thirty feet. She found the brake on the wheelchair and pressed down on it. Her mother was lying on her back. She tried to lift her and couldn't and dragged her the few feet. It took everything to lift her into the wheelchair. She almost slid out, but Bea grabbed her. Her mother cried out again, a yelp of pain, like an animal's. Bea noticed her arm, bent at a slight but sickening angle.

Oh god. Mother. Your arm.

She searched for the seat belt they never used. Bea was crying now, in frustration as much as anything. She found the belt and fastened it with difficulty.

Hang on, we'll get out of this. We will. Oh, I'm so sorry.

Bea pushed her quickly toward the café in the middle of the park. In the parking lot there were people sitting in their cars, engines on, wipers going. The rain coming down so hard. Some of the cars were trying to leave and no one could see and there was chaos in the lot. At the door of the café a man was waving people away.

Full, he said.

It's an emergency, Bea said, checking for her cellphone.

The man wasn't a man. Maybe sixteen, his first job. He quickly disappeared inside, looking for someone in charge. Bea found her cell and dialed 911 and asked for an ambulance. A few people huddled at the door looked at her mother and made sympathetic noises. Drenched, she looked even smaller, as if she would shrink to nothing, melt in the rain like the Wicked Witch.

Mother, I'm so so sorry, Bea said. She was crying harder, kneeling, looking into her mother's eyes, which were blank. She might be in shock.

The ambulance arrived minutes later and had trouble navigating the crowded parking lot. It pulled up and two uniformed people got out. Bea approached them, pointed to her mother. There was a flurry of activity, moving her gently onto the stretcher, buckling the straps, wheeling an IV, then quiet, persistent questions that Bea answered as best she could. Was her mother on any medications, did she have any allergies? Bea climbed awkwardly into the ambulance. Someone folded up the wheelchair for her. She looked at her mother's face, stricken, foreign-looking. One of the paramedics, an expressionless woman in her twenties, her hair soaked, sat beside Bea. The ambulance lurched through the city and Bea swayed with every turn. She looked down at her leg. One leg of her linen pants was torn at the knee. She put her fingers through the hole and touched the blood and brought it to her lips, grateful for the wound.

YOU ALMOST FUCKING *KILLED HER!*

This was three days later, Ariel on the phone. Their mother out of the hospital, back in her faux apartment, her arm in a sling.

It sounds worse than it was.

It *sounds* like you almost killed her. My god, Bea, what the *hell* were you thinking? Do you know how serious a broken bone is at that age?

It was an accident, Air, we were trying to get out of the rain.

Why were you even *in* the rain in the first place? You take an eighty-six-year-old woman out for a walk in a *thunderstorm?*

Bea stared at a point on the counter that could have been a stain or an anomaly in the glazed limestone. She hadn't noticed it before. It might be a tiny fossil, something ancient and extinct, an ice age catching it by surprise. She picked up her glass of wine then set it down again.

She listened to her sister vent for a bit. As a child Ariel memorized monologues from movies. She did an unnerving version of Clint Eastwood in *Dirty Harry* and used to sneak up behind her and jab a ballpoint pen in her neck and deliver that soliloquy—*Being as this is a .44 Magnum, the most powerful handgun in the world and would blow your head clean off, you've got to ask yourself one question: Do I feel lucky? Well, do ya, punk?* And now every real-life rant sounded like a performance. It *was* a performance. Ariel had never stopped performing. She had difficulty distinguishing real life from film. Bea waited as long as she could before cutting her sister off.

Here's an idea, Air: why don't you spend three weeks re-searching assisted living residences, find one that takes people with mild dementia, has registered nurses and a doctor who didn't get his degree from a Guatemalan website, employs two dozen minimum-wage Third World attendants who've been screened for al Qaeda connections, something within driving distance, which this doesn't remotely qualify, and you—

Oh Christ, I don't have to listen to this—

Go and see her six times (more like three) a week and ask how many people Mad Dog Wheeler has bitten then write a cheque for $5,200 every fucking month.

The fact is—

The fact is you wouldn't get through the first *week*. This situation is ideal for you, Air, you get to give advice and keep five hundred miles between you and anything messy. When was the last time you emptied a bedpan?

What the hell are we paying $5,000 a month for—

We're not. *I* am …

Bea had never actually emptied a bedpan. It bothered her that Ariel made her lie. And the money was coming out of their mother's dwindling account, though Bea was managing it.

Jesus, Bea, the money—

You're sitting in another city doing what you do best—giving useless advice and not doing a bloody thing.

Bea punched the red button and ended the call. Her heart was racing. She picked up her wine and took a long sip. Well, family. There was nothing like it.

felony

THE AIR CONDITIONING WAS OFF. The house dark, drapes closed, an interior twilight. The third floor was an oven, the air stale and heavy. Philip had an office with a desk and bookshelves and a leather reading chair with a stack of books beside it. A framed photograph of him on the wall, a much younger version, tanned, slim, laughing with friends on a houseboat. There was a photograph of Katherine, in a bathing suit, posed, a bit severe, devoid of expression.

Katherine once told this heartbreaking story. She was tearfully drunk when she told it, one of the few times she lost that steely control. They'd gone to Paris, her and Philip, before the kids, and they'd been to the Musée d'Orsay and seen Manet's *Le Déjeuner sur l'herbe,* the naked woman eating lunch in the forest with two fully clothed men. And one morning they split up to run some errands, with a plan to meet back at the hotel for lunch, and Katherine went out and bought a baguette and cheese and pâté and wine then laid the bedspread on the floor. She took out all the food for a picnic in their room, then took off all her clothes, like in the painting. And Philip was late, so she was sitting there on the blanket, drinking a little wine, then a little more, nibbling, sipping, waiting for him, and he finally came in with a copy of the *Herald Tribune,* which he bought for the football scores, and she said, in a singsongy voice, *When in Rome,* and laughed and Philip stared at her and didn't get it and wasn't in the mood and she sat there, *so exposed,* she said. And he wanted to go to the Rodin Museum and wasn't really that hungry, he'd grabbed a sandwich from one of those vendors in the park. And she sat there as his gaze wandered away. She got dressed and he went to the Rodin and she went to Père-Lachaise cemetery and pretended to mourn Jim Morrison and they got back in time for a lateish dinner and neither of them mentioned it. *How do you get over that?* she'd said, crying, going through it all again, though it had been ten years earlier. But they did get over it. They wouldn't be one of those couples who breathlessly fucked away their first two years, who went to a fabulous city and didn't leave the hotel room. They would be a different version, orderly and aspirational.

The residue of that moment was here in the house somewhere, a palimpsest that lingered, blurred but never erased.

Philip's laptop wasn't password protected, a surprise. He'd been working on a biography of Wittgenstein for years. He used to describe it regularly in incomprehensible detail, insistently boring everyone within range, though he hadn't mentioned it in a while, more than a year, maybe two. It was sixteen pages long. Another file held notes, almost a hundred pages. The manuscript was titled *Ludwig Wittgenstein: The Burden of Existence.* There were three epigraphs, one from Kierkegaard, one from Beckett, and one from Pink Floyd.

The air in their house was dead. Katherine's closet was familiar. There was a photograph of the family on the wall. It was posed, taken at a studio, the kind that used to go onto Christmas cards.

In the bathroom, the usual prescriptions. Katherine had trouble sleeping. Everyone had trouble sleeping, another silent epidemic, like pornography or debt. But there was an even quieter epidemic, an epic numbing, everyone whittled by time and technology and unhappy commutes and weather that evoked an Old Testament God with too much time on His hands.

The top drawer of Katherine's dresser was filled with her jewellery, a bit baroque, busy necklaces that were jangly in the wrong way. The bottom drawer held sweaters and under the sweaters was red underwear, not the kind you bought at Saks, the kind you bought at a costume store, like a sexy Halloween costume. There was a vibrator and a tube of something—Sensuous Sensations. There would be risk putting those panties on, especially in light of the Paris story. The tube was unopened.

It was a tasteful house, a bit too tasteful, too much time spent finding the perfect placemats, the ideal light fixture. On the wall was a framed black-and-white photograph of Katherine and Philip in a French vineyard. They were younger. Philip had an anecdote to go with the photo, one of those anecdotes that isn't actually a story, a drifting half story designed to showcase his suspect knowledge of wine and equally suspect French. He had a gift for finding academic conferences in exotic places.

She left through the front door. She locked it and pulled the large straw hat tight to her head. She was wearing oversized celebrity sunglasses, her heart smashing at her rib cage like a prisoner. A torrent of emotions: sadness, fear, guilt. The hot air moved slightly, though didn't bring any relief. She moved down the street. She had on grey shorts, a baggy white T-shirt with no logo, running shoes. She could have been anyone.

downlessness

BEA WONDERED HOW MANY INSTITUTIONALLY witty birthday
cards she would get (*The best form of birth control for people over
50? ... Nudity!!!*). It was too hot to have the party outside in
the backyard, which she would have preferred. Even with the
air conditioning turned up, it would get very close inside the
house. She already felt trapped and claustrophobic and she
was the only one in the house.

Bea examined the wineglasses lined up, looked at the line
of bottles—wine, sparkling water—glanced at the clock. Ca-
tered food filled the refrigerator. Bea had supplied the name
of the caterer for Sang and ticked off what they needed, had
bought the wine, had changed Maria's date so she'd clean the
morning of. Happy Birthday. Though Sang had volunteered
to pick up her mother, and Ariel, who had flown in from Chicago, had gone with him, a relief.

The caterer was out in his van, filling out an invoice. He
came back in, a ponytailed man holding a small pastry box.
He set the box on the kitchen counter, and motioned to Bea.

Open it.

Bea opened it to find a brownie with a candle. The man

came over and reverently took it out of the box and lit the candle with a lighter.

Happy birthday!

Bea looked at the brownie.

You're supposed to blow it out.

Bea leaned down.

Make a wish, the guy said.

She gave it a quick blow, smoke trailing up. *I wish the evening was over.*

Your birthday brownie! Enjoy! He left the invoice on the counter and walked backwards for a few steps with an annoying bow, his hands clasped, then turned and left.

Bea poured a glass of wine and took a bite of the brownie. It was awfully good, that elusive texture. She had another bite.

In less than an hour, people would start arriving. The men would be casually dressed, some of them in shorts. There would be roughly three dozen kisses, not all of them a joy, waves of different scents, aggressive high school aftershave, the smell of sweat.

Philip would kiss her on both cheeks and maybe quote a line from an Auden poem. Roger would give her a damp hug, vaguely sexual. Penelope would be sweetly polite, Katherine consolatory. A half-dozen neighbours would come, maybe more, and not all of them would mix brilliantly with her friends. Richard from next door would get someone wound up on climate change.

Ariel would stay up until the last guest had left, and then want to engage Bea on the subject of their mother. Her timing was always exquisite. At the point in the evening when Bea would rather disembowel herself than have another conversation, her sister would pour herself a glass of wine and start talking about their mother not being happy. Not *happy?*

She was eighty-six, a widow for fourteen of those years, losing her mind, almost unable to walk now, flirting with other ailments. Where, exactly, would happiness enter into that picture? And Ariel would say, *Well, happiness is what you have when you're not in a wheelchair accident in a monsoon.* God, she was doing it again—arguing with her sister in her head. She had told herself to stop. It had been a resolution for two of the last three New Years. Anyway, there was no need to argue with her in her head—in five hours (or less) they would argue in person, something sharp and bitter that would echo through the last two days of Ariel's stay.

Would she and Sang have perfunctory sex tonight? Tainted by birthday obligation. Would Sang drunkenly go down on her, ending his unbroken streak of ... downlessness? Perhaps it would become their birthday thing, though it hadn't been. She might drink too much wine, an accident almost, and wake up with a hangover then make a depressing list of all the things she would fail to accomplish in the coming year.

This was a symptom of fifty—imagining everything before it happened, being disappointed by it, and wishing it were over before it began. When you're young, you look forward to things. At fifty, you know how it ends. That's what you lose as you get older—a sense of anticipation. More valuable than she would have guessed. Bea was already weary. She didn't want to sit down because it would wrinkle her dress.

The door opened and in they came, Sang pushing her mother. Ariel was behind them, wearing a black linen dress and heels that would give her an inch on Bea. Sometimes you could see a family resemblance and sometimes you couldn't. It was odd; there were stretches of their lives when they looked almost like twins, then they would drift apart, barely look like sisters really, before being pulled together again. They were somewhere in the middle at the moment. Their hair was pretty close and they both had the Billings nose, optimistically described by their mother as aristocratic. They had good legs. Bea's neck was holding up better. She would hear a lot about how her sister and her and their mother all looked alike.

Birthday girl, her mother said simply.

What can I get you two? Sang asked.

White wine would be lovely, Sang, her sister said. Thank you.

Dorothy?

Her mother stared up, as if reading a menu on the ceiling. I don't like tea, she said. Maybe a martini. A weak one.

They don't come in weak, Mother, Bea said. There's large and small, but not weak.

Large and weak.

Sang went to the kitchen.

So this will be fun, Ariel said.

IT WAS DISTURBING HOW MUCH of Bea's prediction came true. Her neighbour Richard, as expected, launched into climate change—a hoax, he said. Normally this might get polite smiles from people, or they'd quietly move to another conversation. But the temperature in the house had risen quickly to twenty-eight degrees and there was only one fan, which wasn't doing much, and so when Richard aggressively pursued his rote, almost musically cadenced recitation of the earth's macro climate events over the last twenty millennia, his sweaty, sleepless audience responded with more edge.

To think that man is to blame is pure ego, Richard said, addressing a small circle. Don't flatter yourselves. We're a passing fad. Like the dinosaurs. The earth has *always* experienced extremes, there is *proof*…

Bea noticed Roger entering the conversation. He would be three drinks in at this point. You can't be that fucking stupid, can you? Roger said pleasantly.

Richard clearly didn't expect this bluntness. His face reddened. He was sweating in the non-climate-change heat. There are *faulty* measurements, he said, the *data* is incomplete, the scientists have a *vested interest* . . . Richard counted off his points on his left hand.

And you think that 97 percent of the world's scientists are wrong and some idiot Christian in Tulsa who thinks this is just the warm-up act for the Apocalypse is right.

Roger loved to provoke and, even better, to argue. He had a real talent for both. Three philosophy degrees had little practical value, but they certainly made you a capable debater.

There is scientific *proof*—

There is the smug stupidity of a handful of halfwits who think Christ is going to pull up in an suv and give their tiny lives some meaning. Good luck with that. Roger swirled the last of his wine then drank it.

Have you read—

We're past the point of reading, Roger said. Surely you can see this argument is purely theoretical. We're done. We didn't heed our own warnings, we have trouble imagining any future that doesn't involve winning the lottery. Ten years ago, we were warned that we still had ten years to solve the problem and we spent those ten years driving around the suburbs looking for a bigger barbecue. There was a time when halfwits like you were provocative. Now you're the evolutionary equivalent of an appendix, fucking useless, waiting to blow up on a long flight. We're all casualties, you stunned fuckwit. It's a lucky thing that life is meaningless, because it's on its way out.

Roger left to get another drink and the climate change symposium quietly drifted, murmuring. Bea looked out to the backyard. Sang was on his cell, taking short, erratic steps, like following dance steps painted on a floor. Bathed in the dull glow of their unreliable solar lights, he looked a bit blurry. She squinted; he appeared to be melting, another climate change casualty.

Bea had a sudden disembodied feeling, as if she wasn't entirely present. Like one of those films where the character doesn't know she's a ghost. She glided through the living room, invisible. A glass broke. A laugh like a seal's bark. Words arrived in snatches, random and broken. Bea had a muffled conversation with a neighbour, not sure what she was saying, the lipsticked mouth working feverishly. Her own voice sounded as if it was being filtered through wool. The music was tinny. Roger came over to her and quietly ranted, saliva launching from his mouth—tiny drops landing like spores that might reproduce. She suddenly couldn't locate her own voice. Katherine loomed, talking about concussions or orchids. The edges of everything blurred. Bea didn't trust her senses. A thought formed slowly, collapsing repeatedly, like a child trying to build a castle out of dry sand. What was in that brownie?

She hadn't been stoned in more than twenty years. She didn't remember pot being this strong, if that's what it was. What kind of caterer gives someone a brownie with THC in it? If those were even the right letters.

There was a grotesque quality to the laughter around her, something parodic in everyone's movements, their voices distorted, things not entirely at full speed. She was dangerously stoned and tried to will herself out of it. She wondered how much time had gone by, the way she used to wonder in school and look at the big clock and find only two minutes had gone by instead of the hour she'd hoped for. She was frightened of fifty. A reckoning. She didn't believe in greatness, or it would have been worse. Sang did, and carried that wound.

Katherine was telling Bea about their weekend at the cottage, about squirrels and Jet Skis and gin. Bea stared past her to the backyard, Sang standing like a hologram in that ghostly light.

Bea saw her mother, sitting on a chair, talking to a small gathering. Bea imagined she was giving them a fractured description of the twenty-seven hours of labour she'd endured to get Bea into the world. Ariel was standing beside her. Ariel who had emerged in a (now) joyous thirty minutes, squirting out like a lemon seed. Her mother told this story often and always remarked, as she might be now, how usually it was the other way around—the first was difficult then they got easier. But Bea didn't want to come out. And Air would say, You should have opened a bottle of wine. That might have done it. And everyone would laugh as they were now.

Bea had heard the story a dozen times and now seemed to be experiencing it, inching out as her mother screamed. Bea struggled with an image of herself emerging from the womb, seeing those masked strangers murmuring like Druids, that harsh light, this mad world.

Her mother seemed to be drifting farther away, getting smaller. Centrifugal forces pulling at everything that was valuable and you had to hang on for dear life or it would all fly off into the uncaring dark. This was the stoned insight that descended.

Skinny-dipping, Katherine said to her, laughing. I mean, god, when was the last time anyone went *skinny-dipping*.

Bea smiled and said *shrivelled penis* either to herself or out loud and looked at her mother, could suddenly see inside her head, each tiny neural death, a pinprick of light going out.

Sang came into the house and stood on a chair of all things. He was saying something loudly, calling attention. Bea tried to focus. The room was quiet, all the noise leaking out like water down a drain. Sang had once said her breasts gave him strength to face the world. Not now. Now he talked of something something something. They were young, they met at a party, he fell in love. That was the story. He smiled and there was applause and the faces all turned to her, expectant, like birds waiting to be fed. Sang standing tall and lovely, raising his glass.

Peach! Peach!

Bea burst into tears and tried to tell everyone how much this all meant, how much everything meant. She smiled and everyone clapped and she stood in the void.

SANG OFFERED TO DRIVE HER mother home. At the door, her mother clasped Bea's face in both hands, a surprising strength, her own small face looming, whispering fiercely, Live! Before they fuck you, darling.

Bea couldn't have heard correctly. She watched them trundle out then looked at her watch—11:23. She stared at the ruins of the kitchen, the remains of lamb chops, bloody, tearing the red flesh away from the bone with your teeth then holding that Neanderthal evidence. Salads spilled onto the counter, ravaged, and the remains of her cake, slumped like a Dali painting.

They all began to leave, a slow exodus. They approached her and mumbled congratulations, slow, odd kisses, faces in alarming close-up, damp hugs. Her skin was sensitive, alive to every intention. All these wonderful friends who had come to celebrate. She loved them all. The last refugees left, onto a better life, and Bea started to weep.

Are you crying again? Ariel squinting at her.

No.

Jesus, Bea. Where's Sang? He's not back yet?

It could be traffic.

It's after midnight.

Bea shrugged. I'll try his cell, she said. With her own cell. Which was.

Ariel stared at her. Use mine, she said, holding it up. Bea took it, turned it over like something she'd pulled out of an archaeological dig.

Christ, Ariel said, grabbing it back. What is the matter with you? Here, I'll dial.

She handed it to Bea, who looked at it. It rang for days.

Probably driving and can't pick up, Bea said. She debated pouring herself another glass of wine. She didn't want one. Though she often didn't want one when she poured herself another one. Her head was muddy. Would wine help counteract the brownie? She went over and put the kettle on and got a mug out of the cupboard then took some of the lemon wedges that were sitting on the counter and squeezed three of them into the mug.

I think the caterer gave me a brownie with pot in it, Bea said.

Seriously? You got dosed by the caterer? How would you even know? When was the last time you smoked pot?

Dunno. Twenty years ago.

Is there any left?

You want to take it? Don't. I think someone ate it. Jesus.

Bea looked around the room, a mess that was impossible to clean up.

Do you remember that circus Mom used to take us to? Ariel said.

I can't remember anything at the moment.

We left early because you threw up, and outside the tent all those Chinese acrobats were standing there smoking and arguing. They were shorter than me and I was ten.

Can't picture it.

Screaming at each other in Chinese. We thought they were kids enslaved by an evil ringmaster. And that lame trapeze act. The guy fell into the net. *Twice*. And it took him like ten minutes to climb back up.

Bea stared at a plate with the remains of two obscene lamb chops, bloody and torn.

We were sitting so close and when they came up to the audience to take a bow, you could see they were, like, fifty. Sweaty and kind of saggy in those awful costumes.

Bea nodded stupidly. Now she was fifty. She remembered now. On the way home their mother had told them that this is life—it looks fancy on the outside, but you get up close and you see all the cracks. So never get your hopes up.

Bea went over to the kettle and poured water into the cup with lemon. She picked it up and blew softly.

Where the hell is Sang? Ariel asked.

Try him again.

Ariel pressed Redial and Bea walked to the front window. Their car was in the driveway.

Our *car* is in the driveway, Bea said.

What, he's *here*? Where?

Bea looked up the stairs, then went up carefully. She walked down the hall. Had he come in and she didn't notice? It wouldn't have been hard. Their bedroom door was closed. She opened it and went in and stood in the darkness. Sang was in bed, asleep. Maybe he came in the back door. He'd kicked off the top sheet. The fan was going, the top speed, which was like having a weather system in the bedroom.

Bea had already forgotten about her sister and the mess downstairs, and had she remembered them might have thought them somehow indistinguishable, like a car accident on the news, broken glass, twisted metal, a crawl along the bottom of the screen—*local tragedy*. She slid out of her dress and left it on the chair and took off her bra and panties and surveyed herself in the darkness. Trim though middle-agey, a sponginess that hadn't been there yesterday. Now she was a stoned fifty-year-old woman with twelve years left on her mortgage and a fifty-three-year-old husband currently in a fetal pose, folded up out of instinct, protecting something she couldn't name. She remembered making love to him. Another body, or she was another person. A stoned, unwelcome insight landed stupidly: the world was love, or the world was those minutes after a car accident when you sat stunned amid the glass pellets in the front seat, your ears ringing, and nothing moves until a head appears suddenly in the open window and says, Are you all right?

She got into bed beside her husband. He was giving off an alarming amount of heat. She saw waves of it rising off him, visible lines, like in a cartoon, the heat filling the room, suffocating them both.

for art's sake

WHEN SHE WOKE UP, THE covers were off. She still felt stoned. Sang was naked, tumescent, half-smiling, dreaming, hard as a fence post, fucking someone. Not me, Bea thought. This wasn't the erection she'd last seen—softer, distracted, without intent. Maybe he was in love. Or at least his cock was. She wanted to interrogate it, shine a harsh light on that small head, whack it with a telephone book till its sins spilled out.

She loved him, though couldn't remember the last time she'd said it and couldn't remember if it was just the knee-jerk response to his having said it. She thought about when they'd first said it. Twenty-five years ago, somewhere in that first six months, the growing awareness that this was it. He'd told her she had a great laugh. The first of the incremental compliments—I love the way you taste, I love your smile, I love...

She suddenly remembered when they'd said it and she remembered because of how freighted those next days were. Did he mean it? Did she? They said it after making love in a rented cottage on Georgian Bay. The cottage was modest and spare. They were collapsed on the floor of the living room looking through the sliding doors at Lake Huron, dark and oceanic. There were clouds moving slowly and they lay on the floor in that tangle, touching, talking, a breeze coming in and cooling them. They made dinner then made love again that night, carefully, she thought.

In the morning they had to inhabit that space—the space where they were in love. It was oddly worrisome, as if neither was quite sure what they should be doing or saying. They hadn't quite adjusted to the new landscape.

Sang stirred, his slack mouth made an unfortunate sound, and he turned away. The morning light framed the curtains. Bea would have preferred sleep, would have preferred a manufactured dream where she was vaguely triumphant. But she knew she wouldn't get back to sleep. She got up and went downstairs. Ariel had cleaned up the spectacular mess, a surprise.

Bea opened the front door and looked for the paper. It wasn't there, though he sometimes missed the porch or it was under the porch furniture. She stepped outside. It was hot already, the fetid breath of afternoon. The sun stretched across the pavement. She scanned the porch and the paper suddenly arrived, hitting the porch with a thump, making her jump. A man her own age walked on, tossing one toward the neighbour with a hint of violence. His decrepit car idling in the middle of the street. She picked it up and went back inside.

IT WAS THURSDAY, ONE OF her gallery days. Beginning in late May, she only kept it open three days a week and for appointments, though there hadn't been any appointments. The heat hadn't broken. The weather girl had lied, yet again. The mid-morning sun was a hammer and the air felt like a sickness.

She drove the familiar streets, people sitting outside in cafés, coffee in one hand, phone in the other. Shade had become a commodity. People scurried out of the glare like cockroaches, hunched and panicked. She stopped at a red light. On the sidewalk beside her, a disturbed woman was going through a series of contortions, a grotesque dance. She was anguished, dirty, wearing a Harvard T-shirt. She must be on crack, Bea thought, or something worse, if there was something worse, and there probably was. There's always something worse; that's how we progress.

She parked her car and picked up a coffee from the hip espresso bar and opened the gallery. Bea might see two people on a day like this. No one went around the galleries in this weather. Autumn was art season. The jazz station played at low volume. The air conditioning was louder than it should be. It had a slight tic, a metronome sound, something going wrong.

Outside, the streets were almost empty. It wasn't just the city that was abandoned, the days themselves were abandoned, scarcely lived, something to endure until life started again. Bea's view was of another gallery. In it, a woman roughly Bea's age, staring out at Bea, each wondering what they had done to deserve this. How had an early interest in neo-Primitivism led to a prison sentence. You can't leave. Well, you can leave for fifteen minutes, putting up that sign and locking the door. In reality she could probably leave for three hours. She could go to a movie (now *there* was air conditioning). A year ago, she had gone across the street and introduced herself to the woman (Caitlin?). They had chatted for a few moments, and in those moments the issue of friendship sat between them. But they didn't become friends. They simply stared out at one another like zoo animals that had been in captivity too long and had lost their natural instincts.

Her world felt as though it was suspended in aspic, like the awful salad with celery and chicken and miniature marshmallows that her mother had made because she'd seen it on television and her father prodded it with a fork and watched it wobble and shook his head.

AT 11 A.M. BEA ATE her lunch (a barley and parsley salad with too much coriander), more out of boredom than hunger. She looked at the paintings. There were three more days of these oversized stylized landscapes, post-apocalyptic, in dull colours. None had sold. You'd need a gallery-sized wall, for one thing. You'd need seven thousand dollars for another, and you'd need to be clinically depressed. You would also need to believe that these paintings were going to get more valuable. This was a price point where people, most people anyway, needed to believe it was an investment. But he wasn't the next Damien Hirst, just another child of the suburbs with an overdeveloped sense of irony.

By noon no one was on the street. She looked out the window to see Caitlin looking out the window. The hairdresser to the right of Caitlin's gallery was also standing at the window looking out. Everyone looking out at the world, no one actually in it.

She used to bring a book to work, but she no longer read the way she once did. She used to plough through books, beginning to end, a religious commitment. Now she started four or five at a time and was lucky to finish one of them. She drifted and abandoned them then started two more. She liked the idea of reading more than the actual reading.

She liked the idea of a lot of things more than the actual thing. Sex might fall into that category. It had been true of teaching certainly. Her first year of teaching had started with such hope, such energy. She was teaching art history (The Art of Love in the Renaissance) and assumed that everyone in the class had, if not a passion, then at least an interest in the subject. This turned out not to be true. They were tired and disengaged, especially at 8 a.m. Above all, they were teenagers—hormonal, narcissistic lumps. She felt like a doctor checking for vital signs. Her lectures took hours to prepare and so often she felt she was talking to herself. And then she was let go in yet another round of budget cuts (You do realize how little you're saving, she'd said).

When she started her own gallery, she imagined the semi-glamorous vernissages, finding and nurturing (and profiting from) young talent, engaging an art-loving public. Her gallery was on a stretch of Dundas Street that was "in transition," which meant that mentally ill men urinated on your door. It was the only rent she could afford, though the space was actually great, and she had room for larger pieces.

She had brought a box of photographs she and Ariel had taken from their mother's house. She had decided to paste them, chronologically, into a scrapbook. She'd bought three at the dollar store.

She opened the lid of the box and laid the photos out on the largish table in the gallery. A few of the early ones were still in black and white. She picked up one at random and there was her father, so young and stylish, though he was never stylish. Perhaps it was just the times that were stylish and he was caught up in them, a trim suit and white shirt with the top button undone. His hair was black and full and his face had an expression she'd never seen, or at least never remembered, a sense of optimism, joyful. Her mother is standing beside him, pregnant. He's pointing to her belly, his eyebrows arched. *Can you believe this*.

The first step was to establish a chronology. There was a photograph of her and Ariel sitting outside on lawn chairs with candy cigarettes, the ones with the red tip that made it look like they were lit, wearing their mother's jewellery, with highball glasses. The enviable adult world, so anxious to grow up.

They'd emptied their mother's house, when it was clear that she shouldn't stay on her own. She and Ariel going through everything. What to keep? Ariel only wanted a few things; it wouldn't make sense to ship furniture all the way to Chicago. And there wasn't really any furniture they wanted. Their parents had the blurry aesthetic of that time and place—buying whatever maple dinette set was on sale. Bea took a few things: a wooden Shaker chair, a breadbox that must have been forty years old. Odd things. The rest was sold to one of those estate people. The two large boxes of photographs were the only things that really felt like their mother. Though once Bea got them home, they went into the basement and she didn't look through any of them.

She began making three piles corresponding to three different eras: 60s, 70s, 80s. There was a photo of Ariel as a baby, the world as it existed before Bea. Her mother and father seated on the sofa with Air in her mother's arms. It was formal, almost expressionless, like a family mug shot.

There was a Halloween photograph, her and Air standing in the kitchen, posing unhappily. They had both wanted to be princesses and there was only one costume, so their mother had split the costume between them and tried to make up the rest with whatever was at hand. Bea was holding a wooden spoon, a stand-in for Ariel's sparkly wand, though Bea had gotten the tiara. They looked like homeless princesses, glum and resentful.

She looked at a photo of her father's funeral, the cemetery. His death was still vivid, all of them gathered in the church, staring into the open casket. In life he'd been absent, elusive, his impact on their lives diluted. But in death he was suddenly concrete; here was something you could hold on to. He wasn't old (seventy-two) and Bea wasn't young (thirty-seven). His immobile face, so lifelike because it had been immobile in life. He was a man who had simply withdrawn in his last decade, disappearing into his study doing god knows what.

He also had a workshop in the basement, though she never saw him make anything. The tools were ancient, most of them inherited from her grandfather. They were lovely things in their way, well-used, scarred, and sturdy. Lined up on hooks on the wall and laid out on the bench, like a museum. *This was how we used to build.*

Were men getting more useless? It seemed to be the case. It was almost evolutionary. They certainly couldn't fix or build things, the world slouching toward Greece, all the men sitting in cafés drinking coffee and smoking as the country collapsed around them.

Her father used to take her and Ariel to the movies, that was his contribution to parenting. Afterward they went for ice cream, even in winter, to the same place, one of those non-chains that is held up as authentic though god knows. Every Sunday they went. There wasn't always a new kids' movie and they would see random films—*Jaws* (which had terrified her), *Barry Lyndon* (endless, though visually stunning, like a Caravaggio painting), *The French Connection* (a miscalculation). Half the time he made them promise to tell their mother they'd gone to see something else. Maybe that's why Ariel started to do the film monologues, an homage to those afternoons, to all they knew, really, of their father.

Ariel had given the eulogy because their mother wouldn't be able to get through it and might go off script and say something regrettable. Then a quiet drive to the cemetery, the crowd there much smaller, lowering the casket into the ground. A cloudy day with a bitter wind that snapped at the minister's dark trench coat. There weren't any people in the photo, just her father's grave and those clouds.

And now we need to look out for one another. This was what her mother had said when they drove home. As if their father had been doing it up until then. Anyway, Bea was thirty-seven, Ariel thirty-nine. A bit late.

Bea picked up a photograph of her mother holding a baby. It was in black and white. Her mother was holding the baby at arm's length above her and staring up at it, beaming. Bea tried to remember seeing this expression on her mother's face and couldn't. The baby would have to be Ariel. There was a date on the side, and Bea squinted to read it, taking off her glasses. It said September 1960. Ariel was born in 64. So a friend's baby. Her parents thinking of having a baby, her mother with that one-day-I'll-have-one-of-these face.

Bea shuffled through some of the photos and found several more black and whites. The early 60s didn't look like the late 60s. That lovely black and white, those trim, ageless fashions soon to be replaced by a lurid explosion, everything resembling an album cover. She picked up a photo of her father wearing slim, dark dress pants and a shirt with the sleeves rolled up. He was holding a baby—the same baby? Bea brought the photo closer. The date was the same—September 1960. Taken on the same day maybe. The sky was the same (though it was the same in most black-and-white photos). It was the same backyard, not the one from the Euclid house. This one looked poorer. The lawn was ill-kept, some of it dirt, it looked like. Her father had a broad smile. He was holding the baby with one hand under its bum, the other wrapped around it. Both of them looking at the camera. Her father's face held what could only be described as joy. Bea had certainly never seen this version of him. She examined the photograph, turning it over. She felt like an archaeologist who had dug up something valuable but potentially dangerous. The baby might be ten months old, with a sweet half smile, an oddly adult-looking expression, a look of knowingness.

A man stopped in front of the gallery and looked at the paintings through the window, his mouth pursed. He had that art face, the one that says, *What was the artist trying to do here?* In this case the artist was trying to get laid by an impressionable art major.

The man tilted his head slightly, then saw Bea and smiled noncommittally and walked on. It was almost time to close. She put all the black-and-white photos in a pile then texted Penelope to remind her of yoga.

BEA TURNED OUT THE LIGHTS, turned down the air conditioning, turned on the alarm, and locked the door behind her. The furnace of outside. The hottest point in the day yesterday had been 4:04 p.m., one of the facts gleaned from her obsessive Weather Channel habit. So many people thought the hottest part of the day was noon. Caitlin was locking up on the other side of the street. In the late afternoon glare, she suddenly vanished. Bea stared into the blank void. It was as if Caitlin had suddenly become invisible. They both were, she supposed. Unseen in their cloistered businesses, then disappearing in the glare. Caitlin appeared like a special effect as Bea's eyes adjusted. They nodded to one another and moved off in opposite directions. Bea walked to the parking lot, took the ticket out of her purse, and paid the attendant. She got into her car, which smelled of stale coffee, then edged into traffic and crawled then stopped. The fan was turned up to the maximum and blew still-uncooled air on her face, her hair gently waving in that manufactured breeze as if she were moving.

june

EVERYONE TALKED ABOUT THE WEATHER. The first week of June was the hottest on record (going back 114 years, Bea knew). Not just here. It was the hottest in Austria, and their records went back to 1767. An Iranian city had reached 53 degrees C. And what was the reward for surviving June? July, the hottest month of the year.

Bea googled "Arctic Melt." She watched a time-lapse satellite shot of Banks Island that started in 1984, the permafrost receding, slowly at first, an orderly retreat, then picking up steam and making jagged inroads, until finally all that was left was a grey mess of gravel and mud.

July would be a climatic shit show and August would exhaust the northern hemisphere, but it would hold promise at least. It would hold the promise of fall, that crisp air, the leaves turning. Every day brought her closer to September, an escape.

THEY WERE ON AN EVENING walk, holding hands. It was too hot to hold hands and Bea let Sang's hand drop.

Do you ever wonder about the lives inside these houses? Bea asked.

Not really. Sometimes I'll see someone getting out of their car, walking up the steps of their house...Sang shrugged.

Ahead of them a man got out of his car and half ran up the steps and put his key into the door to a three-storey semi-detached. Bea stopped. A light went on inside. The main floor was renovated to an open space; she could see the sliding glass door to the back garden.

This guy, she said.

Sang looked at the car, an Audi, late model, black. The house wasn't in great shape. The garden burned out like so many, the paint tired, steps worn, sidewalk bricks heaved, the retaining wall slowly bursting.

A divorce lawyer who's divorced, he said. They had a house in Rosedale, but the mortgage was too big to swing for either of them after the split. They sold it. She's in a condo downtown. He's here. They're splitting the cottage—she gets it June and August; he gets it July and September.

Bea thought it might be pretty close.

What secrets are in that house? she asked.

There aren't any, Sang said. They're all in the last house—who in the office he wanted to fuck, the lawyer two floors down he sort of flirted with. Now he's on his own, he doesn't need secrets, and he misses them.

It was dusk and Bea felt a drop, almost a mist, prelude to a drizzle. They looked up to the darkening sky.

We should turn back, Sang said.

She remembered walking in London, it was March and never stopped raining. Wet, grey, history-laden London. They were staying in a dismal, damp bedsit in South Kensington where you put coins into a tiny heater. Too cold and clammy and sad for vacation sex. In the morning, they ate an unfamiliar breakfast in the windowless basement. They stood in museums long enough to dry off then went back out into the rain. They ate chips and wondered if they were in a black-and-white movie and wondered how so much history had piled up in this depressing weather.

It started to rain, the drops picking up steam, and they started to walk faster.

Do you remember London? Bea said.

London.

The rain.

God, did we see the sun.

We were worried it was done, retired, moved on, taken up golf, that we would never see it again.

IT WAS SUNDAY, TOO HOT to do anything outside, and Bea worked on Sang about going to a superbly air-conditioned afternoon movie and he said he had work to do, which was probably true, but it was also probably true that he wouldn't actually do any of it. He finally relented and they started throwing out possibilities, each of them exercising their veto almost instantly. Choosing a movie for them was like an Italian election—corrupt and exhausting and far too many candidates. In the end a compromise and no one getting what they wanted.

Sang had developed a complicated, shifting system to gauge the worth of first-run films. He would ask Bea what she wanted. Do you want to be swept away? Depressed? Are you going to be depressed for two *days?* (*Blue Valentine*) His tone bordered on the confrontational. Was it worth fighting traffic, paying for parking, eating too much popcorn just to get depressed by some foreigner's epic despair? Bea countered that they would feel diminished when it showed up on a year-end Best Films list and they hadn't seen it. Sang covered every angle and it was exhausting and annoying and sucked the joy out of going to the movies, many of which had nothing resembling joy in them anyway.

After almost an hour of sporadic debate, they settled on the Nun movie. Once they got there, Sang noticed that the Nun movie started at almost the same time as the noirish detective / revenge movie.

So, if you want, you could go to the Nun, I might check out the detective movie, Sang said. He was holding a bathtub-sized popcorn box.

We bought the large popcorn so we could share.

Maybe just ask them for an empty bag.

This *always* happens, Bea said, exasperated. We have a plan and you don't stick to it.

I'm just not sure the Nun is big screen. Now that we're here.

I didn't want to see the Nun in the first place, Sang. I wanted to see *Room*. The Nun is the compromise because I didn't want to see *Sicario* and you didn't want to see *Room,* neither of which are playing *here*.

Do you want to see the detective too maybe?

What she wanted was to shoot him in a dark theatre and leave him slumped in that plush seat and get up and casually drop the gun in the garbage as she walked (at a normal pace) out onto the busy street. She wanted the security cameras to malfunction and the authorities to be baffled.

I don't want to see *either* of them.

But now that we're here…

Sang had his hand in the tub of popcorn. He kept his hand in the tub at all times, taking it out with a single annoying kernel between two fingers and quickly popping it in his mouth, then his hand right back in, searching for a specific kernel. He was territorial. She walked up to him and took out a handful of popcorn, shoving his hand aside. Popcorn flew up and joined the littered floor.

…we should just make the best of it, Sang said.

We shouldn't *have* to make the best of it, Sang. This isn't a discount vacation we booked online. We can go to any fucking movie we want. How is it we always end up at one that *neither* of us want to see, how—

It happened *twice*…

Bea counted on her fingers. *Skyfall, Elena, Nebraska*—

I *wanted* to see *Skyfall*—

Exactly.

Look, Bea, it's not like I have an evil plan—

I'd *welcome* an evil plan. You don't have *any* plan. You know what movie *I'd* like to see, I'd like to see a documentary on how a dysfunctional couple chooses a movie, how they spend two hours circling around the idea of a movie they both want to see, how they bring out critics' lists, then compare and contrast and somehow pick a movie that *no one*—

For Christ's sake, Bea, it's not that big a deal. It's a *movie.*

Right. A movie. Things blow up. People die. It's not real.

What are you talking about?

Bea wasn't sure. She took the tub away from Sang. I'm keeping the popcorn, she said.

Jesus. Okay, meet you out here in, whatever.

Bea checked her ticket then walked into the comforting darkness of Cinema Six and sat in the plush chair and fumed. She remembered going to movies with Thomas when he was young. Stupid movies, saccharine, manipulative movies with cute dinosaurs where she cried despite herself, angry that they had gotten her tears. They had rarely gone to movies as a family. At first it was just Bea and Thomas. Then, as he grew up and the movies got more violent, when things blew up and villains got eviscerated with power tools, he went with Sang. But when Bea had been sitting in the theatre with the six-year-old version, she longed for the time when she could go to any film at any time of the day, the way she did in university. She wished she was watching *Wild Strawberries* instead of *Rugrats in Paris*. Now that she could go and see anything, it had some-how gotten complicated. She was sitting alone in a cinema waiting for a film she wasn't really sure she wanted to see, and it occurred to her that the movies she'd seen with Thomas had been among the best movie experiences of her life. She some-times looked at him more than the movie, caught up in his amazement. She was angry she hadn't enjoyed it more at the time, all those stupid chipmunks and coy fucking mermaids. And she was angry that she was only enjoying her life as a movie—looking at parts of it from the back row, enjoying it in a way she couldn't when she was actually on the screen, when she was living it.

WHEN THEY GOT HOME, SANG decided to make a complicat-ed lasagna with Chinese duck and shiitake mushrooms and a cheese she didn't recognize. It was absurdly hot for lasagna; this was bloody-minded defiance.

Bea's phone buzzed and she took it out and looked at it. There was a text from Thomas, a multiple-choice question.

> *When did you first realize Dad was a dick?*
> *a. Ten minutes after you met him.*
> *b. Nine minutes after you met him.*
> *c. Yesterday, after he told me I was a useless spoiled fuck*
> *   and I have to pay my own tuition.*
> *d. All of the above.*

Did you tell Thomas he was a "useless spoiled fuck"? Bea asked.

Is that what he said? God. No, not those words, though his version is probably more accurate than mine.

Which is?

That he's drifting through university, drifting through life, and now that he's heading into second year he should maybe start to think a bit more concretely about where he's headed.

So, just basic fatherly advice.

I may have yelled. A bit.

Bea nodded. Sang was chopping onions murderously. He looked up.

He needed it, he said.

Did you tell him he has to pay his own tuition?

I may have. It would be good for him to contribute. *I* paid for everything at that age—tuition, rent, books…

But your tuition was a fraction of his, you know the economics are different. None of them will ever be able to afford a house, at least not in this city. Maybe a bungalow in a dying mining town…

But he's not contributing *anything*. He's like a fucking twelve-year-old who expects his allowance every Saturday. If he had to actually work, it might make him work harder in school.

Well, he has that job.

He's an intern for an online magazine. He makes about nine bucks a day. His life is basically a frat party. I see people like Thomas every day. That's who's sitting in my class—stoned, useless adolescents who don't have any interest in anything past their own immediate needs—masturbate, smoke up, play video games. I stare out at those brain-dead faces and I think about Thomas and I worry that we've raised another First World idiot.

Bea wondered if this was true. He must have been stoned to send that text. She looked at Sang. She'd once watched part of one of his history lectures. She'd gone to meet him for lunch. It would have been six or seven years ago. She'd gotten there early and went to the lecture hall, a large theatre that only had about twenty kids in it. All of them had their laptops open. Sang was talking about the Punic Wars. *Rome was once extraordinarily efficient. It isn't now. It's expensive, crumbling, the traffic is madness, and the cab drivers are criminals, but after a century of fighting with Carthage, it was the centre of the Western world.* She could see two of the screens from where she hovered by the doorway. One student was playing some kind of war game, shooting guys in the desert, the sights lining up another angry terrorist then pulling the trigger and watching his head blow up. A girl was looking at glasses online, trying different pairs on a photograph of herself, her head tilting slightly as she looked at each unsatisfying result then moved it into the trash.

Well, history isn't the most focused of disciplines, Bea said.

They're the ones who are supposed to be focused. History is supposed to be fluid and dynamic and instructive.

I'm just saying it isn't like engineering or medicine or something, where lives are at stake, where they're going to be making three hundred grand a year when they graduate. History is important, but in a more abstract, doomed-to-repeat-it kind of way.

Bea wondered if Sang even had a passion for history at this point. How to maintain that passion in the face of daily indifference from a roomful of stoners watching porn on their laptops. She wondered how much of his chat with Thomas was really about Thomas and how much was about himself.

Do you have any idea what it takes to go in there, day after day, and stand up in a room and talk to yourself? Sang said. It's a formula for madness.

It bothered Bea that he dismissed her own teaching efforts. It's true that it had been years ago. It was also true that she understood precisely what he was going through. But she had empathized all she could.

You tell them stories, Sang said heatedly, and without any video footage, they just can't grasp it. On the first day I ask everyone to write down one line on what they think history is. And half of them write something like, History is stuff that's been totally dead for a really long time.

Like MySpace or *Donkey Kong*.

There is no tense other than the present for these kids. They're like one of those tribes that some anthropologist discovers and they have no word for the future or the past. Everything is the present—they hunt, eat, fuck, sleep, repeat until death.

Well, you take away the hunting and fucking and I'm not sure we're much better.

Jesus, Beatrice, you sit in that gallery and listen to music and read your novel and wait for some halfwit to buy a painting of a dead cow for ten grand and you think that's the world. You and Thomas both live in a place where reality is some country you'd like to visit someday. There are no consequences. Sang started chopping again, rapid, angry strokes. You act like life is a fucking hobby. But every decision you make adds up, and then you get to a point where you realize this is what I've done, this is what I've built, and then you have to live there.

Bea sat in silence, wondering if she wanted to escalate or not. The last serious argument they'd had had been a year ago, at a point when his undeclared mid-life crisis was blooming brilliantly and he'd given her a version of this speech, that he was the only one who was actually engaged in the world, in the *economy,* that Bea and Thomas were tourists.

And now Bea stood in the kitchen, swaying gently, on the verge of domestic blasphemy: You are a pale, desiccated series of grunts and cold silences who lives in a dead sandbox where you grab a handful of Pliny the fucking Elder and throw it in the face of your colleague and fuck you fuck you fuck you.

And what relationship-ending soliloquy was sitting in Sang's head, Bea wondered. Everyone had one, they carried it around in their heads like those Nazis with their cyanide capsules. After their last big fight, they barely spoke for two weeks, gliding around the house like one of those dances where the dancers elaborately avoid one another onstage.

Bea remembered when all they did was touch, that hunger, fucking their brains out, the phrase they used. They had a tiny apartment in Cabbagetown that had an army of roaches. In the morning Sang would go down the street and pick up the odd, heavy croissants from the Croatian bakery and they made coffee with the French press and felt sophisticated and power-ful, an army that could defeat anything in its path.

That lasagna looks complicated, Bea offered diplomatically.

You have no idea.

how to pick a lock with a hairpin

THIS WAS HOW IT STARTED: Sitting in her gallery in deadly June, staring at the sun-bleached desert of west Toronto thinking about how claustrophobic her life had become, how she and Sang had wandered into different parts of the forest, how her son had vanished, how her mother was a sweet, broken harbinger of her own future, how she had somehow slipped into a modern coma that so many people were in, a hazy limbo with undefined borders and lingering ennui, and how all this was being played out in an end-of-days climate that increasingly resembled an Old Testament Hell, Bea googled "escape."

A page came up and she scanned the options and chose "Escape and Evasion." There was a video and Bea pressed Play and a woman in combat fatigues said, Kidnapped? Hostage? Prisoner of War? I will show you how to escape and evade forced captivity.

She was holding up what looked to be a credit card. Maybe you buy your way out, Bea thought.

It looks like a credit card, the woman said, showing each side several times, like a magician. She was rough-looking, pitted skin, narrow eyes, an Appalachian thinness that implied a difficult life. It's *actually* a sleeve, the woman said, and inside you have *six* tools—a Bogota Single, Double, and Triple, the Bogota Sabana, short hook, and a double-ended tension wrench. Stainless steel, flat as a piece of paper. Twenty-four ninety-nine plus shipping.

Bea squinted at it.

When we think of lock-picking tools, the woman continued, most people think of breaking into a place. But they have a more important use—to get out.

A scroll went by at the bottom of the screen—Are You Prepared for the Worst-Case Scenario? What was the worst-case scenario? Bea wondered.

When you enter anything, the woman said—a room, a building, *any* relationship—you need to see at least *two* separate escape routes. Most opportunities for escape occur early on. The farther into a situation you are, the harder it is to escape. Get to know your captor. And don't volunteer anything about yourself. She told Bea that all knowledge can be exploited, every weakness is an opportunity. The ideal escape and evasion tactics are to remain totally invisible, the woman said, while cautiously moving toward freedom.

WHEN THE GUARANTEED FOUR-DAY DELIVERY of her lock-picking kit failed to materialize, Bea went online again, and sent a note to the Kentucky manufacturer. Maybe the woman had been kidnapped and they'd taken away her credit card / lock-picking kit. Bea migrated to another site, an instructional video titled *How to Pick a Lock with a Hairpin*. The first step was to bend the hairpin so it was at a ninety-degree angle. Remove the tiny rubberized end with your teeth. The voice in the video was avuncular rather than criminal. Bea chewed off the tiny nub.

She took her laptop to the back door and sat in the stifling shade and listened to the voice explain the intricacies of the pin-and-tumbler lock, the most common kind. Inside was a series of pins that all had to be pressed to precisely the right height in order for the lock to open. That's what the grooves in a key did. To replicate a key, you needed two things: a small lever and a pick to manipulate the pins. And you could find both with a hairpin, apparently.

Now we are ready to pick the lock, that reassuring voice said.

She inserted the lever hairpin into the lower part of the keyhole. There was room at the top for the pick hairpin. You needed to put pressure on the lever to turn.

All locks have inherent imperfections, he said. This was a surprise. Bea would have thought this was an area of exactitude, perfectly machined parts fitting together then that satisfying click when it locks shut.

Ignore the pins that easily rise and fall, the voice said.

This was simple enough.

Focus on the seized pin.

She did, nudging it, worrying it. The hairpins seemed so fragile. She pressed the pin up slightly and let it fall. The first two gave easily. The seized pin was harder.

Slowly and carefully force the pin upwards, the man told her.

The sun came over the fence, bleaching the screen of her laptop. She was quickly coated in sweat, and the hairpin slipped out of her fingers and landed with a tiny ping on the patio brick. She reinserted it, probed, listened to the pins, a primitive language. It took more than an hour, but she was in.

OVER THE NEXT TEN DAYS she would find out that lock picking was a seduction, that you probed and caressed. The pressure on the lever was almost constant, with the smallest worrying motion. The pick moved inside, deeper as the pins gave way. Then that satisfying click as the barrel rotated.

She bought a lock at the hardware store and carefully removed it from its plastic, then practised on it for five hours on the dining room table until she could open it in reasonable time (eleven minutes). She took it back to the hardware store and told the pimply boy in the red company shirt that it was the wrong kind of lock, apologizing.

She went to eight hardware stores, buying locks, practising on them, then returning the locks. It had been difficult at first, but with practice it got easier. She ascribed different qualities to the different locks. The Yale was solidly American, an eastern seaboard aristocrat, with the flaws that aristocrats have (underestimating those beneath them). The Kaba brought essential Swiss traits; it was precise, emotionless, but, because of that, more predictable than some. Efficiency above all. The Kaba rebuffed her, not unkindly. The British Chubb brought centuries of tradition, though the Brits were too trusting perhaps.

The hairpins were elegant but ultimately too limited. There was still no word from her Kentucky captive, so Bea bought a lock-picking set on Amazon for twenty-nine dollars—the Klom sixteen-piece Deft Hand Lock Pick Tool Kit—"Good for amateurs and professionals alike."

SHE WOULD LEARN THAT MOST break-ins occur during daytime. Daylight offers something that darkness doesn't: anonymity. At 3 a.m. you had the cover of darkness, but you were alone and suspicious. Walking anywhere during the day, you were simply part of the urban scenery. You could walk the same street fifty times, at different times of the day. You were invisible.

So when Katherine and Philip gave her a key to their place and asked her to water their only, clearly dead plant while they were away in Iceland for six days getting some relief from the heat, Bea didn't use it. She picked their lock with her tools, and with that almost innocent act, she embraced her new life as a break-in artist.

scrap heap of history

BEA HAD TOLD HER MOTHER they'd go somewhere nice for lunch. She got in the elevator with two men who stepped in carefully, as if they were wading across a river. Everything moved in slow motion here. She asked which floors they wanted and one of them, thin and hunched, looked at her with a panicked face.

Two, he said. Then, as if she had broken him down under interrogation, blurted, Three.

She pressed both two and three. Her mother was on four. The other man just stared at her. Neither man got off on two or three and the doors stayed open for a longish moment, despite Bea's pressing the Close button. She got off at four and went down the hall, along the patterned beige carpet, under harsh light and a floral chemical smell.

She knocked on her mother's door and waited a few seconds and knocked again then took out her key and opened the door. Her mother was sitting on the sofa wearing a black Megadeth T-shirt.

Where did you get that T-shirt? Bea asked.

Her mother looked down. James. Our anniversary.

She stared at her mother. Her long-dead, rock-averse father who never remembered their anniversary rose out of his grave to give her a Megadeth T-shirt.

Well, that was nice of him, Mother. Her mother's face was dark and helpless, the last of her anger still a faint imprint. Was this T-shirt someone's shitty joke? She looked at her uncomprehending face, the fog of war, all the battles with ourselves now.

It was, Bea guessed, thirty-five degrees in her apartment. A wave of hot, stale air.

My god, Mother, it's an oven in here. Where is the air conditioning? Bea walked over to the window unit and looked at it. It wasn't on. She turned it on and it coughed and turned over like a car on a cold day, then caught. It was very loud, louder than she remembered.

Let's go out. A nice lunch.

Sandwiches today. The chef's disease.

What? We'll go out, Mother. We need to get you dressed.

On their way out, Bea registered a complaint with the woman at the desk who had the optimistic title of concierge. My mother's room is unbearable. Dorothy Billings on the fourth floor. You need to deal with this immediately.

The woman nodded vigorously, made some conciliatory noises, and wrote something down.

THE RESTAURANT WAS WHEELCHAIR ACCESSIBLE and cheery and too expensive and luxuriously air-conditioned. Bea ordered a glass of white for herself, feeling guilty, breaking her six o'clock rule.

She ordered a kale and gorgonzola salad for herself and a pasta dish for her mother that didn't look too complicated or messy, something she could eat with one hand. She couldn't bring her mother back to the home, not with that heat. The air conditioning had been on for fifteen minutes before they left, still blowing warm air. Her room was dangerously hot. This was how old people died.

I'm calling them, Bea said. We're not paying all that money for you to sleep in an oven.

Her mother ate a bite of her pasta and looked around the restaurant.

Is that Alma? she asked.

No ... I don't ... Oh hi, Bea said into her phone. This is Beatrice Billings, Dorothy's daughter. Yes, hello. I picked up my mother today and her room was an *oven*. Her air conditioner wasn't on and I turned it on and it isn't working. How long has it not been working?

Her mother was saying something about Alma's many shortcomings—loose as a shingle in a hurricane.

Bea was transferred to three unhelpful, medicated-sounding people (were they stealing people's drugs and taking them themselves? Apparently it happened all the time), and was then put on hold, giving her time to think about a course of action. She'd have to take her mother back to her own house. They could put her in the guest room. Should she be reasonable with the Galileo people, who were, after all, working for low wages in what was undoubtedly a stressful environment? Should she assume this was a brand new problem, and they would fix it right away? Or should she escalate, as Ariel would surely do if she were here, go to the nuclear option immediately—*I'm pulling her out of here today, I'm launching a formal complaint with the authorities, I'm talking to our lawyer about a negligence suit, I'm hiring a hit man to pick you all off one by one ...*

Mother, you can't sleep up there. You'll have to— Oh yes, hi, she said to the phone. She explained her mother's situation, exaggerated her condition slightly (*we're at the hospital right now, getting treated for heat prostration*), demanded immediate action.

What she got from the Galileo voice at the other end was a patient though not quite apologetic response that declared this to be unfortunate but that there have been some problems with the air conditioning units, and every repairman in the city is booked for the next two weeks and people rarely fix these things these days anyway, and they had looked into ordering new units to replace some of the ones that had been less than completely optimal, but again, due to the weather, there wasn't a unit to be found in the city. Everything was on back order and we would all just have to be patient and wait for the Chinese to manufacture another three million units and that shouldn't take long ha ha and that we were all in this together and they were providing the best care they could under the circumstances.

Under the *circumstances,* Bea said, angry now, I'm going to stop payment and I'm going to put in a formal complaint to the appropriate authorities, not that they'll do anything, but when one of those old women dies of heatstroke, it'll be entered as evidence in the lawsuit and I don't have to tell you that the two million dollars you have in legal insurance (a random guess) will give you about six months of mediocre, self-serving legal advice and then you'll need to run about two hundred bake sales a day to keep from losing the building.

There were institutional murmurs on the other end— Dorothy was a beloved client and they would do everything in their power ...

Bea pressed End and went back to her kale, her heart thumping. Dorothy the beloved client announced loudly that Alma was a cunty cunt and went back to the kindergarten mess of her pasta. Bea wasn't surprised at anything that came out of her mouth these days, but this was new territory.

She checked her phone to see a text from her son. *Tonight baby all night long.* This had to have been sent in error. Perhaps to his friend Rebecca. Bea didn't even know if she could call her a girlfriend. The text must be ironic, a quote from a song, a private joke.

Bea only knew Rebecca from Facebook postings and from an awkward conversation when she'd called Thomas on his cell and he'd picked up—a surprise—and almost immediately and arbitrarily put his girlfriend on. *Not a good match* was Bea's first impression. Though no one said that anymore. There were no more matches. It was as if the human race had ceased to pair off. They hooked up, had booty calls, meandered, didn't notice they were single, preferred screens. We might not need climate change, Bea thought, we may die out all on our own.

Her relationship with Thomas followed the same arc as her relationship with Sang, so intense at first (eighteen-hour labour, grunting, twitching, screaming) then inseparable, then lovely, then drifting apart. Thomas drifted toward Sang at first, then toward sex and freedom and stupidity, moving like the tide, that lunar inevitability. And now he seemed to have severed all ties save for the financial. For a year in high school he'd been secretive, moody, dense in the way of the habitual pothead, an ennui that was layered and punishing.

Those early years when he was helpless (as opposed to useless). The days endless, the stolen minutes, the relentless accounting of dependency. Though she remembered little of it, like a childhood illness.

She had longed to deliver the speech that would sustain him, light his path with a mythic tale. But life arrived in mundane tasks and he disappeared into his bedroom for a year, like a bewildered pet not sure of its new owner. Then he emerged one day and fluttered off to university leaving that dark space with its dark urges, suddenly gone.

Bea sent a text—*And how is Rebecca?*—then turned her attention to her mother, who was lost somewhere, her eyes a bit red, her mouth a thin, wavering line.

Bea had brought some of the photographs in an envelope. Maybe it would help her mother's memory. She took the photos out of her purse and showed her mother a picture of her and Bea and Ariel standing on a giant deck in Quebec City, the St Lawrence River behind them. Bea was twelve.

Remember this trip? Bea said, showing the photograph to her mother. You and me and Ariel. Quebec City.

Her mother stared at the photo. Quebec, she repeated.

She and Ariel were studying French in school. They drove to Quebec City in their ancient, rattling Plymouth Valiant, with its heroic name, though the car was rusting and unreliable. It had taken most of the day to drive there.

Remember we stayed at the Château Frontenac. Bea showed her a photo of the grand hotel. It was a surprising indulgence. On vacations, they usually stayed at cheap motels on the edge of town where you parked in front of your room, cigarette burns on the carpet, smelling of bleach. The Frontenac was like a castle from a children's book, filled with curious spaces and staircases that she and Ariel explored. They observed the people and made up lives for them—reclusive millionaire, international jewel thief, spy. In restaurants she and Ariel rated the french fries, comparing them to those at home, drawing up an elaborate chart that had various headings (*crispness, saltiness, ambition, likeability*), each given a number value.

Their father wasn't with them. There was already trouble in the marriage, a silence that had slowly descended. There weren't the fights she'd heard at her friend Jenny Albracht's house, her alcoholic German father yelling and throwing whatever was handy, the walls of the house marked and dented with his anger (her brother had a scar on his forehead from a hurled ashtray). But there was a cocoon forming around the Billings family, they were being wrapped in something that dampened talk and emotion. It left a hush. Her mother was a middle-aged woman trying to keep up a brave front, giving her girls a sense of the world that was larger than their silent bungalow on a pleasant enough street. Her parents' love for one another unglimpsed. She wondered what it had looked like at its peak. Those photos suggested it had once been a glorious thing. But Bea didn't remember anything glorious. By then it was simply a partnership to face a world that only understood these Noah-like pairings.

She took out the black-and-white photographs and found the one with her mother holding the baby.

Do you remember this? Bea said. This is before Air. The neighbour's baby? The house isn't the one on Euclid, so wherever you lived before we were born.

Her mother's face collapsed, retreated.

Do you remember where this was?

Summer, her mother said.

Yes. Summer.

Bea's phone buzzed and she checked it, a text from Thomas, a response to her inquiry about Rebecca, *scrap heap of history*.

So, Bea said, returning to her mother. It was summer …

Holy Name.

Holy Name, Bea repeated. Was this a church? Her mother's mental deterioration had gotten more acute in the last few months. Less lucidity and more non sequiturs.

A church? Bea asked.

But her mother was lost somewhere. Bea looked at her, the napkin tucked into her blouse, her face suddenly empty, as if every trace of her life had been suddenly heaved over the side. All that turmoil. We store it in our hard drives; you can't erase it. All her mother's life adding up to this, another world she hadn't anticipated. Though even if she had, how could she have prepared for it? You can only prepare for the life you've just left.

the pull-out method

BEA WAS SURPRISED THAT THERE were locksmith clubs. But there were. Hundreds of them across the continent, all peopled by hobbyists, allegedly. She'd found seven local clubs online, and chose the one closest to her to avoid traffic. She told Sang she had joined a book club; this week they were discussing Ishiguro's *The Buried Giant,* a book she'd read part of.

The host was a retired mailman named Murray. He was short with a thin, helpless-looking moustache and his bungalow was a swath of unfortunate smells—fried meat, air freshener, cat piss, the off-gassing of cheap carpets. There were eight people there. She introduced herself, gave the wine she'd brought to Murray, who looked confused by the gesture, and sat on a saggy sofa next to a very tall young man who introduced himself as Will. The rest of the group looked near retirement age.

Murray stood in the middle of the living room, holding up a lock. Wafer locks are barely worth the name, he said. He went on to tell them it was what you bought when you wanted the illusion of security. The cheapest lock, the equivalent of putting up a sign for an alarm company when you didn't have an alarm.

You can use a bump key on a wafer, he said. Give it a whack and there you go, Bob's your uncle.

Bea noticed that everyone else had brought a lock with them.

And now Will is going to say a few words about impressioning, Murray announced.

Will might have been twenty-five. When he rose from the couch, it was like a water bird taking flight, awkward and flapping. He was slightly hunched and had a pile of untended blond hair.

So. Impressioning, he said. He explained that it involved fitting a key blank into a lock then turning it to bind the pins. Then you wiggled the key to produce marks on the blank. Then you filed the blank to the marks. Usually some tuning was necessary. You tried the blank, noted the markings, filed it, re-try, it doesn't work, re-file.

One of the things about impressioning, Will said, is, like, it's *totally* stressful. The blank can crack. On the blade, right, near the shoulder, which is pretty much what you'd expect. You hear that crack, and it's whoa, step away from the lock. Will had both hands up and took a step back. You do *not* want to break it off in there. I don't have to tell you how hard it is to get it out. You take it out gently, and duplicate it, by hand if you don't have a machine, but I got a key micrometer on Craigslist for basically the cost of *Call of Duty,* like the early version, used. Here's the thing you can do and it's old school but sometimes, anyway, you hold the cracked key over a candle, key gets that black smoke mark, you clamp the cracked blank to a new blank and file until you hit the black smoke, you actually see that black shit in the filings, right, so that tells you right there, stop. No means no.

Bea didn't grasp any of this. She looked at the audience, and it appeared they weren't too sure either. Will seemed not to notice or not to care.

It's not hard to cut too deep, Will said sadly. I've done it. You don't have to throw out the blank, but probably in the end that's what's going to happen. If you took it to max depth, like number *nine,* and you haven't found the shear line, then, like, seriously, you've gone too far.

Is there a special tool? Bea asked.

What you want, said Will, is a number four Swiss-cut file. That's the bomb. You want a little roughness. It's, like, *super* delicate so it's kind of weird, like you would never guess. It only files going forward, so you want to go in hard, out easy, right, like zero pressure on the back-stroke.

You can get it online? Bea asked, taking out her phone to make a note.

Jeweller supplies. Out of, like, Ohio, somewhere like that.

Number four.

Definitely. That's where you start. And you have to try the pull-out method.

The *pull-out* method? Bea hadn't heard the term in thirty years.

The pull-out only works if you cut it down to a number one, so you knife-edge the blank, wiggle to check zero cuts, apply a little turning juice but pull out the blank at the same time. But you *totally* need to scribe the blank after you find the pins or you're basically, like, lost in space. You need that for filing, right. But the pull-out leaves marks.

Marks, Bea repeated, typing into her phone, not having a clue what he was talking about.

Yeah, you see the marks and you're like, *there,* right?

Bea nodded.

Don't try it on wafers.

No wafers.

It's in the wrist, Will said. You want to handle the head then go with that quick ... He twisted one of his thin wrists. Ooh baby.

Ooh baby, Bea repeated, and checked her watch.

BEA RETURNED TO THE CLUB the following week, and the week after that. Murray was the host and not all the same people were there, but Will was a regular. He was the de facto group leader. He was without anything resembling leadership qualities, but he was clearly the most knowledgeable, and there was a purity to his enthusiasm. Bea was after practical information, and Murray and the others were hobbyists who might have gotten caught up in a dozen other arcane hobbies. But Will was a purist. He loved locks. He talked about what they represented and how walking around with the skill to open them changed your relationship with the world.

Basically, the world is property, right, Will told her at one meeting. I mean, that's what drives *everything*—cities, countries, wars. *History*. People have stuff, they need stuff, they take stuff then try and keep that stuff. The way you hold on to stuff is lock it down, right. Put that shit where no one can get it.

Murray's house had substandard air conditioning and the heat crept up at every meeting. Bea took a sip of her wine.

But if you can get in there, Will said, I mean basically *anywhere,* then you hold the key, right. It's why they call them *keys*. I'm not going to go into some guy's place and steal his flat screen or anything. But I *could*. I'm not bound by the same rules. If I don't take shit, it's because I don't want to, not because I can't, and that's a big difference.

It gives you power.

Spiderman.

Maybe more like the Queen—it only exists until you decide to use it.

You can see how I'd maybe prefer Spiderman.

She finished her wine. Three of the people were wearing the T-shirts Murray had had made that said *Easy Entry* on them. She wondered if this was her last meeting with the club. The heat had taken root in Murray's house. There was a shortage of oxygen. She was perspiring beneath her linen shirt.

The thing is, Will said, the worse the outside gets, the more we're going to want to be inside, right. The more valuable "inside" will be. And not everyone can get inside. But I'll be one of them.

Bea nodded and thanked Will and waved good night to everyone and stepped out into the heavy air.

open house

The realtor pounding the For Sale sign into the dry ground
had laboured in the heat. It wasn't perfectly straight. There
was a small, cheery photo of her on it. The grass was brown,
the trees lifeless. A windless Saharan day, as dead as sand.

The next day, Bea returned. The front door had that realtor's padlock box on it, the back door was unencumbered.
There was no sign of an alarm. She had read online that the
vast majority of people who had alarms advertised the fact.
The point of an alarm wasn't to catch burglars, it was to get
them to skip your house and break into the neighbour's. The
back door had a Weiser lock that gave her a little trouble. Inside, she stopped, listened, her reptile brain tense. She felt sick
and weightless.

By the door there was a box of photographs in frames:
mother, father, two children. The woman was late forties. She
looked organized, a government employee, booked vacations
a year ahead, scheduled sex. Who knew what was behind her
smile. There are no unhappy pictures. That all happens outside
the frame. This family was in the process of moving some of

their things out so the realtor could stage the house, remove the clutter and personality and replace it with a better life.

Beer in the fridge, no art, a few books. In two days, all of it would be gone, their lives stripped to a marketable essence. Like locusts had come through. You work so hard to create something, then God sends His judgment.

Where were these people going? A transfer out west, downsizing to a condo, a divorce. People from the Old World used to move here to have a better life. Now we move to a worse life.

She never left the main floor. Her heart was beating fast, she had trouble breathing deeply. She assessed the furniture and countertop and cutlery, trying to divine their particular brand of unhappiness. A dog barked outside, then its owner's sharp, angry command, also a bark. She quietly left.

under all is the land

BEA WALKED SLOWLY, PRESERVING ENERGY, trying not to over-heat. A hot wind blew, belligerent gusts. The air was cloying, the oxygen gone. Clouds mushroomed in the west, the light dour. A damp procession of people shuffled in the heat, irritable, murderous. The whole city soiled, like something you'd found in the back of the refrigerator. Temperatures inside the Arctic Circle had reached 31 degrees C. There was a YouTube video of a polar bear standing on its hind legs then falling over, dead, a victim of the heat, apparently, though it may have been Photoshopped. A local lawyer beat another lawyer to death in an argument over a parking spot.

Bea had a list in her pocket—pharmacy, liquor store, strawberries if they were local and not outrageously expensive. There was a sandwich board propped on the sidewalk ahead of her, OPEN HOUSE. Everyone moving out, escaping. The sandwich board had Roger's name on it—Roger Hannister, Agent—and the address and an arrow pointing west. Roger had abruptly left his job teaching philosophy and jumped into real estate, leaving muffled rumours of something inappropriate. The rumours, of course, were true, more than one complaint, a trail of indiscretion. Security actually escorted him to the door, as if there was something he could steal from the philosophy department.

Now he was hosting an open house. Bea turned down the street and walked to number fifty-three. It was a generic three-storey semi-detached. The front lawn was dry prairie grass with an iron flamingo sculpture spiked into the parched earth.

Through the picture window, she could see Roger inside, pointing up to the crown moulding. A couple was nodding noncommittally. The air conditioner was especially loud, wheezing with effort.

Roger came out to the porch and took out a cigarette and lit it and exhaled upward then levelled his gaze and noticed Bea.

Bea smiled. Asking one point one, hope for one point three, she said.

Oh Bea. Wake up and smell the bull market. One point eight, counting on two point two.

Seriously, this is what two million buys these days?

Perfunctory bathroom reno, ran three dehumidifiers for four days to deal with the mould, no insulation, fixtures are shit, furnace is shit, joists sag. Took three mice out. Coat of paint, some rented furniture from that bandit on King. Voilà.

The couple Bea had seen inside came out and walked by Roger. Thanks, they said in unison.

Buyer, no buyer? Bea asked after they'd crossed the street and climbed into a Toyota.

Married six years, have a two-year-old, already thinking about schools. Don't have two million because no one has two million. On their way back to their apartment, which is hotter than Satan's helper, she's going to say, Well, honey, if we got your parents to put in a little to bring the mortgage payments down, then I think we could swing it and the baby's room is so *so* perfect and I'd paint it that colour I showed you on the colour chart thingy that you weren't looking at…Roger took a big drag and blew it out. So, long shot. They can't afford it, want it, need to decide if they want to be fucked by debt or fucked by a rented oven above a shawarma hut.

These are life's choices?

Life is about progress, Roger said, and real estate *is* progress— you can live in the house you can afford or you can live in the house you think you deserve. George Bernard Shaw said that the reasonable man adapts himself to the world but the unreasonable man persists in trying to adapt the world to himself; therefore all progress depends on the unreasonable man. Real estate depends entirely on the unreasonable man, or, more often, the unreasonable woman.

I want the tour, Bea said.

Roger smiled. Are you looking for a new house or do you just want to make me your bitch?

Mmmm, bit of both.

Roger took a drag and flicked his cigarette toward the road. It occurred to Bea that if it landed in that dry prairie grass, the house would be engulfed in flames within a few minutes. Everything so dry. You heard sirens every day.

Roger held the door for her. Do you know what the real estate motto is? he asked.

You have a motto? Like the Boy Scouts. What is theirs? "Be . . . Be something." Bea couldn't remember: Be helpful / virginal / adept / tragic?

Under all is the land, Roger said. That's the first line. Brilliant, really. Upon its wise use depends the survival of our civilization.

You're what's holding up civilization.

I'm all that stands between you and chaos.

Roger was chaos, Bea thought, though perhaps he was like a vaccination—his smaller chaos a bulwark against greater chaos.

They walked through the underwhelming living room, past a small dining room disguised by a rented nine-thousand-dollar table and chairs, a narrow fourteen-foot refinished barnwood top on steel legs and twelve elegant ant chairs that didn't take up any space. The kitchen was routine, the cabinets probably twenty years old. On the table was a pile of handouts that showed the house's specs. There was an open bottle of very good Bordeaux and six wineglasses.

The backyard— Bea started, looking through the sliding doors.

The backyard is shit, Roger said. But it has possibilities. Real estate is about possibility, it's about metamorphosis. There are forty-eight thousand agents in this city and each day they leave their house thinking their lives will change with one big sale. They stand in front of the mirror and straighten their tie and check for porridge in their teeth and give themselves a Dale Carnegie pep talk. And four thousand prospective buyers leave their houses hoping they'll find the perfect place and when they do, they won't have to commute so far to work, then they won't be so tired, and they'll start having sex again and their marriage will be saved, and their children will go to a good school and get into Harvard and meet future world leaders. The buyers want a new life, the agents want a new self. And each day these armies clash in their thousands.

Roger led her upstairs. There was another couple in the hallway, doing the math.

Bathroom is serviceable, Roger said. Kid's room is fine. But here … Roger led her up into the third floor, into the master bedroom. It was loft-like, with a deck at the back and an en-suite bathroom. This is where you manufacture the fantasy, he said. You only need one good room. Think of the sex they'll have here, like in the movies, in soft focus and slow motion with Celine Dion singing in the background.

Roger sat on the bed, the Versace sheets with a Roman pattern. Bea wondered if he expected her to sit down as well. She stared through the sliding door.

Then out to the deck for a post-coital cigarette, Roger said. He got up and straightened the sheets imperfectly. They gaze down at the neighbourhood, he said, on all those lives that aren't lived as fully as theirs.

This furniture is rented?

Even the sheets. Their stuff made you think of sick days and daytime television.

Bea opened the closet door out of instinct. Inside, half the extensive rack was empty. The rest held a woman's clothes. He'd already moved out.

Why are they selling? she asked. Divorce? She absently flipped through the rack as if it were a sale at Nordstrom.

Everyone is selling. Divorce is what holds the market up.

There's a million houses on the market, Bea said. Is there that much divorce?

People are moving up north, Roger said. An exodus. People with cottages are moving there permanently. You can't find a cottage for sale within a five-hundred-mile radius. They've all been snapped up. They'll conduct their business online, raise chickens or goats, drink well water, learn to make clothes out of hemp. It's five degrees cooler up there, the last to die.

Bea wondered how long these people had stayed together because of the house, knowing they'd have to sell then each of them rent somewhere. Years going by in miserable stasis, knowing the relationship was gone, not able to let the house go too. And now nothing of them remained—the furniture all gone. But something remained, the trailing scent of discontent. Bea closed the closet door then walked onto the deck into the hot air. Roger followed her. It was a nice view. The city sloped down toward the lake.

In every one of those houses, there is need and desire, Roger said, pointing outward. That's the modern condition. Half the city thinks a new house would change something fundamental in their lives.

Bea nodded. It was incredibly hot on the deck. No one would ever use it. People thought they would, standing here like Bea was. They thought they'd take their gin-and-tonics up here and sit down and gaze over the city. But you did it once or twice, then trudging up two flights of stairs to deal with that heat became a chore and you just went into the backyard. This had once been the perfect house for the divorced couple—the house that would change their lives, that would give their lives meaning. Roger had confronted the meaninglessness of life; he'd been a philosophy professor, it was his job. And now houses were supposed to give life meaning.

They moved back inside and Roger slid the door closed and they walked down to the main floor. Roger poured a glass of wine and handed it to Bea. She stared at it. It was 4:05, a bit early. And the warmish silky red wasn't right for this weather.

Oh, no thanks, Roger. Too hot for wine.

Roger shrugged and poured more into the glass and took a healthy gulp. The couple who had been upstairs emerged from the basement. They were forty or so, wrung out. They'd probably been to a half-dozen open houses today.

How old is that furnace? the man asked Roger.

Fifteen, an adolescent.

The man pursed his lips and nodded. Well, he said, thanks. His wife nodded and they left.

Roger waved his free hand around the kitchen. Real estate is the new religion and kitchens are Jesus, he said. The house can be shit, but if the kitchen is glorious, she sees herself making dinner like Nigella and her husband comes up from behind and gives her a hug as she sorts the juniper berries for the rack of venison and the dinner guests are all elegant and they're toasting someone who just won the fucking Nobel…

Is this the story you tell them, Rog?

You can't describe the fantasy for them. You have to get them to imagine it on their own. That's how the best advertising works. How about you, Bea? Do you see yourself here? Do you see your new life?

I don't know that I have the energy for a new life, Rog. If real estate is a religion, would that make you a priest?

Roger the atheist. He'd once told a United Church minister that half the world's problems stemmed from a bunch of ragged desert tribes fighting over whose imaginary friend had a bigger dick.

Real estate *deserves* to be a religion, Roger said. It is concrete, has actual value, provides genuine, measurable comfort, and soothes our soul in a way that stubborn myths and horseshit miracles can't. Heaven is an affordable four-bedroom detached in a neighbourhood with good schools.

What do you make when you sell this? Bea asked.

Roger rotated his hand in mid-air, back and forth. Fifty, sixty, the agency takes some of it, useless tits. More work than you'd think.

Bea knew from Penelope that Rog had sold one house last year, a down-market bungalow that probably netted him twenty grand.

Roger looked at his watch. I'm going to lock up.

This seemed ambiguous. Everything Roger said seemed ambiguous. Lock up with the two of them inside? Take a closer look at the Versace sheets.

I should run.

Errands.

Strawberries. Not the ones from Chile that taste like potatoes.

He walked her to the door.

We'll have to get everyone together, she said.

Yes. We should.

He bent down and kissed both her cheeks, lingering slightly, she thought. She turned and walked down the sidewalk and could feel his gaze.

AT THE ASIAN MARKET THE produce looked soft and forlorn. She asked if they had any local strawberries and the man nodded vigorously and pointed to the plastic cartons of whitish strawberries that had been half ripened in a truck a thousand miles away and tasted like cardboard. Even they were expensive now. Crops were failing in the south, the soil dried up, everything grown in industrial greenhouses. What is the point of them? she said, more to herself. Point, the man repeated dully.

She squeezed a few apples that yielded too much. She couldn't wait for the crisp apples of autumn, then wondered if there would be any this year. The cauliflower was bruised-looking, the peppers starting to pucker. She picked up some beets, both red and candy striped, thinking she'd make a beet salad with goat cheese and walnuts. She didn't have much of an appetite. She left the store and walked west toward the pharmacy. The sun had come out and bleached the street. She took her straw hat out of the cloth shopping bag and put it on. The light was in her eyes and even with her oversized sunglasses she couldn't see the faces of people who approached on the sidewalk. They were pale silhouettes. They reminded her of the photographs of Hiroshima victims that had been imprinted on the landscape; a human form, but lifeless.

filing the marks

BEA HAD EMAILED WILL, WHICH felt illicit. His email was on
the group list that Murray used to send out to everyone. She
wanted to talk about locks but wasn't up to the oppressive interior of Murray's house, or the weight of that odd society. So
she emailed Will and asked if he wanted to meet in a café. She
was surprised when he agreed, and wondered why he would.

In the living room she lingered at the door. In the canvas bag
was a lock she was bringing for Will. Sang was on the couch,
reading. He was teaching summer school, three courses, one of
them an evening class.

I'm off to book club, she said.

You talk about the book for an hour, have a glass of wine.

You sound like you don't really get it.

Yeah, I mean I get it, it's not for me, but I get it. Wine,
books, a kind of friendship. Women of a certain age.

There's one guy. Will. He's like six foot four, one of those
guys who's hunched over, probably was that tall in grade six
and he tried to hide it and now he can't straighten up. I have
this weird feeling he's a virgin.

How can you tell he's a virgin?

It's an aura. It just kind of emanates. Bea wafted her hands upward, fluttering. They're all virgins now. They have online porn, they don't have to have awkward prom sex in the back seat of a car with someone as inexperienced as they are.

The lock was heavy in her bag. Like the head of an enemy.

Do you think Thomas is a virgin? Bea asked.

I can't imagine that he is.

When you had the sex talk, what did you say?

The sex talk? He was fourteen. I don't know. Be nice, wear a condom, something.

Do you think he is?

Is what?

Nice.

I don't think he's mean. I can't imagine he's predatory or anything.

We don't really know, though, do we?

We have an idea.

Bea had a sudden apocalyptic thought, something she was increasingly prone to, about mothers being told their son had done something awful, killed someone, and every mother saying there must be some mistake, going back to the five-year-old version that held their hand in the park, knowing that that version could never do anything bad.

I hope so, Bea said.

Sang went back to his book. Bea left. She got in the car, took the lock out of the bag, and looked at it. A Schlage single-cylinder deadbolt five-pin tumbler, C keyway standard. She could open it with her kit in less than a minute. To her surprise, she had become adept.

THERE AREN'T A LOT OF rules for filing marks, Will told her. Basically, there's one: you see a mark, that's where you file. You can start off hard, but when you're close, I like to go one stroke at a time. You go past the shear line and that's all she wrote.

The light came in the window and lit his blond hair into a religious glow. The others in the café were closer to Will's age—twenty-five?—than Bea's.

There are skinny pins and fat pins, he said. If they're skinny, just use the tip of the file, that's enough. Fat, you can go a little crazy, they don't mind. If a pin stops marking before you get to the shear line, don't freak. That's life.

Will had an expectant look, the hint of a shrug, inviting questions.

What got you into this? Locks?

Will tipped his head. I don't know. You see it in all those movies. Someone takes out a bobby pin and gets into, like, Fort Knox.

She liked Will, liked his dedication. She wondered how unfortunate his life had been up to this point, what had driven him into the damp sanctuary of Murray's house. Around them, young people showed each other stupid pet videos. Their silence was comfortable. Bea drank her tea.

She took the lock she had brought out of her purse and handed it to Will like an offering. He turned it over, examined it, then explained it as if it were a religious text, how it came about, what it meant, how to interpret it. He spent twenty minutes going through the details. He took the key that Bea had and inserted it and turned it and they watched the bolt shoot out with that satisfying click. He handed it back to Bea, then talked once more about marks, leaning in, as if he was sharing a secret.

The thing is, he said, marks, sometimes they're, like, kind of mysterious. They don't always mean what you think they do.

THE RAIN WAS HOT, THE devil's shower. Bea found parking not far from the entrance. She signed in, those familiar, faintly searching faces in the lobby. She went up to her mother's room and let herself in. Her mother was there, she was always there, staring outside or at a screen or into the middle distance.

Mother.

Her mother looked at her, something dark moving swiftly across her face then organized into that blankness.

I brought lunch. Bea put the bag on the small table. From that French place. You like their sandwiches.

French.

I got you that brie one.

Breed along with Mitch.

The word association seemed to be increasing. *God grant me the humidity to change the way I change the tampon.*

They watched a baking program where three pleasant middle-aged women were making blueberry scones, and ate their lunch. Bea kissed her forehead and patted her cheek lightly when she left.

Good dog, her mother said.

it's perfect for you

IT WAS A LISTLESS SATURDAY, the sky distant and grey. The subway was surprisingly full, damp strangers trying to keep some distance. Bea had no money to shop, but wanted the experience, to go through the motions.

In Saks, Bea lingered over clothes she couldn't afford and didn't need; if she bought them, then she'd have to get the life that went with them. But they spoke to her. It wasn't glamour she was after; she was past that. It was something else, something vaguely therapeutic, inclusionary and suspect, something she didn't want to examine in the light. She held up a Yamamoto dress, minimal, midnight blue, skewed cut, not too formal, almost practical. She looked for the price tag and, when she found it, closed her eyes and made a wish: $335. She opened her eyes and the tag said $1,449. A saleswoman came by and smiled sweetly. It's a lovely piece, she said. Let me know if you have any questions.

Will it make my life look bigger?

Thank you, I will, Bea said.

She moved around the store, cataloguing what she liked, what would look good. She was discouraged not by the fact that she couldn't afford these things, couldn't really afford anything, but by the fact that she wouldn't get any use out of any of them. She still looked good in jeans. Maybe put her efforts there.

She browsed aimlessly, noting a few outfits, calculating whether she could afford them if they went to 60 percent off. She saw a woman pick up the Yamamoto dress and hold it up, appraising it. She held it against herself, twisting slightly. It looked to be a size six, the one Bea had looked at. The saleswoman came over and they chatted for a moment and both of them laughed about something and the woman touched the saleswoman's arm. Bea envied their easy familiarity. She hadn't wanted to engage the saleswoman herself, but now that someone else had, she wished they'd somehow hit it off.

The saleswoman led her to the change room with the dress. Bea lingered, waiting for her to come out. Her phone vibrated and she took it out of her purse and looked at the number: her sister. She thought for a moment about whether she really wanted to deal with Ariel right now. They were capable of arguing over anything: whose city had more lesbians; whether Darwin or the Beatles had more impact on humanity; private versus government garbage collection. Bea didn't even know which they had. And this was part of the problem; with her sister she could get into fights over issues she had no interest in, or any real grasp of, and she hated it when she found herself vigorously defending public health care or Britney's sex video or arguing over who was the best Batman.

She pressed Accept.

Hi.

Hi. I spoke to the people at Galileo. I think you probably know what they said.

That Mom's never been happier.

Why didn't you tell me that she was staying with you? That her so-called apartment is a *disaster?*

Her apartment was too hot. Everything's too hot. You've probably noticed. So until I got a guy I found on Craigslist to fix her air conditioner, I had her with us.

I shouldn't have to find this out from the woman working the desk, Bea.

The Yamamoto woman came out of the change room to check the dress in the brighter, less flattering light of the store. The mirror in the change room made everyone look like Kate Moss. She did an ironic twirl in it and she and the saleswoman both laughed. She stood stock-still in front of the mirror, as if she were examining someone else, then turned with military precision and marched six steps away from the mirror. She stopped, turned around, looked at herself, then marched back toward the mirror like a runway model. Bea couldn't tell if she was doing something with her face. We get what we need from mirrors.

We have to find a new place for her, Bea. I mean, she's obviously not happy there …

The woman smoothed the dress, running her hands along her sides as if she were slimming herself. She's going to buy it, Bea thought.

Bea? Are you listening? Not happy?

The issue, Air, is: Will she be happy at the next one? And the answer is no. Because the next one is going to be worse. Any day now they're going to phone and say, Oh, Dorothy is lovely, but she needs more care than we can provide here and may I recommend a maximum-security madhouse. And what exactly are you using as a definition of happiness, Air?

Oh, I don't know. Maybe not dying of heatstroke. Do you know how many old people died in Paris in that horrible heat?

It was, like, all of them basically. We could hire someone to come in.

The woman walked toward the change room and stopped. The saleswoman said something that Bea couldn't hear. *It's perfect for you.*

How much can you and Levi contribute to this upgrade, do you think?

We've been through this before, Bea. You know how Levi is, it's like a no-fly zone. And he doesn't have as much money as you think.

Levi's money was something of a mystery, family money that came from fertilizer or something.

I mean, the whole estate thing was a nightmare, Air said. They take so much, and it's so complicated. And he has that brother who's a psychopath, like practically out of *Fargo*. And my business is still in start-up mode and every bit of profit goes back into it. I mean, I'm taking a salary of *nothing*.

Ariel had opened a children's clothing store at a point when parents everywhere were suddenly questioning the value of pima cotton hats that resemble pandas and cost forty-seven dollars.

The woman came out of the change room and handed the dress to the saleswoman, who folded it elegantly and placed it on the counter then laid and smoothed tissue paper beside it. She placed the dress on the tissue paper and wrapped it, then delicately put it in the large shopping bag, and Bea felt that something was being taken from her.

... and this heat means no one is buying clothes for a one-year-old, Air said. It's too hot to even *think* about layering ...

The woman opened her purse and took out her wallet. She started counting out bills; she was paying in cash. Bea counted. She was paying in hundreds. Who carries a pile of hundred-dollar bills around? The saleswoman looked mildly surprised. Bea thought the tenor of that relationship had subtly shifted.

…we have these sweaters with a moose on them, so darling you'd go through childbirth just to have a reason to buy one…

The saleswoman came around the counter and handed the bag to the woman, who took it and turned and walked toward Bea. The saleswoman was scrutinizing her, her look of curiosity changing into something closer to suspicion. As the woman got closer to Bea, she could see that she was older than she'd thought. Over forty. Good skin. Her blond hair was expertly streaked, her shoes expensive though practical, Prada walking shoes.

Bea turned to follow her, the phone at her ear.

Maybe she could come out and stay with you and Levi for a bit, Bea said, knowing the answer to this would be a long, defensive no. She followed the woman, walking twenty steps back. The woman went down the escalator, stopped at the perfume counter and sprayed mist from a tester and walked through it. She quickened her step, the martial step of someone who wants to get home and try on her new dress again in the familiar mirror of her bedroom, walking in it, stopping, turning, examining the back, the side, lifting it up playfully.

…and I mean, you *know* this, Bea. Empathy isn't necessarily his strongest … and the timing …"

The woman slowed by the watch case, looking down through the glass. Bea looked around. What would the value of everything on this floor be? The Donna Karan Liquid Cashmere Perfume, the Montblanc TimeWalker watches. Millions certainly. Tens of millions. The whole floor sparkled. The air sparkled. Perhaps that was the most valuable thing, the cold, soft air. It was caressing, not the vulgar blast you got in a theatre. It brushed against her face, cooling and soothing.

The woman exited onto the street and Bea followed, that hot air welcome for a minute before it oppressed.

...you know what, I would like that, Ariel said. I really would. And you know what else?

Mom would like it, Bea said to herself automatically.

Mom would like it. She would.

The woman stopped at the light, waiting to cross, and Bea stopped and stared up at nothing.

Where *are* you, it sounds like you're in traffic...

When the light turned green, Bea followed. She didn't really know why, an instinct.

Bea, are you even *there*...Look, I don't want to be a bitch and I know you're dealing with this as well as you can...

The woman walked west on Queen. Bea assumed she had a car parked nearby, a sparkling suv. But this seemed unnecessarily far to park.

...it's just that right now is maybe the *worst* time...

I have to go, Air. I'm in traffic. Distracted driving. I'll kill someone, honestly.

She pressed End, and put the phone in her purse.

Bea Bea BEA!

She hadn't pressed End. Her sister braying out of the phone in her purse like a hostage. She took the phone out and stabbed at it with her index finger as if she were killing ants and put it back in her purse.

She followed for another block. The phone rang. It had to be her sister. Bea kept her eyes on the Yamamoto woman. She didn't pick up but launched into an animated conversation with Ariel. Oh Air, great to hear from you, it's been, what, almost two minutes since we talked, and it was *so* good to have the same conversation we've had six hundred times, and you know, I've been thinking the best thing might be to put a pillow over our mother while she's sleeping, but maybe we should get a second opinion. Anyhoo, give my best to Levi even though he's a dickish tightwad with deeply rooted narcissism issues and what are the odds of two narcissists getting together, but I guess neither of you would really notice would you ha ha, and I hope the market for fifty-two-dollar T-shirts the size of a napkin with cute sayings on them—"Colicky and Headed for Harvard"—I *really* hope that market comes roaring back!

Bea suddenly wondered if the phone was on somehow. There wasn't any kind of automatic answering thing, was there? Who knew with phones? You could send a man to the moon with one now. Oh Jesus. She fished it out of her purse and turned it on, and would it have turned on if it was already on and her sister was sitting there listening to this shit?

She walked toward the art gallery, down a side street, half a block back, perspiring like crazy. The houses were a mix of gentrification and the original immigrants, old couples sitting motionless on their small porches. The woman walked through the gate of a modest two-storey house, a postwar semi with little exterior renovation. The woman wasn't a gardener if the front yard was anything to go by. She took out her key and let herself in. It wasn't the house of someone who paid fifteen hundred dollars in cash for a dress at Saks. Bea wondered if there was a partner in there. Something was in there.

it's perfect for you, part two

SANG WAS STILL THERE WHEN she left, sitting at the kitchen table, looking at his phone.

I'm off to see the Georgia O'Keeffe exhibit, she said. All those oversized vaginal flowers.

Kind of one-note, Sang said.

In a groundbreaking kind of way.

I like the cattle skulls better. They say something.

What they say is death. The flowers say life.

They give birth astride of a grave, the light gleams an instant, then it's night once more.

Who said that?

Beckett. Who else.

You're sure you don't want to come? It's free with our membership.

I've got work, Sang said, turning back to his phone. I can always go out and look at the flowers in the garden.

More death than life out there.

Bea left and drove downtown. She parked three blocks away. She was wearing the large straw hat, the celebrity sunglasses, a white T-shirt. She had a large cloth bag with a beige linen shirt in it in the event she had to change. She walked slowly to the Yamamoto house, her heart already speeding up. She passed a handful of barely clad, glazed pedestrians moving like zombies.

She'd strolled the neighbourhood for the better part of two days. Yesterday she watched them load up their car—a slightly battered Honda. She guessed they were going away for at least three days. Somewhere in the country probably, somewhere north of here, on a lake. Her husband was perhaps five years older, Bea's age, blandly handsome, longish greying hair.

She walked down the narrow passage between their house and the next, and opened the back gate. The fence was eight feet tall. There was a large garage, no indication of an alarm. She opened the gate timidly and walked in. The backyard was nicer than the front. The lawn furniture appeared to be hardwood. It wouldn't have been cheap. There was a large tree that blocked the alley and a smaller tree to the side. With the high fence there were no obvious sightlines for the neighbours.

She knelt down in front of the lock, a Schlage single-cylinder, probably a 2¾-inch deadbolt. Right in her wheelhouse. Her heart raced. She tried to will it to slow down, took deep yoga breaths, and pulled a wooden chair up to the door and went to work. One of the pins wasn't on board, which was good. She probed and caressed and applied subtle pressure on the cylinder. It took four minutes, then that lovely quiet pop.

She let herself in. The rush of relief that no alarm sounded.

On the table by the front door, she picked up a letter addressed to the two of them: Richard and Jenny Semple. Dick and Jen. So that if someone came by—a sister, someone was watering plants or whatever—she could say, Oh didn't Jen tell you? Hi I'm Anne (or Faye or Helen), I'm doing some design work for them.

The living room had tasteful, expensive furniture, a Barcelona chair, a Jacobsen egg chair. There was a lot of art, and some of it was quite good. In the kitchen, copper pots and French cookware and Danish flatware with a geometrical flair. The dining room table was oversized and would have cost ten thousand dollars, Bea guessed.

The exterior of the house bordered on decrepit. It had very little curb appeal, as Roger might say. Drab and under-maintained. The house didn't match its contents.

The basement door was off the kitchen and she tried it and was surprised to find it locked. She looked at the lock, a Weiser single-cylinder, a tube lock, more lock than you normally saw on an interior door. What was in the basement? It was a house that held secrets, though she had a frisson of teenage fright—basements were where horror dwelt. You went down there with a flickering candle and then there was a scream.

Bea pulled up a kitchen chair and sat down with the lock, an enjoyable puzzle. She took out her kit and went to work. There was no pressure here, she could take her time. It was stifling inside the house, they'd turned off their air conditioning. She had a hair band on to keep the sweat out of her eyes. It took three minutes.

She turned on the light at the top of the stairs and stood for a moment. She wasn't sure she wanted to go down there. What if there was a kidnap victim in a cage, or a freezer filled with remains. Would a sociopath shop at Saks? She seemed normal, at least until she pulled out those hundreds.

She went down.

There were shelves lining the walls, industrial steel shelves that were two feet deep. The windows had blackout curtains on them. There were appliances still in their boxes—microwaves, toasters. She examined them. Expensive stuff. A red-enamelled espresso maker that would have cost at least four thousand dollars. In the corner, three flat-screen TVs. She opened a closet door and jumped backwards. Two haz-mat suits hung there, looking like mummified humans. There was a forty-pound bag of rice on the floor and three cases of bottled water.

She tried to find the narrative. They were thieves.

Bea suddenly felt spooked. For a moment she was rooted in place. The basement was a warehouse of sorts, filled with stolen merchandize. And two haz-mat suits as a hedge against the apocalypse. She went back up the stairs, turned off the light, and closed the basement door.

She sat down at the dining room table and thought about their lives. She wondered how they'd met, how they'd started on this path. Some people just seemed to find the perfect partner. Happy their whole lives. A rare thing. But you saw them sometimes, you could tell. Had they met at a party? *What do you like? Oh, Fleetwood Mac, walks along the beach, breaking into houses.* It was odd they didn't have an alarm, but maybe they felt it would draw attention. This wasn't a street where you saw signs for home security.

Bea went upstairs to their bedroom. The second floor had been renovated so that there was a large master bedroom and a large bathroom. The original plan would have been two small bedrooms and one very small bathroom, built eighty years ago. They'd knocked out walls and one of the small bedrooms was their walk-in closet. Clearly no children.

Bea walked into the closet. Jen had two-thirds of it. Bea moved hangers along the rack, quickly assessing her wardrobe. A lot of Armani, some elegant pants. She found the Yamamoto dress and pulled it out. She was tempted to try it on. She gazed at the line of shoes, opened a few drawers.

There was a noise from downstairs, something outside (inside?). Bea's heart leapt again, a sudden stab of deep, intense regret. She looked out the window. A blue uniform appeared on the sidewalk and she felt nauseous then realized it was a courier. He'd been on their creaky porch.

She took the Yamamoto and walked back downstairs and laid it on the pristine kitchen counter.

This isn't stealing. You can't steal something that is already stolen, or at least bought with stolen money. This probably wasn't true. She folded the Yamamoto and quickly put it in her straw bag. She put on her sunglasses and straw hat and left through the back door and walked through the yard into the alley. With her head down she walked as slowly as she could manage. Her whole body was wet with perspiration, flowing freely. When she got to her car, she started the engine, turned the air conditioning up to the maximum, and sat. After two minutes, she pulled away slowly.

The house was modest because they couldn't pay cash for it. But they would have paid cash for the renovation, for that furniture, all those clothes. The eight-foot fence gave them privacy as they unloaded things from the garage.

They were in this together. They broke into places, stole things, felt that adrenalin rush together. They might have sex inside the place they were breaking into. Then they came home, had a drink, talked about it, relaxed, laughed.

What would they do when they realized someone had broken in? The back door and basement door unlocked. They were already preparing for disaster and now this new wrinkle. They'd see the markings on the locks, slight but unavoidable. For a moment they would be filled with fear, expecting their house to be emptied. Then a quick casing of the place to find nothing gone and a new, much greater fear. Who broke in? *Why* did they break in? What did they want? In a week or so Jen might notice the missing Yamamoto. Then what?

Their new fear would be open-ended, Hitchcockian—it would continue to haunt them. Even if nothing like this ever happened again, they would always be carrying this; someone knew they were thieves. A thief knew they were thieves. And what would a thief do with that knowledge? Nothing good.

They would get rid of everything in the basement, probably not getting a good price given the fire sale. They'd get an alarm system, better locks. They might even try to sell the house, though it would be difficult to move, such an odd hybrid. A gay couple might want it. Bea guessed they had a substantial mortgage. They could buy another down-market home and pay cash to have it renovated. They weren't big-time, these two. They knew that whoever broke in could come back, could call and blackmail them perhaps, could tip off the police. Bea felt a terrible guilt. She had introduced uncertainty and dread into their lives. Though this was what they did to other people: violate something precious, take away their sense of well-being. Sanctuary was fundamental to humans; we build houses and churches to shield us from the Lord's burning rain.

Bea drove home, blooded.

IT HUNG BEAUTIFULLY. THE MATERIAL, which Bea had originally thought was a very fine wool, was in fact a complex combination of wool, silk, elastine, and some kind of engineered Japanese fibre made from god knows what, and it managed to make her look both slimmer and more intelligent. It gave her a *gravitas* that hadn't been there when she stood in front of her bedroom mirror critically judging her naked body, the pale, uncertain contours. It was remarkable that a dress could fill you with a sense of purpose.

Sang was gone, teaching. A lovely light came through the venetian blinds, striated shadows fanning out on the floor, magic hour light.

Bea moved across the room, past the mirror, examining herself as she walked. She took off her heels and walked by in the other direction in a pair of flats, which seemed more Japanese, and glanced at the mirror as if she had just suddenly noticed herself. She adjusted the shoulder, smoothed the sides, and walked toward the mirror, examined the pores of her face from one inch away, then walked back and looked over her shoulder at her ass.

She thought of the photo of her and Ariel dressed up as their mother. Skirts tied around their waists with string, blouses that hung down, sleeves rolled up. They wore their mother's jewellery, necklaces and jangly bracelets that slid off their thin wrists. They started out in her shoes but abandoned them because they were impossible to walk in. They poured lemonade into highball glasses and took out candy cigarettes, and talked to each other in adult voices, stylized banter taken from old movies on tv, bits borrowed from their parents or neighbours. Ariel sashayed, smoking her candy cigarette with one hand supporting her elbow, withdrawing the cigarette and blowing imaginary smoke upward. Wearing their mother's clothes made them think they had access to that rich adult existence that sprang to lurid life when all the children of the world were asleep.

Bea put the heels back on and went downstairs to the kitchen. The clock on the stove said 5:38. She poured a glass of white wine and swirled it and took a sip and walked around the house in the glorious Yamamoto.

Sang would be home around seven. They didn't have anything planned for the evening, didn't have anything planned for any evening. They might need to order takeout, unless Sang was stopping at the supermarket on the way home from work, which was unlikely. She suddenly felt a vicious desire for a cigarette. If Roger was here, she would bum one, light it up, blow out that comforting smoke, and be filled immediately with searing regret.

The doorbell rang. Bea's heart jumped. The irrational thought that the woman would be there, the thief, demanding the return of her dress. Her instinct was to race upstairs and change. She lifted the blind slightly and looked out the window. There was a delivery truck parked on the street. She put down her wine and opened the front door.

There was a man in blue pants with a matching blue shirt that had red lettering on it. He might be twenty, handsome, aware of it, a boy who still thought his high school charm was a valuable asset.

Ms Billings?

That's me, she said, taking the package from his outstretched hands. An offering.

Sign there please.

She heard her cell ring. Her busy life. The phone was on the dining room table and the ring reverberated, louder than normal.

Oh, hang on, she said, I have to get that.

She could see from the display it was Sang.

Hi, listen, I'm going to have a drink with Gordon, he said, waiting a beat. Wakowski. Remember you met him at that faculty thing. Bea tried to picture a Gordon. Has a book deal, Sang said. I told you about it. Another valuable addition to the seven hundred Kennedy books. So.

Bea had trouble keeping his colleagues straight. She only saw them once or twice a year at most.

We don't really have anything for dinner anyway. Delivery guy is here.

Delivering what?

Love.

Did you buy something online?

Who can keep track. Maybe. She rarely bought anything online, other than lock-picking kits (three now). She didn't trust those sizing charts, and you had to see it on anyway. The odd book. Did we order something? she asked. A part for something? Things were always breaking down—dishwashers, ceiling fans—then you ordered a part from a German website and by the time it arrived, you'd replaced whatever it was you were going to fix.

I don't know. Probably. Oh, there's Gord, so I'll see you later, then.

Bea pressed End and went back to the door. The dress moved with her like a dance partner. She wasn't wearing panties.

My apologies, she said, taking the pen and signing a scrawled version of her signature on the tablet.

The man nodded and took it and walked back to his truck. The package looked to be a part for the bathroom faucet they'd ordered. It would be another month before Sang tried to install it himself, then another couple of weeks before he called a plumber.

She walked to the kitchen and caught a glimpse of the dress as she walked by the hall mirror. She had wanted to be at the centre of something. Everyone does. Then they end up being the centre of their own life, and it isn't enough. She had a sudden ancient longing, a memory of her fifteen-year-old self standing in a new dress that her mother had helped her pick out, going to a school dance, the dress hinged to a sense of possibility. Something good would happen to her, something warm and inevitable and miraculous. But nothing good would happen in a stolen dress. It was Exhibit A.

She went to the refrigerator and took out the wine and poured a little more in her glass. She opened a can of tuna and added some leftover couscous and drizzled a little of the wasabi vinaigrette that hadn't been a hit, then went downstairs and sat on the couch and turned on the TV and started watching a show about stolen art. Apparently the world contained a trillion dollars of stolen art, hidden in basements or attics or country homes. Stolen Van Goghs in locked rooms where thieves sat and admired Vincent's lunatic brush.

Bea took a bite of her tuna, careful not to spill any on her dress. If she stained it, she'd have to kill herself.

two

agreeable theft

EVERY HOUSE HAD ITS OWN smell, complex layers—volatile compounds baking in the heat, the accumulated dinners, traces of cleaning products, the broad, democratic scent of a family, the wolf pack happy in its redolence.

The curtains were drawn against the midday glare, the air conditioning off. She moved quickly and soundlessly up the carpeted stairs. The second floor was an oven, the most over-used metaphor these days. The master bedroom was spacious, the closet uneventful, the medicine cabinet untroubled. Everything tingled. Her senses feeding information to the amygdala, the autonomic nervous system on the verge. Adrenal glands aching to release all that wartime adrenalin. Her senses were heightened. She heard things, noticed things she might not have (a crooked coat hook). Her nerve endings were sensitive to the smallest movement, a change in the air, a smell. She'd become an animal, all sensation and survival. Her movements economical, a predator's movements. Though she was prey as well, every sound a threat.

She moved down the hallway to the study and sat in the desk chair. Their computer was password protected. She searched the drawers, then looked in the filing cabinet for a list of passwords. No one could remember all their passwords and you couldn't have the same password for everything. The filing cabinet didn't have anything obvious. In the drawers small stacks of papers, neatly arranged. Extra pens still in their packaging. An ordered life.

She hadn't chosen them randomly. The Thorolds, Gilda and James. They lived eight blocks away. A couple who were roughly her age. They had a son who might have been fifteen, a dark-haired boy whose expression was blank in the school photo that sat on the desk, tight-lipped, hiding braces, hiding something.

The front hall closet was neat, a few of the coats in dry cleaners' plastic. The living room furniture was antelope-coloured, a glass coffee table. They had neither good nor bad taste—the neutrality of a show home.

The basement didn't smell of mould or mildew. There were coats in storage, a small bathroom, the laundry room. In the predictably neat furnace room there were four plastic tubs with lids stacked on top of one another. She opened the top one and found neatly folded Halloween costumes, a princess, a tiger. The second had Christmas decorations, as did the third. The bottom one had flannel sheets. When she pushed it slightly, it didn't move. She took the sheets out. There was only one. Beneath the sheet were silver bars. They were flatter than the trapezoid gold bars you see in heist movies. She picked one up. It felt like five or six pounds. She counted them—twelve. What was the price of silver? She had no idea. Less than gold, but still quite a bit.

Why did they have silver bars? Bea walked to the back of the basement to a door with a small padlock on it. She picked it quickly and opened the door and stared at the contents for a full minute, cataloguing. Hand tools, cans of food, solar blankets, matches, lighters, survival manuals, a crossbow. A hedge against the apocalypse. This family was far better positioned for survival than her own. They would be bartering silver for food in the post–climate change wasteland while Bea and Sang starved. There would be no more history and no more art. Everyone preparing for the worst. How many other homes contained this? She put the bars back in the tub and put the lid on and went upstairs.

On the second floor, in the boy's room, homework arranged on his desk. In his closet there was a stack of shoeboxes and she opened the top one. Inside was a pair of new sneakers. She opened the next one and found the same pair of sneakers, then realized they were a size larger. There were three identical pairs, all in different sizes. They had bought them on sale. He would have the same running shoes for the next three years, incrementally less cool each year, a curse.

Thomas had had a fixation with sneakers, checking German websites to find something that no one in the school could possibly have. When he went away to university, it changed her relationship with Sang. They no longer had that foil, they had to communicate directly with one another. Thomas had taken up so much space, most of it when he was an infant. It was an odd inverse mathematical relationship: the larger they got, the less space they took up, until they were completely grown, then they moved out and didn't take up any space at all. And what had she and Sang filled that empty space with?

She remembered the day in the supermarket when he was three. She was in a rush, distracted, frustrated, hauling Thomas through the store and grabbing things off the shelf. She stopped to read the ingredients on some package, to make sure they weren't filled with DNA-altering chemicals, then looked up to find him vanished. It was like a special effect. She thought she'd only taken her eyes off him for a second. The aisle was empty. That instant desperation, a desperation she'd never felt, sudden, stabbing, already a worst-case scenario. She ran to the end of the aisle, looking for him, but he wasn't there, ran to the aisle beside theirs, where there were people, but no Thomas. Then back to the aisle on the other side. A woman looked at her. *My child,* Bea said. The woman managed a look that was both empathetic and judging. Someone had taken her son. Right from under her nose. There were a million movies about this. Children disappearing, aging on milk cartons, their features updated each year by a software program. She was in tears, racing up the aisles, sick to her stomach. *Please God.*

He was standing in the frozen food section, his face pressed against a cold pizza clutched in those small hands. The relief was greater than anything she'd ever experienced. She collapsed, her knees buckling, and the sobs came out, heaving, huge, as she moved toward him on her knees then held that uncomprehending bundle, squeezing him. And these thoughts prompted a sudden onset of sobbing as she sat on this boy's bed. Bea cried for a bit then sat up suddenly, not sure if she'd been sitting there for two minutes or twenty.

She went downstairs, softly, despite the fact that no one could hear. She had left her basket on a chair. In it was a baguette, a prop. She put her hat and sunglasses on, looked around, and walked to the back door. The backyard had a small garden that lacked imagination and a patio made of rose-coloured interlocking brick. There was a table made of some kind of engineered wood and four plastic chairs and a large umbrella in its own stand. The wisteria was dull from lack of water.

The fence was six feet tall, made with overlapping boards, so she couldn't see into the lane. She listened at the gate, her ear near the wood. After ten seconds of silence she lifted the latch gently and opened the gate. She stepped into the alley with as natural a movement as she could muster. A woman was standing to the left, ten feet away, motionless, checking her cellphone, waiting for her dog to take a dump. She held a small opaque plastic bag in one hand. She looked up, squinting.

Oh hi, the woman said.

Her Portuguese water dog was hunched and constipated. It looked embarrassed, though the woman didn't.

Bea's heart was galloping, a wild thumping, preparing for flight. Adrenalin ricocheted around inside her like a stray bullet. Her breathing instantly shallow. Hi, she said as casually as possible. Did this woman know the Thorolds? Never volunteer anything; it implies guilt. Not dog-walking weather! she said, too cheerily.

The woman smiled. No, it's *hell* for him. A black coat. What is it—*forty?*

She wasn't sure if the woman was assessing her.

Is that Panier Cirque? the woman asked.

What?

That baguette?

Oh, no. No, it's Paris Ici. More authentic.

I'll have to try them. Though with baguettes you have to eat them like ten seconds after you buy them, don't you.

Bea nodded vigorously in agreement. This one was four days old. She was sweating heavily, grateful for the heat for the first time; everyone was sweating in this, even the innocent. *I don't know what came over me.* These were the words she was bound to utter at some point, in front of a police officer, a judge. And it was true. She didn't know.

The water dog finally completed its task and the woman put her cellphone away and put her hand in the bag.

The joys of dog owning, the woman said, stooping down.

Good luck with the walk, Bea said, and turned to walk down the alley.

Thank you.

Bea could feel the woman's eyes on her as she walked. She struggled to walk normally. Her gait was jerky and she tried to smooth it. Another thirty yards Sweat poured down her back, though it wouldn't show up dramatically on the white T-shirt. The woman was probably looking at the house then looking at her then back to the house, trying to do the social math—she must be a friend, maybe a relative? When she got to the sidewalk, she turned south and allowed herself a glance down the alley. The woman and her dog were gone. Perhaps she'd gone home, was calling the police. Or knocking on the Thorolds' door. Wouldn't she have said something? Bea's heart hadn't settled down. She was suddenly exhausted. She saw her car and it seemed like a mirage, shimmering in the distance. It took forever to reach it. She opened the doors and put the bag into the back seat then got in the front and started the car. She drove quickly down the street, turned south and drove to the lights, and turned and zigzagged away from the crime. Was it even a crime? She hadn't taken anything. At a red light she took off her floppy hat and examined her face in the rear-view mirror and wasn't sure what she saw there.

a different kind of different

THEY WERE SITTING IN A restaurant where everyone was twenty years younger than they were. It was on a list somewhere. Bea had saved dozens of lists—ten best Pinot Noirs, the year's greatest indie films, the city's best pulled pork sandwich, five albums you can't live without. She attached them to the fridge with square magnets that had images of famous revolutionaries on them and the lists fluttered every time she opened the fridge door. She rarely acted on any of them. But now she and Sang were sitting in front of two Negronis, listening to music neither of them could identify, basking in the suspected hipness of a restaurant that was number eight on someone's list. Outside, the evening heat was still barbarous. A stream of people moved past the window, shiny and exhausted.

Bea had first reserved, then told Sang they were going out to dinner. He didn't want to go. Work, he was tired, it's too expensive. She insisted, kept at it, feeling something was at stake. They had to get back to a place where they at least talked. A nice dinner, sex, something revived. He'd followed her out to the car like a child heading to the dentist.

Do you think we had more fun than this crowd? Bea asked.

What, when we were this age? Sang looked around. God, I hope so. How old are they, anyway? Are these people thirty?

Bea surveyed the room. A lot of beards and too-tight sports jackets on the men. The women were tattooed, Tibetan symbols, Celtic crosses, short calligraphic paragraphs in another language. They wore loose, layered singlets and everyone's hair seemed dyed. They were animated, laughing, poking each other.

They look like an ad for happiness, Sang said, rather than the real thing.

What are we an ad for?

Sang took a sip of his Negroni and made a face. I'm not sure about it, he said. They had agreed to try things they'd never tried before, so they both ordered Negronis, a name they knew though neither was sure what was in it.

I like it, said Bea. It tastes Continental. She took a sip then picked up the menu. Remember, it has to be something you've never had.

This isn't one of those places that serves insects, is it?

Bea shrugged. Here's one: goat varutharacha . . . The syllables came out hesitantly. Curry. You could have that.

I tried goat. That Jamaican place. It's not there anymore. What is shirasu? Oh, here they say, dried baby anchovies. Yeah, maybe not.

They have suckling pig. You rarely see the word "pig" on a menu.

You want to avoid the farm narrative, all that death.

The music seemed just a tad loud, Bea thought. She read through the menu, staring down below her glasses so she could read the print, which was smallish, and went on a bit.

She was wearing the Yamamoto, fearfully, guiltily. Sang hadn't noticed it. It was flattering, the midnight blue so complex it had a personality. Though it wasn't the right dress for this restaurant, this crowd. It was hip in its way, with its Japanese aura, its asymmetric cut, but to these people it probably looked like gingham. Too formal, too rehearsed. She checked the door nervously every time a couple came in, expecting to see Dick and Jen.

She envied them, that solidarity, joined in everything. What intimacy. Though maybe their relationship was more like those couples who own a convenience store and all that shared work only induces a trudging familiarity, moving toward death like hamsters sharing a wheel. What Dick and Jen shared was illicit; each of them held the key to the other's downfall. Though perhaps that was true of most couples.

Do you want red or white? Sang asked. Should we get a bottle?

I think I'm white tonight.

Do you know what oca is?

No.

How about romanesco? Salsify? Jesus, can there be that many vegetables we've never heard of? Are they inventing new ones?

Salsify? Really? It sounds like a verb. Bea checked to see if there was any description and there it was: *the consistency of a root vegetable with artichoke flavour believed to help with snakebite.*

Sang sat motionless, looking up, listening. Is that Gateway Drug? he asked.

What?

The song that's playing. Is it the band Gateway Drug?

Oh, how the hell would I know, Sang.

They hadn't been to a restaurant in almost a year. She remembered a restaurant they used to go to when Thomas was very small, a huge Greek place that didn't mind unruly children. There was a fountain in the centre of it and when Thomas was two, he'd wandered over and she and Sang both felt the other one should be watching and they were at that moment when they were a bit overwhelmed with their child and they weren't having sex and there was an unspoken accounting over the parenting chores with each feeling they were doing more than the other and neither of them was watching him and he fell into the fountain. Bea rushed over and pulled him out, seized with panic, though the water was only six inches deep. He was crying, that look of betrayal (a look he'd managed to keep). A woman sitting near their table told Bea it only took two inches of water to drown.

What do you think Thomas will remember from his childhood when he's our age? Bea asked.

I don't know. What do you remember?

Sometimes I feel like I remember everything. That I've compressed the files for storage but that everything is there. It seems more eventful than Thomas's somehow. It bothers me that he's so far away and we know so little about his life.

Sang returned to his menu.

Who he's dating, what his grades look like, who his friends are. I mean, we really don't know anything. I send him texts and I get back these haikus.

Sang looked up. Were you that different at that age? Didn't you just want separation?

Maybe, I don't know. I just feel like I'm losing track of him somehow.

She went back to the ambitious menu. There were paragraphs about provenance and sidebars on cooking techniques. It was like an annual report.

Oh god, Sang. Look at this—casu marzu.

Which is . . .

Sheep milk cheese with *live* insect larvae. You *have* to order it. I'm serious.

You're joking. Where?

Look, right here. She pointed to it on his menu. You have to try it. I hear they make the best casu marzu in town. She laughed. Seriously, if you eat it, I'll blow you.

Sang examined her. This was uncharacteristic. Bea went back to the menu and Sang stared at his wife.

The waiter came over. He was in his twenties with an unruly man bun barely held in place with chopsticks. His forearms were covered in dark-blue ink that told some kind of story.

Any questions about the menu? he asked.

How long have you got? Bea said.

Ha ha, it is a bit of a walk on the wild side.

I'll have the casu marzu, Sang said. Medium rare.

Yeah, so it doesn't actually come in—

It was a joke.

Right, but, like, you *do* know that it's—

Larvae.

Yeah.

Can't get enough of that shit, Sang said.

Wow, okay, living the dream. Casu marzu for the man. He turned to Bea.

How old would you say the suckling pig is? she asked.

Well, I think the deal is about two weeks, which I know sounds kind of young maybe…

Yeah.

But I mean, it's not as if it was going to have, like, a brilliant career or anything.

No. No, still. Bea looked back at the menu. She didn't want the image of that piglet yanked from its mother's teat then clubbed for her dinner. Piglet and Pooh. The tandoori eel, it's not slimy, is it?

Opposite of slimy. Totally.

Bea moved her head back and forth. Okay, the eel, then.

Eel and bugs, the waiter said. He gathered up their menus. How are the Negronis?

I'll have a glass of that New Zealand white with the eel, Bea said.

Give me a wheatgrass beer to go with the bugs.

Excellent choices.

Was that Gateway Drug? Sang asked the waiter. Playing just before.

Like the last song?

Yeah.

I don't know, man. I think it might have been Average Cock, but I can check for you.

No, that's okay.

He walked away and Bea laughed. I can't believe we missed the last Average Cock concert, she said.

She listened to the song that was playing, dirge-like, vaguely Germanic. It reminded her of music they'd heard in Europe, before Thomas was born. Waking up in a small hotel in Burgundy, wine-stained, a glorious night, the cool white cotton sheets, the blankness of morning.

She looked around the restaurant at the thirty-year-old couples who had $180 to spend on dinner on a Wednesday night. Maybe Thomas would be one of them at some point. He would emerge from his attenuated teenaged existence and become whatever these people were.

She hadn't seen Thomas since Christmas, when he was home for five days and stoned for two of them, it appeared. He was uncommunicative and gangly and vague, and she wondered if they'd lost the knack for being a family.

She wanted to tell Sang that she was unable to imagine their son sometimes, unable to imagine a next phase. Thomas with a

132

wife, with a baby. And they would be the doting grandparents. Maybe there wasn't a next phase. He would move to Hong Kong to work in arbitrage and never come back. Like raising a bear cub, the mother fiercely protective then the cub grew and moved on and you never saw them again. She wanted to tell Sang that she was worried, that this fear ate at her, that the world seemed too dark and punishing a place for anyone's child. But she couldn't bear the thought of saying it out loud.

There was a din in the restaurant that was comforting, the sound of people, all those arguments and flirtations bouncing off walls that were partly covered with large, dark murals, slightly Daliesque, surreal and swirling.

She looked around at the other diners, at the end-of-days wait staff, tried to glimpse the plates going by. The morose playlist droned.

Are you feeling adventurous or doomed? she asked.

Bit of both.

SANG WAS UP MOST OF the night, vomiting, shitting. In the morning he was ghostly. He seemed to have lost ten pounds during the night. He was damp and wasted and bitter.

You wanted different, he said.

bumping and shimming

THE DAYS PASSED IN A pale, boiled blur. July lingered. Bea visited her mother, sat in her gallery, called Penelope and Katherine, cased houses, walking the stained concrete, her eyes moving behind the sunglasses. The weather settled in like an ancient feud. Every week more casualties. Afternoons smelled like rotting meat. Inside condos with high fees and a reserve fund that couldn't cover the looming infrastructure problems, couples re-examined their relationship in the sick heat, like a thumb testing the sharpness of a blade.

IT WAS THE LIGHT SHE loved: ancient, sepia-coloured, an Egyptian evening coming through the blinds. Bea took her place among the yoga penitents. Pen was already there, lying in *shavasana*. Bea rolled her mat out and lay on it with her secret knowledge. No door was closed to her. This was her current sin. Her bitter grandmother had told her that God sees all sins. Bea wondered at the sins around her, held at bay for an hour then flooding back like the tide.

The instructor, whose name she couldn't recall—their names jumbled, though at least two were the names of teas—

told them to wiggle their fingers and toes, feel the life coming back, concentrate on their breathing. She was a woman of about twenty-five, aggressively illustrated, and the elaborate hibiscus on her calf at Bea's eye level appeared to be masking an earlier, more sinister tattoo. Bea thought she might be one of those small-town girls who flee a terrible home life and come to the big city and pursue health and mindfulness and whatever with the same fervour they'd pursued drugs and ill-advised sex with a droopy thug back in Palookaville. *You can't kill your thoughts,* the instructor said in her rhythmic trill, *but you can leave them on their own for an hour and return to them, stronger, more rooted.* In her decade of sporadic yoga classes Bea had never successfully cleared her mind of anything. She lay down and all her problems flowed to her head.

When they stood up, Bea surveyed the class. Fifteen or so people. Penelope was sandwiched between two shirtless middle-aged men, neither of them in good shape, pasty lumps lolling through the sun salutations, sweating heavily. It was hot in the room, the consuming heat of India. Were they hoping to meet women here? Drinking that awful tea after the class, cooling off, insinuating themselves.

It bothered Bea that although she had been coming to this particular class for two years and the order of the poses was rigidly fixed, she often didn't know what was coming next. How could she not have memorized it by now?

She moved through the poses, thinking of the photograph of her father holding the baby. Could it have been theirs? It would explain those photographs, that joy. It would explain something about her parents' marriage. Another sadness her mother carried.

She tried to observe her breathing like one of those CSI programs, her breath rambling down the bronchial tubes and filling her lungs, sending oxygen past the cilia to the bronchi, then the tiny alveoli (?), which pushed it to her capillaries, which raced down her still very viable legs. She dimly remembered this sequence from a biology model she'd made with Thomas in middle school, a model that had involved a lot of glue and coloured construction paper and she had ended up doing most of it.

In her final *shavasana* Bea lay there remembering Thomas as a three-year-old, a sweet-faced boy, his rosy cheeks when they went down the small hill on the sled, the exhilaration in his face. The simple joy of speed. Those years of fish sticks and daycare and going to the beach covered like Muslims against the sun. Everything about being a family made sense then.

A heaviness came over her. Usually she got up quickly and showered, but today Bea needed another minute or so, may have said those words softly then drifted off.

When she woke, the room was empty. It had been one of those deep sleeps where she woke up both refreshed and paralyzed, unsure of her surroundings. She might have been asleep for ten minutes or three hours. She rolled up her mat and hurried down to the showers. Pen was in the change room, wrapped in a towel, putting her panties on.

God, I was completely out, Bea said. I could have spent the whole day there.

I'm always afraid I'll fall asleep and wake up and the place is locked. That no one comes to wake me.

A yoga hostage.

They went down the street to a restaurant neither of them were thrilled with but it was walking distance. They sat inside for the air conditioning. This was the new frontier for restaurant critics—*a rich, satisfying mélange of argon, nitrogen, and neon with bold oxygen notes*. A waitress came by. Water for both of them, a few minutes to look at the menu even though Bea knew she was going to have the Greek salad, the safest thing on the menu.

Roger told me he has this fantasy of having sex in one of the houses he's selling, Pen said matter-of-factly. Or not selling.

With you? Bea immediately realized this sounded shitty.

No. Apparently it's a client, a tall, middle-aged professional. That's the description I got.

He tells you all his sexual fantasies? I thought it was middle-aged eastern European housewives.

It's everyone I'm not. I think it's basically a legal disclaimer. This way, if he has an affair, he can say he warned me. Partly, I think he was hoping I'd make more of an effort. It's a sort of threat.

Bea imagined effort to be a large part of sex with Roger.

How's Sang?

Teaching through the summer, going through the motions, bit of a zombie apocalypse phase. We hardly speak.

I don't have to speak. Roger delivers an angry monologue every three days and that seems to be enough. Pen toyed with her salad, which was what she did with most food. I'm not sure I'm crazy about that instructor.

What's her name? Jasmine? Hibiscus? I get her mixed up with the other one, the one who tells you to let the energy in the room invade your spirit.

I don't think I want Mr Beluga invading my spirit, Pen said.

You wonder why he goes shirtless.

Maybe we should admire his lack of vanity.

I'd rather admire it from a safer distance.

A stream of cars went by, horns honking. Men leaned out the windows, waving flags that Bea didn't recognize, yelling in a language she didn't understand. This could only be soccer, some distant victory uniting the diaspora.

BEA HAD AGREED TO MEET Will at a café downtown in the early afternoon. She went straight from lunch and planned to have dessert with Will. The café was half-full, a dozen millennials buried in their laptops. Will wasn't there yet. James Taylor was going on about something. Bea ordered a cappuccino then sat in the back of the café. Her stomach was unsettled. She stared at her phone. Her screen photo was of Thomas at the age of four, beautiful, a face that shone with innocence. Who knew how precious that commodity was? She felt she'd squandered it. Even his tiny three-year-old erection in the bathtub was innocent. God knew how guilty it was now. But Thomas at four, at five, maybe six, was the embodiment of innocence. Every year after that a little was chipped away. By violent shows, overheard comments, the vulgar soliloquy of a friend's older brother. The glimpse of something online. You needed to lose your innocence to survive, but they seemed to lose it so quickly and in such twisted ways. They were cynical and corrupt but somehow still innocent of the real world.

Will was only three or four years older than Thomas. Perhaps he was closer to thirty; it was hard to tell with young people. They all dressed like urchins. She was interested in what locks concealed. She measured herself against those lives, an anthropologist. For Will it seemed closer to religion.

Will came in, a loose-jointed gait. He waved and stood at the counter and waited for a coffee and picked out two expensive, well-intentioned cookies. He approached, apologizing for being late. The subway had stopped, *just stopped*.

They don't even bother telling you why anymore, he said. He sat down, settling into the seat in his awkward Great Blue Heron collapse.

Once he was settled in, Bea examined him and jumped right in. Are you ever tempted? she asked him.

Tempted?

To use your skills. To break into some place. Even if you didn't take anything. Just to stand there, inside.

Will looked down. I mean, you get caught, your life is basically fucked.

There's that. Yet without that possibility, all those lock-picking clubs may as well be knitting circles.

I guess.

Maybe the issue is really power.

Will shrugged.

But at some point, we use that power, don't we, Bea said. Isn't that human nature?

They chatted about locks and Will deflected any personal questions. He was still going to Murray's and gave her reports on what happened at the meetings, though Bea didn't have any interest.

Will talked about bumping and shimming, but it seemed his heart wasn't in it. You need to deliver a solid whack to the back of the head, he said. The energy is transferred to the driver pins, they're, like, *freaked,* they jump out of position and you're in.

Will picked up a cookie and bent over to take a bite. His long blond curls drooped down, obscuring his face. He looked like a dog.

So the thing is…He looked up. So you said, aren't I tempted. I haven't told anyone this. Well, the answer is yes and no. I mean, I did break into a place, but I didn't take anything. I just wanted to see what it was like.

My god. And what was it like?

Kind of scary and kind of amazing, Will said.

Where did you break in?

One of those big houses in the Annex. I couldn't see any sign of an alarm system. I'd walked by there, like, twenty times, different times of the day. And the guy, he's old, I don't know, fifty, and he leaves every morning at seven thirty. Then his wife goes out around nine thirty. So two days ago I followed her. She works at the art gallery, one of those volunteers at the AGO. She walks to work. I followed her there twice.

Bea was mildly stung by the fact that fifty was old. It probably was. At least, it used to be. Still.

They didn't look like dog people, you know, Will said. They looked like the kind of people who'd forget to feed it and would argue about whose turn it was to walk it. The lock on the back door is a Weiser SmartKey. I can open this at home in like twenty seconds. But I'm way more nervous than I thought. I can't get going. I'm like working it around in there and…you know, nothing. It takes four minutes, the longest it's ever taken. I almost quit. I thought it might be a sign, you know, like turn back while you can.

But you got in.

Yeah. And it's huge, this place. And they've got all these paintings. And I felt like I was in a museum after everyone had gone home. Like it's just you, and you wander around all that shit and it's kind of weird but amazing.

You went upstairs. Bea imagined the house, imagined going up the stairs.

Yeah, and I'm tiptoeing even though there's no one in the house. And I go into their room. It's at the front of the house with a big bay window. She has a closet that's bigger than my bedroom.

You went through their drawers.

No, no.

You did, Bea thought. You took her panties out and held them to your face and breathed them in like oxygen.

How long were you in? she asked.

That's another weird thing. I thought I was there for like two hours. But I set the stopwatch on my phone and when I was back out in the alley, I checked it and it was nine minutes, thirty-eight seconds. Like time stood still or something.

And you weren't tempted to take anything? Not even some little souvenir, something that didn't have any real value.

Will looked down. He put his hand in his pocket and pulled out a small jackknife. On the side it read, *I've been to the Grand Canyon.* There was a distorted photograph of the canyon on it.

Grand theft, Bea said. Well, it sounds incredible. I'd never have the nerve.

Will took a bite of his cookie, crumbs raining down.

Here's the thing. This couple, they were one of these kind of perfect-looking couples. There's no sign of any kids or anything. And so I'm in the house, and I go up to the third floor and they have this exercise room, weights and one of those things where it looks like you're cross-country skiing. And there's a big TV. I see this self-help book on the exercise thing, you know, like *Be Your Own Best Friend,* whatever, and I pick up this book and look around and I had this strange feeling, I can't really explain it, but I suddenly felt like I understood these people, like they tried to have kids maybe and it didn't work and he didn't want to adopt and she's doing this volunteer work and he stays at the office too late and you get this feeling, it's like the ghost of what their lives might have been is in the house and you can feel it.

Will took a sip of his coffee. His face was struggling with both pride and shame, trying to find the right expression.

You're not going to do it again, Bea said. He'd been researching it. He'd been in. He was hooked. She should tell him not to. This was her job.

No. No way. He ate the last bite of his cookie.

Bea watched him chew (again, so doglike). He would find a way. Not this week perhaps, but one morning, next week, or the week after, he'd wake up with that itch.

Don't do it, Will. Promise me. Look me in the eye and say the words. She reached out and held both his hands, leaning in. Say the words.

the invisible woman

THE WEISER PIN TUMBLER LOCK gave up early. The living room
had two Le Corbusier chairs and one of those pre-faded faux
Persian carpets that are almost as expensive as the real thing.
There were copper pots hanging from the ceiling. On the wall
was a very large painting—two figures in black moving toward
the viewer. Everything a bit too tasteful. It didn't look occupied.
As if someone had bought a life and wasn't sure how to live it.

She had walked the street two dozen times. He left for work
at 7:30 a.m. (a lawyer?). She was gone by nine, which could
mean retail. There were no kids, no alarm.

The radio was on as a deterrent, a dull ruse to suggest someone was still here, listening to an oldies station turned down
low, the sixties-sounding DJ introducing a Turtles song with
a slight rasp.

Their closets were orderly, the bathroom cabinet free of
drugs. Magazines fanned out on the coffee table. Putting up
a brave front. A mausoleum, dead already, leaving no imprint
on this world.

Walking along the street in one of her anonymous uniforms
(straw hat, sunglasses, loose T-shirt, shorts, running shoes), no

one had noticed her. Here was the gift of invisibility that fifty conferred. She had nodded to a few people she passed. No one acknowledged her. She wondered how far she could take this gift. Perhaps she could break into houses while the people were actually there, sitting in their living room, glued to the flat screen, or sitting at the dining room table eating a wordless dinner, Satie playing in the background. She could walk by them, slip up the stairs, take their jewellery. She could grab the Bordeaux on the table that had been opened twenty minutes earlier to breathe and glide out the door. She could steal their secrets, their senses, their will, and they might never know any of it was gone. This was the Zen pinnacle. A breakthrough: I am the Invisible Woman.

photo finish

AUGUST BROUGHT ROTTING AIR AND violence. A man killed his neighbour's dog with a shovel. A wife in the suburbs ran over her husband in their van. Suicides were up. Air conditioner repairmen were gods.

Bea's gallery was empty. In October people would start thinking about art. At least, they would start thinking about it as much as they ever did, which was never. But in fall people feathered their nests, they gathered what they needed to comfort them through the winter: booze, a bigger TV, abstract expressionism.

Bea sat in the gallery and scanned the new exhibit—a local artist, angry and ironic, her work a feminist riff on marriage and family, happy-looking households interrupted by violent splashes of colour and wild animals charging. Too obvious for a collector, but she could maybe rent them to a hip restaurant for a few months.

Bea was wearing the Yamamoto. Why not? It was elegant. It suited the job, or at least the idea of the job. If the gallery was regularly filled with interesting people rather than spectacularly empty, it would be perfect.

She'd brought the photos and she picked up one of her mother wearing a minidress. She did the math: if this was 1967, her mother would have been thirty-seven. Could she have been hip, sort of? It was hard to imagine.

Her cell rang and she picked it up and saw Ariel's name.

Hi.

So how's Mom? Ariel asked.

Good, fine. You know, the same basically.

When was the last time you saw her?

Bea hated the tone; it sounded like she was checking up, supervising.

When was the last time *you* saw her? Bea asked.

Okay, I didn't mean it like that. Don't be so defensive.

Bea looked at the minidress photo. It looked like a cocktail party. A few people in the background smoking.

Do you remember Mom wearing a minidress? Bea asked. It has a geometric pattern.

What?

I'm looking at a photo of Mom; she's wearing this minidress. Holding a cigarette. She looks sort of, I don't know, almost hip.

It's not ringing a bell. What year is this?

Not sure, maybe '67, somewhere in there. Summer of Love.

I would have been three.

She would have been thirty-seven.

Thirty-seven back then was older than thirty-seven now.

She looks so young. She has great legs. In the photo she's talking to a guy with sideburns. It's kind of hilarious. The colour in the photograph has that blotchy Technicolor look— that orangey-red tone.

Why are you looking at photos?

I'm at the gallery. No one comes in, so I brought a box of those photos we took from Mom's house. I'm going to sort them and put them in an album. Old school.

There must be hundreds of them.

I'm not going to put them all in the album. Just the Greatest Hits.

Am I going to get equal billing?

Equal Billings. I'm cutting you out completely. I'm going to reimagine our family without your needy-ass self at the centre.

Fuck off.

How is the children's clothing business?

Oh, god, the summer's been a disaster. No one is buying. *No one.* I went to a thrift store and it had a French Bonpoint sweater, one of those blue-horizontal-stripes-with-a-boat-in-the-centre sweaters that would have cost like a hundred and twenty bucks new and they're selling it for four dollars.

Bea had the depressing image of her sister sitting in an empty store five hundred miles away while she sat in an empty gallery. The Billings sisters waiting for their lives to come to their natural, unremarkable conclusion.

Maybe find cheaper lines. You know, cheap chic for toddlers.

Yeah. The Walker Evans line, coal-streaked onesies made out of potato sacks.

Bea laid out ten photographs in rough chronological order, the black and whites giving way to lurid colour. Her mother's life stretched out over four decades. What had happened to that baby? There weren't many possibilities. Had it died, and did that sorrow underpin all the other sorrows her mother accumulated over the next five decades? Air was going on about something. Bea looked at the minidress photo, examined it for signs of mourning.

Bea, are you even listening? What is the point of telling you *anything* . . . I mean, my life is basically *fucked* and what are you doing? Pasting those stupid photos in your scrapbook?

Sorry, sorry, Air. No, it was a customer. Someone wanting information on the artist. Sorry, I'm here now.

I said Levi and I split up.

What? Jesus, Air. When?

Well, two months ago more or less, but I only moved out two weeks ago. We dragged it through a marriage counsellor, but it was just so we could find a soft landing, I think. It was never going to fix anything. I've got an apartment, not far from the university, and it's nice and everything, but basically I wake up and I'm a fifty-two-year-old woman living by herself in an apartment with a dying business.

Air burst into tears.

Oh Air, I'm sorry. I'm so sorry.

He's such a shit.

Bea wondered how emphatically she should agree. She had never warmed to Levi. She couldn't imagine anyone warming to him and it had always disturbed her that Air was the sole exception. He was aloof and self-centred and petty. But you had to be careful; you trashed someone's husband then they got back together. You needed to show solidarity, though not get too original. There are some things you can't retract. *How you spent eighteen years with such a limp lame selfish narcissistic dickhead who redefined the word "useless" and who has the emotional range of a cuttlefish and who has never given a single thought to anyone other than himself and who will die unmourned and who has the diet of a nine-year-old and the temperament of a teenager and whose lack of curiosity in anything on this earth made me want to hit him with a nine-iron is a mystery to me. You are childless because of him, childless because he is a spineless child.*

Oh Air.

AT HOME BEA BROUGHT UP the other box of photographs and cleared the dining room table. She took photographs out one by one and placed them in her decade-divided chronology.

There were seven more black and whites that featured the mystery baby. Bea wondered if there had been dozens of them but her mother had gotten rid of them. Gotten rid of the evidence. There was a photograph of her mother and father in matching bowling shirts. There were Christmas photos when Bea and Air were young, their unimpressive tree, her father in his chair with a half-opened present on his lap, a doll on the carpet, Ariel already tired of it.

She tried not to linger on the photos or it would take forever, but there were photos that triggered vivid memories—a shot of them on a seashore during what might have been September (a real September, not the one they would be getting this year). They were bundled up and the sea was grey. Maybe Cape Cod. They had red checked coats and were flying a kite. It was a good picture, almost brilliant. It captured something, something of the family and of the era. Bea wondered who took it. All the family was in it. Their mother running alongside, their father staring out to sea. It was in colour, but had that hand-tinted look.

Sang came in and looked at the photos. Are these the photos from the basement?

I'm organizing them.

Sang picked up the photo of her father. I don't remember him being that happy, he said.

Neither do I.

I'm out tonight.

Bea picked up a photograph of Ariel on her way to the school dance with her date, Dennis something, both looking strained. Their mother must have taken it. She remembered Dennis's bad skin.

Air and Levi are splitting up, she said.

Is that good or bad?

Bea looked at him.

I'm serious, Sang said. With divorce you never know if you should be offering condolences or congratulations. I mean, Levi was a piece of work.

Everyone's a piece of work, Bea said.

Didn't she basically complain to you all the time about how cheap and emotionally distant he was? Two things that might be related.

Everyone complains about their husbands. That doesn't mean they want a divorce.

Maybe she'll be better off.

She's fifty-two, not an ideal age to be looking for a prom date.

Sang nodded, weighing this. Just going up to change, he said. A faculty thing.

Sang went upstairs and Bea went online, trying to search birth records. She tried the arcane government site, following their breadcrumb trail, guessing at the baby's sex (male), first name (James, after her father), and birth year. If the baby was ten months old and the picture was taken in September of '60, then it would have been born around December '59. She looked at the photo closely. It could be older or younger; she couldn't really tell about babies' ages anymore. And she couldn't tell if it was a boy or a girl. As tended to happen when she did anything online, she became frustrated and bitter and gave up, vowing to return with a more strategic assault.

Have you seen . . . Sang bellowing from upstairs. She couldn't hear the rest. Something lost, something that was suddenly crucial.

I can't hear you, Sang.

He came partway down the stairs. Have you seen my yellow shirt, the linen one?

I don't know that yellow is your colour. Sort of a jaundice thing happens with your skin.

It was hanging up.

Bea gave every piece of her clothing a two-year window of opportunity; if she hadn't worn it in two years, it was gone. And when she dropped it off at Goodwill, she felt liberated, as if she had unburdened herself, another sin floating upward to be catalogued by God. But Sang was a hoarder; he had clothes from twenty years ago. Partly it was his belief that all fashion was cyclical and those unfortunate bell-bottoms he discarded would come back in ten years to taunt him. And he was proud of the fact he could still wear jeans from the nineties.

Bea may have applied her own philosophy to Sang and given some of his stuff to the woman collecting household items for Syrian refugees.

You haven't seen it, Sang said, an accusation rather than a question. There's other stuff missing. You didn't accidentally give it away.

No, she said. Which was true. It hadn't been an accident.

You know my philosophy about clothes.

Bea examined a photo of her and Ariel in matching winter coats, posing, snow in the background. They had matching hats, fake fur around them, like they'd just stepped out of *Doctor Zhivago*.

I am Israel when it comes to clothes, Sang said. You know that: why give up territory.

Israel, Bea repeated absently. She checked the back of the photo to see if there was a date or the place. Sometimes her mother wrote it on the back in her impeccable cursive, but it was blank.

So you didn't give it away. My yellow linen shirt you didn't like.

I don't know, Sang. Maybe it got mixed up with the stuff of mine I dropped off for the Syrian Relief whatever.

Here's the thing, he said. You think I hang on to stuff for twenty years because of some deep psychological issue with attachment, some Psych 101 horseshit about having things taken away and now I—

I don't judge. I'm not Palestine in this scenario.

Sang came down the stairs and stood behind her.

Have you ever wondered why you throw things out at the very first opportunity? Slightest problem—*colour's weirder than it looked in the store, I don't like the way it feels when I move, they're hard to walk in, I have one sort of like it already* . . . This was in a voice slightly higher than his normal voice.

What is your point, Sang?

My point is you can't apply your own twisted philosophy, that whatever dress you bought on sale didn't change your life the way you'd hoped, and now you don't want to be reminded of every stupid decision you've made . . .

A dress *can* change your life, Sang. It had changed hers.

I make *good* decisions, decisions that stand up over *decades*. Those clothes are a reminder that I understand myself at a deep fucking level, that the yellow linen shirt that I buy today will still be an object of desire a decade from now.

Bea turned to face him. He was in his underwear. Had he been trying on clothes upstairs?

Have you been trying on clothes?

No. And even if I'd been *trying* to try on clothes, half of them have been given away to Syrian fucking refugees.

Bea looked at a photo of her and Ariel, at a cottage somewhere, one of the gloomy rentals her mother had found through their Italian neighbours. The entire country was filled with pristine lakes and they usually ended up in some damp bungalow a mile from the shore. In the photo they had marshmallows on sticks, burnt to a crisp. Ariel was smiling, showing two missing teeth.

So let's say, Bea said, there is a Syrian man in this city who left everything behind and managed to escape persecution or even death in his native country and managed to get here through impossible odds and a dangerous voyage in a leaky boat and six months in a crappy refugee camp with no plumbing or running water and now his life has been made better by a yellow linen shirt bought on sale fourteen years ago...

My life was made better by that shirt.

Bea looked at him, standing there, almost naked, furious, suddenly not sure where to put his hands.

Tell it to the Syrians.

Outside, there was the deafening sound of emergency vehicles, a series of them screaming west. The freeze-frame of traffic, then everything starting again. September would arrive in a few days, a month that used to fill her with a sense of renewal, but you needed that crispness, the first cool notes of fall. The air was thick with the grit of summer, the city weary of itself. She carefully put the photos back in the box.

you are here

THERE WERE PAW PRINTS IN different colours that guided you to
the animals. Bea hadn't been to the zoo in a decade. She pushed
her mother along the sidewalk that had large blue cat paws on it,
past an empty giraffe compound and an empty orangutan cage.

How is Mrs Wheeler? Bea asked. Still biting people?

They had to have her put down.

Bea looked at her mother, not sure if she was making a joke
or was getting Mrs Wheeler confused with their dog Shepherd
whom they'd had put down when Bea was nine. Also a biter.

A bit harsh, Bea said.

Nature, her mother said pleasantly.

Bea had worn a Lycra jogging top underneath her linen
blouse and she took off the blouse and folded it carefully and
put it in the compartment in the back of the wheelchair. The
path undulated over small rises and pushing the wheelchair
uphill triggered rivers of perspiration.

They stopped in front of the lion enclosure and gazed into
it. Bea scanned the dry grass, empty of lions. There were
flat-bottomed clouds moving slowly, almost African-looking.
There weren't a lot of people. A few exhausted-looking moth-

ers with toddlers. Peacocks wandered. The smells were layered and vivid, a mix of dung and rotting vegetation, the musk of stale sex, stagnant water.

I guess the lions are all sleeping inside, Bea said. The heat.

They keep themselves to themselves, her mother said.

They walked past zebras bunched in the distance, past a pacing cheetah, some antelopy-looking things. The sun flickered out of the clouds, making it hotter.

Are you thirsty? Bea asked. She looked in the wheelchair compartment for the water bottle she'd brought and realized she'd left it in the car. We could get a cold drink, she said. Or an ice cream. Bea suddenly felt like one. And she needed to get water for both of them.

They stopped in front of the hyena cage because it was in the shade. She took off her mother's straw hat to adjust it. That grey, vulnerable head. Inside, thoughts rolling like lottery balls. There were no hyenas. The cage was dark, spartan, and smelled of bleach. The smell reminded her of the Dickensian rest home her grandmother used to live in. Her mother's taciturn mother, Beryl Compton, was from Liverpool when it was cheerless and grey, before the Beatles rescued it. She'd lived through the Depression and two wars and lost her husband and lived to ninety-four, thirty of those years spent believing each was her last, and the sixty previous years spent in privation. A sharp tongue made sharper by gin. Her middle years had been an oppressive lull, her husband gone, two children, no money, old at thirty. She came to Canada and saw those first sunny suburbs and was never able to forgive the people who lived there. Certainties stored inside her like nuggets of coal. They saw her one Sunday a month, going into the dimly lit, musty home with a sense of dread to hear a lecture on how suffering was good for people.

It hadn't been good for Beryl, and it hadn't been good for Bea's mother. Bea wondered if she would walk into that same wilderness herself. Beryl had had no choice, her suffering was unavoidable, historical. Her mother had limited choices. She'd been a wife when it was an occupation, *full-time, unpaid position, involves light housework and annoying sex*. Bea was free to create her own suffering.

There was a map posted on a nearby board faded by the sun. Bea walked up to it, squinting in the sunlight, and found a round red dot—*You are here*.

It was difficult to see, even with sunglasses. Bea thought she saw a quick movement off to the side, animal-like, a darting into the trees. Perhaps something escaped. The smells were orchestral. Layered in with the dung and rot she caught the encouraging smell of something fried, the comfort of sizzling fat. She stopped and sniffed. Something disappeared to her right, a slithering then a vanishing. Maybe they'd all escaped. Within minutes the grounds would be filled with frightened prey and out-of-practice predators. Lions dragging ibexes down by their throats, their necks turned up in that *Guernica* anguish. All that pent-up instinct, the path covered in blood.

The orange roof of the concession building came into view, a relief, and Bea wheeled her mother up to the counter.

Two ice creams please, Bea said, then looked down at her mother. You wanted an ice cream. Two ice creams, and two bottles of water.

She paid and opened her mother's water bottle and gave her a long sip then finished the bottle herself. She wheeled her mother to a small orange plastic table and they sat down. Bea unwrapped the ice cream and handed it to her mother.

Her mother's arms were spotted and fragile, the broken arm even thinner. Healing was a slow process. There wasn't the urgent rally that occurred when you were a child, the red and white blood cells racing to the scene like emergency vehicles, every scrape and cut magically vanished in days. Our bodies become bureaucracies; a bruise lingers for months because we can't get white blood cells there, a new ache barely acknowledged among the din of old aches, a backlog.

Did you love Dad? Bea asked. A brash question, but Bea felt the need to assemble her mother's life while she could. Her memories were vanishing, occasionally lighting up her cortex in a brilliant, unreliable flash.

Her mother took another lick of the ice cream. People didn't love in those days, she said.

Really, Mother. No one?

Movie stars. She waved her ice cream in a circle.

Bea stuck with it. But in those photographs, she said, the black-and-white ones, with you and Dad holding that baby. You were in love then. Weren't you? You *looked* like you were in love. You'd only been married a few years.

Her mother stared past Bea, busy with her cone.

It was a neighbour's baby?

A boy, her mother said. Her face collapsed slightly, her mind grinding through poorly stored histories. Oh god, Bea thought.

A boy, Bea repeated.

Her mother focused on the ice cream.

Your boy, Bea said.

The light in our hearts.

The light ... What happened to him?

Her mother looked at her ice cream for a full minute, then said, He brings the darkness into light.

Was she quoting Scripture? Bea wondered. She had never been religious. She looked at her mother's face. She looked as though she was somewhere else. A tear formed and rolled down her cheek.

Bea took a napkin and wiped her mother's face. Oh Mother, she said. I'm sorry.

Bea couldn't bear to ask anything more. It had been their boy. She looked over at the next table. A toddler was sitting on one of the plastic chairs in the shade, his mother looking for something in her giant bag. The boy had a limp french fry in his hand. A peacock strutted up in that regal, lunatic gait and nabbed it with its beak and ate it. The boy's mouth opened in surprise and he stared after the idiot bird, parading down the path. His mother finally emerged from her bag with a small toy and put it on the table and the boy glanced at it then stared after the peacock.

The sun disappeared behind a cloud, the light flattened into grey relief. Bea got up heavily and put her mother's straw hat on her then put on her own.

It's late, she said.

BEA RACED TO HER DOCTOR'S appointment, more than an hour late, but her doctor usually ran at least an hour behind, probably more this late in the day. She couldn't find parking and had to park seven blocks away and the hurried walk made her perspire heavily, her linen blouse heavy and wet. The waiting room contained several elderly people, huddled and wheezing. Her doctor, Margaret Ma, was a humourless Asian woman she'd inherited when her original doctor decamped to Darfur. Bea checked in with the receptionist and sat down in the only seat left, wedged between two heavy women.

Her phone rang and Bea took it out, surprised to see Thomas's name.

Hello.

Hi Mom, it's me.

How are you, honey? Bea got up and went into the hallway.

You know, the usual, okay.

School?

You know, you have this idea that everything that sucked about high school won't suck in university, but, like, it still does. It just sucks in a different way.

Sucks in what way?

Do you know how many kids are in my Revolutionary Politics class?

Bea waited.

Three hundred twenty-seven.

That's a lot of revolutionaries. I hope they all find work.

The prof needs to use a mic, but the sound system is so lame you can barely tell he's speaking English. Half the class is asleep.

The image of 150 sleeping revolutionaries seemed like a metaphor for something. I know some profs are boring, Bea said, trying not to sound lecturing, but you have to try and get what's best from every class...

Yeah, you gave me that speech.

Life—

I *know,* life can be boring too sometimes, but—

If you're bored with *everything,* then maybe the problem isn't with—

Mom!

It was true they'd covered this ground before. But it was never clear how much Thomas absorbed. She waited for another shoe to drop; he must want something to have called. Bea paced near the doorway.

Beatrice Billings. It was the receptionist. Dr Ma will see you now, she said.

Oh, hang on, sweetheart, she said into the phone, then

covered it with her hand. Thomas's calls were so rare she didn't want to cut it short. Listen, she said to the receptionist, I have an important call, can I trade with the next person?

The receptionist looked at her uncomprehendingly but called out another name and a woman stood up.

Hi, sorry, I'm at the doctor's office.

Uh-huh. So how's everything with you guys?

Thomas never asked about their lives, even in a polite rhetorical way. Did he think something was wrong?

We're good. Your father's busy at school, I'm at the gallery three days a week.

Uh-huh.

Are you still seeing that girl…Bea wasn't sure of her name. *Sharon?*

Bea didn't think that was it. Yes, Sharon, she said.

She's totally crazy.

Wasn't the other one…

Rebecca?

Possibly, Bea thought. She wasn't sure. Yes, Rebecca, she said. Wasn't that her problem as well?

She makes Sharon look sane.

When you say crazy, do you mean eccentric, or…

I mean batshit.

Thomas, the idea that you think every woman is insane is troubling to me. I know that online—

Okay, I totally don't want to have the online porn talk again, Mom.

Bea didn't want to have it again either but felt it needed to be brought up.

They only let in crazy women, Thomas said. There's some kind of screening process and all the sane women are sent to Yale or something.

Bea decided not to pursue it. How is your French? she asked. Is it getting better?

Bea had gone to McGill, had lived in Montreal for several years, and her French had gotten respectable, though now it was pretty much gone. She wished she'd kept it up.

C'est pire que jamais.

Pratique, pratique!

Yeah, whatever. It's like unavoidable.

You should embrace the opportunity. I did, but I wished I'd done it even more.

They chatted amiably about the weather. The summer had claimed more than five thousand people in Montreal, old people in those third-floor walk-ups without air conditioning, sitting there, quietly expiring in front of the TV. Assisted living residences, hostels, and no-star hotels had all become killing grounds.

How is it in your apartment? Bea asked.

Hot, but sort of okay. The one above us is brutal. There are people sleeping in Mount Royal Park, like *thousands,* not homeless, just people without AC. It looks like a refugee camp.

Thomas wasn't equipped to deal with the world, let alone the end of the world. There was something in his voice, something only a mother could hear. He was lonely, not the kind where you miss your mother's cooking; an existential hollowness that descends at night, lying in bed, looking at questions too large to frame, unable to see where the light could possibly come from.

They finished chatting and Bea hung up, worried. The woman who had gone in in Bea's place came out and Bea got up.

The receptionist called out, Pat Bezic.

A large woman got up heavily, likely hip trouble.

I believe I was next, Bea said to the receptionist, feeling conflicted. Pat was in obvious discomfort. I'm sorry, she said to Pat's blank face. Please, go ahead, I'll wait.

You sacrificed your turn, the receptionist said.

I didn't *sacrifice* it, Bea said. I traded places.

No trading.

What do you mean, "no trading"? What difference could it possibly make?

It's a rule.

Really, Bea said, angry now. If it's a rule, it has to be written down somewhere. I'd like to see it.

The receptionist was officious, her life spent surrounded by sickness and fluorescent lighting. Unwritten rule, she said.

If it's an unwritten rule, then it isn't a rule, it's a whim. And Dr Ma is running two hours late.

The receptionist shrugged and made her wait for another woman to go in after Pat Bezic then murmured something into the phone to Ma.

Bea finally went in and Ma had her laptop open, reviewing Bea's medical history.

Any complaints? Ma asked.

Where to start, Bea thought, but said, No.

Smoking.

No.

Alcohol still two glasses of wine per week.

Yes. It was closer to two glasses a day, but when she'd initially told Ma this, she was so alarmed that Bea pretended she'd misspoken and downgraded it to weekly.

Drinking is bad.

Actually, red wine is supposed to—

No change. Nothing unusual.

Life is unusual.

Ma ignored this and opened the door. Undress, she said, and left the room. Bea undressed and sat for a longish time on the fresh paper on the bed thingy. Ma came back and started in without a word, taking blood pressure, probing ears and throat, tapping her back. She examined Bea's breasts for lumps, her hands kneading absently, her face turned up, trying to divine whether there was cancer in there. She stopped and came back to a place and rubbed, not gently.

You feel something? Bea asked. She was instantly panicked.

Ma's face was noncommittal.

But it's probably nothing, Bea said. A weak, fearful attempt at humour, what Ma was supposed to be saying.

It's always probably nothing or probably something, Ma said.

Ma's idiosyncratic English and factory pragmatism unnerved Bea. Ma finished her examination and looked at Bea.

It's nothing? Bea asked. She knew eight women who'd had breast cancer. Nine. The world had cancer and now it was Bea's turn.

Ma shrugged. She typed something into her laptop. You are serviceable, she said.

family man

BEA FINALLY FOUND THE MISSING child online. She'd had to create an account on a genealogy website and one that specialized in old newspapers, but her archaeological dig finally yielded bones: Patrick James Billings, born November 23, 1959. There weren't any details, though, just proof of his existence. The obituary read, "Patrick James Billings, b. November 23, 1959, d. December 9, 1960. He was the light in our hearts and we will hold him there always." Her mother had been quoting the obit maybe — he brings the darkness into light. Her fractured memory of it.

Barely a year old. An accident perhaps, or disease, crib death. It didn't say.

Bea brought out the photographs, the seven that had Patrick James in them. She examined them, looked at the boy, wondered about the man. Her brother would be fifty-six now if he'd lived. A silver-haired man with a family and a Volvo and plans to go to Florida in March. Perhaps he would be divorced by now, bitter and lost and drinking at noon. She turned the photo over. On the back was an address she hadn't noticed before. It was written in pencil, faded almost to nothing. 188A Shaw.

BEA BROUGHT THE PHOTOS WITH her. She went around the back of 188A Shaw and opened the back gate and examined the yard. She held up one of the photos and found the angle. It was the same yard. It hadn't changed much. It had the feel of a rented house, that benign neglect.

She'd watched the occupants. They left together in the morning and came back together after six. Early thirties, a hip-looking couple who might own a struggling graphic design company.

The lock wasn't challenging—a Kwikset pin tumbler, maybe ten years old. Inside, the air was stale and musty and the house smelled like rubber boots and eggs and dead flowers. The main floor was quite dark. It still had the original layout, with three small rooms and a convoluted hallway. How did people live in such small rooms? So many of these old houses had been renovated, the walls taken out, opened up. The living room was claustrophobic, filled with a heavy coffee table stacked with design magazines and books, an old couch and two green armchairs worn through at the arms. There was a painting on the wall, an orangey-red print of an abstracted prairie that she quite liked, the wheat fields broken up into geometric patterns.

Bea walked down the hall to the dining room, which would probably have been her parents' bedroom years ago. Big enough for a queen bed and little else. The kitchen was tired-looking, a seventies reno that was collapsing.

The current occupants were David Lilly and Edith Small. The house seemed temporary. They didn't have kids.

She went up the stairs, which were angled downward where the ancient floor joists sagged. The small rooms on the second floor were dark and jumbled, filled with old furniture. The bathroom was tiny. She checked the medicine cabinet, which had a surprising number of prescription bottles in it. Everyone was medicated these days. It was worrisome that 80 percent of oncoming traffic consisted of drivers who either were on something or had forgotten to take their meds.

She went back downstairs and into the dining room and sat on one of the chairs. This would have been her parents' bedroom. She looked up at the ceiling they would have stared at when they couldn't sleep. They would have been in their twenties, the last decade when a crappy flat can feel romantic. Revelling in themselves, fucking like they'd invented it, though that was never gifted to the previous generation; it always belonged to the present. Then that beautiful boy. Did he sleep in this room? Would they have put the crib against that wall? Those early months when families are simply mammals, huddled for protection, so physically close, before the children grow up and launch into their teenage orbits and the parents drift to their separate side of the cage.

They might have had one of those old black-and-white televisions with the antenna you had to adjust to bring in a signal or you had to wind aluminum foil around it. And then you'd only get three stations. The boy was their entertainment. The way you invest so much of yourself in that first child— you will be better, you will succeed, this child will never know misery. But we all know it eventually.

Patrick James may have died here. Bea felt a welling of tears. She started crying and it triggered something and she began sobbing heavily, her body in spasm. She wasn't even sure what she was grieving. That lost boy, a brother she'd never met, the happiness her mother was denied, her father's sterile existence. Or her own unhappiness. The emotion was inchoate and primal and it shook her. She looked around the small room where her parents' lives had begun and been undone. Her sobbing subsided slowly, the way a baby's wailing slows then finally stops, the breath coming in those mad, uncontrollable, subsiding gulps. She wiped her nose on her T-shirt sleeve.

A key in the front door.

Bea could hear it turning, embracing the pins individually, sending them upward, the deadbolt sliding back in, the handle turning, the sound of the door opening. Every operation distinct, in slow motion. She was rooted to the chair. She tried to hold her breath, to stop the heaving denouement of her crying jag. She wiped her wet face with her hand. If there was a moment to run, it was at the first scrape of the key. It was too late now. She sat there, petrified, like one of those mice confronted by a poisonous snake—they just give up. *I am invisible.* She closed her eyes.

Shit shit shit. It was a woman's voice. Bea could hear books and magazines being lifted up and smacked down hard in the living room ten feet away. She was looking for something. She'd gotten to the office and realized she'd forgotten something critical and she'd raced back and now she was looking for it.

Fuck. The woman stomped along the hardwood, out of the living room. Bea was sitting at the head of the dining table. She didn't move. These old floors creaked with every movement. All she could do was stay as still as possible, to get her breathing under control and use her powers of invisibility. What a pathetic sight she would be. She'd left her bag with her straw hat and sunglasses on the counter in the kitchen. They would be impossible to miss.

The woman raced up the stairs and Bea opened her eyes, not sure what she would see. She should race out right now, but she couldn't move. *I am the air, the light passes through me. I walk among you: the Invisible Woman.*

Thank you *Jesus,* the woman said, crashing down the stairs. She'd only been up there a few seconds. She must have looked into the bathroom at the top of the stairs and found whatever it was she needed.

She rocketed out the door and Bea heard the key once more, turning quickly, the pins settling in, the bolt sliding, the key withdrawing. She realized she'd been holding her breath and she let it out now. A film of nervous sweat covered her body. Filled with relief, still stunned, she examined her arms, her corporeal self, the faint hairs, a mole she'd once been worried about, a vein that seemed absurdly prominent, a junkie's vein.

She got up quickly and left the dining room, grabbed her bag, put on her hat and glasses, and left through the back door. Her heart was pounding and her breathing was ragged and shallow, her face still wet. She closed the door behind her and walked into the infected air.

all very Rome

THEY LISTENED TO THE RADIO as she drove, her mother in the front seat, silent, staring. Bea turned onto their old street and parked in front of the house. Her mother hadn't lived here in fifteen years.

Our house, she said. You remember.

Her mother stared at the modest two-storey building. The windows in need of paint, weeds pushing out through the cracked cement walk. It was a small house, wedged between the neighbours' houses like a subway commuter. The light was dull.

Where we all grew up, Bea said. Where you lived.

Bea remembered her and Ariel drawing things on the sidewalk in pastel-coloured chalk. An Italian boy from down the street with the trace of a moustache came over and took a piece of chalk and wrote the word "fuck" on the sidewalk in big letters and said, Ask your mother what this word means.

Her mother's face had an untroubled emptiness. There were small blue veins at her temple that Bea hadn't noticed before. Her skin was still lovely.

Ariel and I, Bea said. You and Dad. We still had Shep then.

Her mother nodded.

Bea wondered if the new owners had renovated the house. The basement had been their play space, though it still had a cement floor then and was mostly a storage area. She and Ariel used to make up games down there, secretive and hushed, involving imaginary enemies. Sometimes their pets were involved in the games. Ariel insisted on pets, one after the other. The backyard was a cemetery for hamsters and budgies and guinea pigs, a cat and a turtle, their names lost now. Ariel involved them in her intricate, narrative-driven games, but had less interest in feeding them or walking them or doing whatever you were supposed to do with them. Though it wasn't hard to lose interest in a guinea pig. Shep ate one of them.

Her mother made a noncommittal sound then rapidly said, Ann Jamieson drank by herself tipsy-tipsy-face-like-a-gypsy.

Bea wondered if these stream-of-consciousness snippets represented the things that had been important to her, or were they simply random images, whatever her brain had access to at a given moment. Bea had started writing them down.

Their neighbours all seemed fine when she was a child, and she had assumed every household was a version of their own. It wasn't until she was a teenager that she was able to divine the separate madness inhabiting every home—alcoholic mother, violent father, damaged child, the envy and pressures, all the domestic rage and sadness barely contained.

Bea pulled away. Before turning onto College, she saw Sang, walking briskly. It looked like him. Had he responded to her invitation to dinner? It *was* Sang, wasn't it? Bea had a secret life, why not Sang. Except his wouldn't involve sitting in empty houses, weeping. The space between them had seemed like a desert, but now it suddenly looked like something else.

She drove to the Café Napoli and parked on the street. She wrestled her mother out of the car and pushed her to the restaurant. It was pleasant, already half-full, the specials written in chalk on a blackboard. There were four tables on the sidewalk and one was empty and Bea asked if they could sit outside.

Mother, you'd like it outside, wouldn't you?

Her mother stared at the passing cars.

So we'll eat outside, Bea said to the waitress.

It was noisy with the cars, but Bea hoped the extra stimulation would be a help. The sun was low in the sky and had found the edge of the clouds and the street was golden. It was still hot and humid. Within a month they would miss the heat that oppressed them.

Their dinner came and they ate in silence. Bea examined her mother, too delicate to survive, though something hard and dark beneath the surface, something that led people through pogroms and putsches. *Every morning you made breakfast and we sat quiet as church, the sound of crunching toast and the radio, Father reading the paper. You helped us with our coats and bent down and put your hands on our cheeks and told us never to get into a stranger's car. You sent us off to school then sat in that kitchen with your tea and listened to the radio and talked to a neighbour on the phone and walked to the grocery store and made a recipe you'd found on the back of a package of miniature marshmallows.*

Bea wondered if she would see Sang walking by with a woman, off for a bite after a quick fuck. Her phone rang and she took it out of her purse and saw Ariel's name.

Hi.

Bea.

I'm sitting at the Napoli, having dinner with Mother.

Why go there? The food is terrible.

Nostalgia. I thought it would be nice. We drove by the old house.

How is she?

Same. Here, you can talk to her. Bea handed the phone to her mother. It's Ariel, Mother.

Ariel, her mother repeated. Bea pressed the phone to her mother's ear and heard her sister's voice.

Mother, wouldn't you rather go somewhere *nice* to eat?

There's cars, her mother said.

There was a stilted conversation and Bea could feel her sister losing patience at the other end. Her sister was good at nagging Bea about spending time with their mother but not great at actually spending time with her herself. Bea finally took the phone back.

You're sitting outside? Air said. It sounds like you're in traffic.

We are. It's all very Rome.

Did you bring a sweater for her?

It's the warmest September since the Big Bang, Air, and stop supervising. I'll call you later.

She hung up and they sat outside in the unseasonable sun amid the traffic. Her mother took another tentative sip of her wine.

Remember you tried to grow tomatoes in the backyard like the Italian families, Bea said. Except theirs were the size of grapes and hard as potatoes. The house down the street had huge red tomatoes, vines wrapped around wooden arbours, grown by a wiry guy in a singlet who drank homemade wine on his porch. They had chickens in the backyard and zucchinis and basil in pots. The wife only wore black, forever mourning something, though maybe just preparing for the inevitable. Her husband died on the porch, sitting there. The twelve-year-old Bea saw him, slumped in the August heat, one arm dangling to the side.

Bea looked down the street and saw a black pile on the sidewalk. She didn't think it had been there a few minutes ago. It looked like a dead bear, an impossibility. A man stood over it. He knelt down, then stood up and looked around.

What is it? Bea asked.

A dog, the man said.

It's dead?

The man nodded uncertainly. The heat? he said.

Bea scanned the street. I think someone was parked here, she said, pointing to an empty parking spot. They left the dog in the car.

They dumped it onto the street? the man said. Jesus.

Bea felt a sudden piercing sorrow. She went back to her mother. The waiter came over.

What the hell *is* that? he asked.

A dead dog.

Seriously? Why is it on the sidewalk?

Because we live in the Middle Ages, Bea said.

Because, Bea thought, someone went for a pedicure at two o'clock and ran into an old college friend afterward and they went for a spritzer and her dog sat in the sealed car for five hours and slowly boiled to death.

Bea paid the bill and pushed her mother to their car, past stores that had been here forty years ago, odd little shops that sold communion gowns and unfashionable clothes and practical shoes. The separate immigrant dreams, holding on to the old country as they pushed their children into the North American abyss.

TRAFFIC ON THE WAY BACK was at its incomprehensible worst; it took more than an hour to creep home. She opened the door and Sang was sitting on the couch, watching a football game with the sound off, drinking a glass of wine and grading students' papers, the first tentative, half-plagiarized papers of the semester. A Miles Davis record played on the cool, bright-red retro turntable he'd bought. Everyone cheated now. The whole world would soon be filled with professionals who only knew about half of what they needed to.

Had it been Sang she'd seen? Here he was. Though he could have fucked an undergraduate in her student flat, taken the subway, and gotten back here before her. *Why were you in Little Italy?*

You got my text? Bea asked.

Text?

Dinner. With my mother.

No.

We ate at the Napoli.

Sang nodded. Had my class. Remember.

We rarely go to that part of town anymore, she said.

The Napoli isn't worth the traffic.

No. Probably faster to walk at this point.

Sang nodded, buried in his marking.

Bea went to the kitchen and took a bottle of white out of the fridge. I think I'm getting a migraine, she said. It was more just a colossal weariness, but it was too unspecific a complaint.

Isn't wine, like, the worst thing for a migraine?

That's red. White dulls the pain. Four out of five doctors.

Bea sat at the kitchen table and opened her laptop and googled "U of Toronto." She clicked onto courses, instructors, History. Tonight Sang would have been teaching the course on local history, Toronto's something something. She scanned the course names. Here it was: Hogtown Confidential: Toronto's Hidden History. Course instructor: Sanger Bennett. Offered in the winter semester only, starting January 8, Thursdays, 7 p.m. She glanced up at Sang. He was sprawled on the couch now, looking at his phone, scrolling, given up marking.

How is your class? she asked.

Usual.

You don't have that one special student?

What?

You know, you used to say you'd find the one student in every class who was listening, and you'd talk to them.

Yeah. I don't know if there are any more special students. Now there are students who have done fuck all all semester and they come to your office and say they need an A to get into an MBA program at Queen's and then you get twenty-seven reasons why they didn't get to class and they know their essay wasn't maybe their best effort and how important is this shit going to be in real life anyway, right?

So?

So what?

So do you give them the A?

Sang shrugged, now looking for something on his phone. You can give a mercy B, he said, not a mercy A. That's the unwritten rule.

Prepare them for life.

Nothing prepares you for life, not even life.

cottage country

IT WAS A CHUBB LOCK. You didn't see many, a bit stubborn, almost resentful, though she was probably reading too much into it. Inside, the walls were dramatic colours: blood red, apple green, a light grey for contrast, a midnight blue. There were faint rectangular outlines where paintings and pictures had hung. It had been on the market for three months.

Bea walked up the stairs and stopped and looked down. The hardwood was scratched in places where furniture had been dragged. The wall colours suggested that the reno was at least twenty-five years old. It hadn't aged well. There wasn't any furniture. The emptiness had an odd weight.

She went up the stairs, took a quick look around the second floor. The air was thick and dead. She walked up to the third floor. It might have been a study, someone working from home, gazing across the street every morning, content.

Perhaps they had moved to a cottage on a small lake to the north. Bought a canoe, dug a well, bought books on animal husbandry and making bread and growing herbs. A family huddled near the lake, the slow boil that would take us all.

A loud noise startled her. A heavy thump, something dropped.

She froze, unable to move. It was in the other room, less than twenty feet away. She didn't think she should call out. What would be the point? She was the intruder. She forced herself to move, walking slightly sideways, trying to see through the open door into the next room. A scratching sound.

She looked around the corner and jumped back. A raccoon. It seemed larger inside somehow. It froze and stared at her. She looked up and saw the hole near the top of the wall. Noises came from the wall. A family. Bea eyed the stairs and edged toward them, though it brought her closer to the raccoon.

She inched to the top of the stairs then raced down, rocketing down to the main floor to the back door. She stood there a moment, looked outside. She opened the door quietly and closed it behind her. Nature was taking over, like those ancient cities in the jungles of Thailand. A vanished civilization now consumed. The house would be covered with creeping vines, choked, the chimney filled with bats, rats in the basement, squirrels in the attic, raccoons in the kitchen. She'd seen foxes on their street, two coyotes strolling confidently in daylight, a deer in the grocery store parking lot near the ravine. They sensed that we were on our way out.

form follows function

THEY MOVED SLOWLY ON THE Chicago River, sitting on the up-
per deck of the boat to get the breeze. Dark-grey clouds lolled
to the north. The afternoon heat lingered over the water. It
could have been July. It could have been Iran. A class of school
kids twitched and squirmed and looked at their phones. Bea
examined her sister, her hair twisting in the wind, one hand
continually pushing it off her face, which was drained-looking.
She'd lost a little weight. *I'm a mess,* she'd said tearfully on the
phone. The architectural river tour was a ritual of sorts; they
did it every time Bea came to visit, weather permitting. It was
relaxing, and slightly cooler on the water. Their guide this time
was a man in a Cubs cap, wearing khakis and a red polo tucked
in over a substantial belly. There are thirty-nine of these types
of bridges, he said as they glided beneath one, more than any
other city on *earth.* He didn't look like an architect. He looked
like a football fan. Everyone in Chicago looked like a football
fan to Bea, the brisket faces, hearty, wide-beamed men who
looked as if they came from another era. Bea loved Chicago,
its iconic buildings and immigrant brawl. But you couldn't
break into houses here; you'd be shot.

They slowly glided toward another bridge and Bea examined the intricate ironwork as Ariel talked about Levi.

You know, you think somehow things will change, Air said. There should be a mandatory class at university that explains how relationships in fact *don't* grow. They solidify on about Day Six and what you see on that *day,* that is what you will see for the next twenty years...

The tour guide had a hand-held mike, his voice competing with Ariel's. *You got your beaux arts buildings...*

So if that thing he does with his teeth, Ariel said—kind of click the front ones together when he doesn't agree with you but is too passive-aggressive to say so—if that bugs the shit out of you on Day Six, then it's going to make you murderous by Year Eighteen. He will not get cooler, more understanding, less selfish, his dick isn't going to flourish...

The massive warehouses drifted by, the sturdiest buildings in the nation.

I think the problem, Ariel continued, well, basically everything was a problem, but the *root* is that Levi inherited exactly the wrong amount of money. If he'd gotten a pile, then maybe he would have been more generous or less worried, or at least less obsessive. But you know, he got enough to live on if he doesn't actually do anything. I pick up a Starbucks every morning to take to the store and he downloads this article that says a daily Starbucks habit costs like sixteen hundred dollars a year and he puts it on the refrigerator. If he'd inherited less, then he'd have to work like a normal human being instead of spending his time in front of the computer finding bargains on AA batteries and one-ply toilet paper and streaming *The Walking Dead*. He's one of those guys who checks online to see who has the cheapest gas in town. There's an army of them, they have websites, and he'll drive to, like, *Waukegan* to save four cents a gallon and not see the irony. Oh god, Bea.

Ariel buried her head in her hands and started heaving and Bea put her arm around her and stroked her head.

Air sobbed and sucked in her breath as the guide stood rooted, staring up, stuck in his monologue, a meaty hand wiping his brow.

Tip of my tongue, he said. Help me out here, folks…Louis Sullivan! That's it. I can't believe I forgot his name. He put a finger to his temple and pulled the thumb trigger. You may be familiar with the phrase "Form follows function," he said. That was our Louis. Except it's actually "Form *ever* follows function." Lotta people don't know that.

But I mean, he has to give you half, right? Bea asked.

Ariel burst into tears again and Bea looked at her sister and hoped with every fibre of her being that she hadn't signed a pre-nup. Bea remembered going out on her first date and Ariel giving her advice—first base, second base, et cetera—and Bea got a bit lost with the baseball metaphors. *They only want to slide into home.* All those bases finally ending in this.

The boat floated past neoclassical, beaux arts, and Mies's International Style as Ariel went on about Levi. His last name was Soderstrom, the umlauts long gone, and the Soderstrom family was a bit severe, Bea recalled. Assembled for the wedding, Levi's family looked like a Swedish version of *American Gothic*. A handsome clan, though chilly. Stiff Lutherans who didn't mingle well. Ariel was thirty-four when she got married and their mother actually heaved a sigh of relief when the vows were spoken, happy that Ariel had snuck in under the wire, able to start a family if they got started *right away,* a fact she brought up three times during the course of that day.

Air told her their marriage counsellor wasn't even a real marriage counsellor. You could get a discount if you went with a grad student and Levi couldn't resist a bargain. Ariel only found this out when Levi was late and Air chatted with the counsellor, who did look alarmingly young, and was alarmingly young (twenty-four), and had never actually been in a serious relationship and said her work had made her think twice about getting in one.

Bea remembered Ariel laughing at the beginning, though. Remembered Levi actually being kind of funny, especially about his humourless Scandinavian family. He'd done something with computers, but he quit (or was let go) and stopped laughing and slowly returned to the fold, became a Soderstrom, that genetic destiny hardening within him like cement. Bea only saw him once a year or so, and each visit she noticed there was less of him: less laughter, less spontaneity, less flexibility.

Air was getting some money, but Levi had bankrolled her business, which had zero equity in it, and that would be part of the deal. And the family trust was so cleverly and intricately constructed that it wouldn't be part of any settlement.

The Wrigley Building went by, an empire built on chewing gum. Bea recalled from an earlier tour that it was the first office building in the world to have air conditioning. What did the white-collar world look like before air conditioning? Men in suits sweating like galley slaves. Which is what they were doing now. Men without their jackets, stains spreading like Rorschach prints on their shirts after walking two blocks.

Ariel sat up and wiped her eyes and blew her nose. She looked the way she had looked when that boy shot Old Yeller. Air and she and their mother sat in the theatre and waited until the credits finished rolling because they were all crying so much they wanted to stay in the dark. It was a repertory theatre—the movie was twenty years old when they saw it, part of some ironic festival—and there were only about six other people. That's when Air made Mother get the dog, Shepherd, so she could love it and never shoot it. Except Shep was the kind of dog you wouldn't mind shooting. They'd gotten it from the animal shelter and it had been mistreated, apparently.

BEA STAYED FOR THREE DAYS, sleeping on the couch in Ariel's apartment. They got up late, went to a local yoga studio, ate at two of Air's favourite restaurants, drank too much wine, and reconstructed odd events from their shared history.

They remembered a trip to a cheesy resort north of town named for a happy animal. It was on a lake and you ate at picnic tables inside and everyone got the same dinner, as though it was a massive dysfunctional family. A teenaged boy who was showing off for Ariel jumped off the roof of the boathouse on a water ski, but he mistimed it and the boat yanked him down onto the dock and he had to be taken away on one of those stretchers where you're strapped down because it may be a broken back or you're paralyzed or something and Bea remembered his eyes looking at her, the only things that moved.

IT WASN'T UNTIL THE LAST day that Bea brought out the photos. They were sitting in Ariel's living room, drinking wine in the early evening, an uncertain sun illuminating the carpet in slow flashes. A languorous light. The air outside was heavy, industrial. A fan circled overhead.

So I've been going through Mom and Dad's photos, Bea said.

Ummm, yeah, you said.

And there's some great shots. There's a shot of us in maybe Cape Cod, only it's autumn, an actual autumn. We're on the beach flying a kite. One of those photos where you feel like there's a narrative you can't quite pin down.

Not ringing a bell.

That's the point of photographs. Anyway, there are some in black and white, that go back before us. Some of them are just Mom and Dad, their wedding pictures, a few shots of them standing in front of a car. They're so young. I'll scan some of the coolest ones and send them.

Ariel nodded, sipped her wine, waited.

But there's these photos with them and a baby, Bea said. From 1960. September '60. Bea shuffled through the black and whites. And you see Mom holding it up, that face. So, I thought, you know, 1960 baby lust. It's the neighbour's baby and she wants one too. Bea found that photo and showed it to Air. But then there's this one, she said. She held up the shot of their father holding the baby, facing the camera. It's the same baby, the same day. And look at Dad's face. He's *thrilled*. And I couldn't really imagine him being thrilled by someone else's baby.

Ariel examined both photos, brought them closer then pulled away, almost at arm's length. I can't imagine him being thrilled by his own baby, she said, squinting at the photo. It looks like Dad, the baby.

Yeah, well, babies can look like anyone, but here's the thing. It was their baby.

What? You *know* this? How?

I checked online, found the obit.

Did you ask Mom about it?

I tried, but I felt so shitty. But you know, anything we want to know, we need to ask it soon, or it's gone.

A boy. What was his name?

Patrick James. He'd be, what, fifty-six now.

So what *happened?*

I don't know. He died.

Ariel held up the photos of their parents with the baby and looked back and forth between them. So we're Plan B, she said.

183

Air, I don't think—

Think about it. A boy. That's why Dad's thrilled. He's got a son who looks like him and he's thinking of all the things they'll do, they'll go *camping*—

Dad hated camping.

—they'll play catch in the backyard, whatever, then the son dies and they are so bereft they're comatose and it would be Mom who finally said, "We have to try again," and he'd go along with it and when she's pregnant, neither of them really know how to feel. It's complicated and any joy they feel for the new baby is marred by the grief they feel for the old one. She gives birth and out pops a girl. Out pops me. And nothing can replace that lost boy, but if something *could,* at least for Dad, it wouldn't be a girl, it wouldn't be me. What happened to that baby? We need to talk to Mom.

I don't know, Air. I talked to her and I still feel like shit. I mean, it's her *most* painful memory. This is the only upside of dementia, that you forget the worst things.

I don't know if you forget the worst things.

Who knows what we hold on to.

We hold on to the things that formed us.

Ariel poured more wine for both of them. Through the window Bea could see dark, rolling clouds and people on the street moving with purpose, the muscular pulse of Chicago.

Ariel looked at her. Nephelinite, she finally said, deliberately pronouncing each syllable.

What?

Neph-el-in-ite. Volcanic rock. Go ahead.

Air, I'm not in the mood.

You're conceding, then.

No, I'm not conceding…

Nephelinite, last pronunciation.

Oh for fuck's sake. N-E-P-H-E-L-I-N-I-T-E. Nephelinite. Your turn.

It was a game they had played when they were kids. They used to play it whenever things got too tense or too crazy or too anything. They had both been spelling bee champions, sharing what was an almost autistic ability to see an unfamiliar word in its component letters. They had been champions in an era that didn't prize spelling bees. They'd once made it to the city finals and were the last two standing. Bea had been pushed up two grades because she had demolished her classmates (Air had envied her nickname, Spelling Bea). And Air had whispered to her that they should both misspell the next word on purpose and it would be a glorious tie between the Billings sisters. So Bea, who had drawn "recalcitrate," a word she'd never heard before but somehow instinctively knew how to spell, replaced the *i* with an *a* on purpose, and even as she was delivering her word, she had vague misgivings about the pact with her twelve-year-old sister. When Air marched through "hyperkinesia" without hesitation or error and the judge nodded and everyone clapped, Bea burst into tears, not at losing but at the betrayal, and Air took her aside and said, Stop being such a baby, it's over now, it doesn't even matter who won. Ariel's version of this was quite different, as it so often was.

Okay, Bea said, ah, Proterandrousness.

Really.

Proterandrousness.

Use it in a sentence.

Sitting in front of his computer screen, Levi gave off an unmistakable air of proterandrousness, Bea said, adding, The quality possessed by hermaphroditic plants.

Bea wasn't sure of the definition. As a result of this game, both she and Air had a store of arcane, hard-to-spell words, the way some Scrabble players memorize words that start with *x*. But the definitions had jumbled; they hadn't played in years.

Last pronunciation, Bea said, then her voice was suddenly dramatically quiet. A hush falls over the auditorium: Proterandrousness.

It's not even hard. It's just long and you think I'll lose track because I've had two glasses of wine.

Bea gave her an expectant judge's face, eyebrows raised, head tipped. We're waiting, Miss Billings, she said.

Jesus. Okay. P-R-O-T-E-R-A-N-D-R-O-U-S-N-E-S-S.

Bea nodded.

Okay, Ariel said. Crassulaceous.

Is that even a word? Bea asked. It wouldn't be the first time Ariel had made up a word. It sounded made up. Definition, please.

Crassulaceous. A member of the Crassulaceae family.

Better the Crassulaceae family than the Billings family.

The clock is ticking.

C-R-A-S-S-U-L-C-E-O-U-S. The eldest, and in many ways most annoying, daughter of the charming and talented Crassulaceae family.

Fuck off.

F-U-C-…

BEA TRIED TO EMPATHIZE WITH her sister. She'd been broken up with. Everyone had. She remembered a boy in first-year university, Jarett, whom she hadn't been attracted to initially, whom she was drawn to in small, measured moments. This made the breakup much worse. She had inched toward him, perhaps to the brink of love, and it meant that the contented, almost-in-love silence that followed that last, somewhat tepid sex wasn't in fact a contented, almost-in-love silence, but an I-should-have-ended-this-sooner silence on Jarett's part. And the mathematical parsing of the relationship that Bea went through afterward more than once meant that he had been pulling away from her, perhaps at the same rate she was inching toward him, and she wondered how long they had liked one another roughly the same amount, and estimated it was less than three days. The sentences and silences Jarett used during the actual breakup seemed trite and false and she tuned out partway through and felt she was having one of those near-death experiences where people rise out of themselves and are viewing their dead body on the road. She heard only random words and phrases—*freedom, love but not in love, young, I just think*—as well as a quote from a Leonard Cohen song. She felt betrayed, not just by him, but by herself for not having seen this coming. She resolved, long before he got to the part about hoping they could still be friends, never to break up with anyone this way. Though, less than a year later, she basically used Jarett's lame, hurtful breakup speech as a template for her own clichéd, rambling, silence-filled breakup with a boy named Abbott Sims whose penis was shaped like a shiitake mushroom, and once, when seriously stoned, she wondered (possibly out loud) if it would be more appetizing sautéed in butter with a little thyme.

But marriage breakups were different. Love wasn't always the issue. It was logistics and money and property and, at this point, the sudden, vivid spectre of being alone. To find oneself one of those women to whom everyone keeps saying, *You're so fabulous, I can't believe they aren't crawling all over you*.

THE CAB WASN'T AIR-CONDITIONED AND they weren't moving fast enough to get a breeze. The Chicago traffic was dense and angry and gun-laden, a symphony of horns. Bea would be a damp wreck before she even got on the plane. At least it was only a short flight. By the time they got to O'Hare, she had to run to the gate, a middle-distance sprint through those caverns. She was sweating heavily when she slumped into her seat after wrestling her bag into a too-small space in the overhead compartment.

As the plane banked north, she observed the city laid out below, its insistent grid receding from the lake. Every city was an argument with itself. How many murders did Air say there were last year? Every day someone got shot or stabbed by someone they knew. The Willis Tower gleamed then vanished and all she could see was the grey lake below.

Form follows function. What are we formed by? We construct the world we need. A family constructed on the ashes of another, imagined family, a family their father resurrected in his tiny study every night, leaving his wife to deal with the one they were saddled with. Maybe everyone had this, the family they imagined before marriage, the one they envisioned after the birth of a child, the one they could see on the horizon, past the arid indifference of their partner. Each step, both real and imagined, sparking a recalibration, as possibilities rose and disappeared.

not everyone's cup of tea

THE DAWN WAS LISTLESS, THE sun slanted on the wall. Sang's face was slack, unprotected, guilty. Bea looked out the window at the elm tree, palsied in the slight wind. She got up, showered, resolved to make the day count. Downstairs, she made a cappuccino and read the headlines on six different pages of the newspaper. A photograph showed a cruise ship lying on its side in shallow water.

On her way to work, she took a different route, imagining she was in another city. The song on the radio had played at her high school dance, a waltz, no one really knowing the steps, just clutching one another on the dance floor, turning small circles, not knowing whether to talk or not, the lights playing off all that longing.

Bea picked up a coffee, let herself into the gallery, turned on the lights, examined the walls, turned on the radio, settled in.

Saturdays were hopeful. People wandered into the gallery on Saturdays, couples out for a stroll. They looked at art and stopped at cafés and read magazines and newspapers and tried on shoes. They went to afternoon films and shared popcorn in the dark then went home, ordered takeout, watched TV, drank wine, made love. This was the order of things.

THEY WERE GOING TO A play with Roger and Pen, and Katherine and Philip. They always had plans to see more theatre and never went, but Pen had gotten the tickets. Bea liked the feel of the theatre, the sense of camaraderie. It felt like a society, where the cinema was a group of alienated individuals sitting as far apart from one another as possible. Though she was perhaps a better fit for the movies.

She and Sang sat in the living room, waiting for Roger and Pen to pick them up. Sang had a largish vodka on ice. He swirled the ice aggressively. He didn't want to go, felt he'd been ambushed.

How long has it been since we went to the theatre? Bea asked.

Not long enough.

Five or six years ago she and Sang and Thomas had gone to see a bloated musical that no one wanted to see, but she'd gotten cheap tickets and that was that. Sang was resentful and terse, driving like a teenager. On the way to the theatre the car behind them slammed into their bumper and a man got out of an SUV and he and Sang yelled at one another and the police arrived and coordinated the exchange of documentation for insurance purposes. Sang was silent the rest of the way and his silence and body language suggested he blamed Bea for the accident because if she hadn't bought the stupid tickets, they wouldn't have been rear-ended by a fuckwit suburban hockey dad. By the time they got to the theatre, the show had already started and the usher wouldn't seat them; they had to wait for the intermission. They ordered drinks and stood by the door and listened to the muffled generic music for forty minutes.

After the intermission, Sang refused to come in and sit down. She and Thomas sat together listening to lusty baritones belt it out while Sang stayed in the lobby and drank vodka for an hour. She'd had to drive home.

It wasn't *Phantom,* was it? Bea said. When was that, five years ago?

I should have been consulted, Sang said.

For tonight, or for *Phantom?*

Both.

If you'd been consulted, you would have said no. You always say no. It's almost a principle with you.

There's a reason theatre is dying. It's pure fucking artifice.

Why don't you wait until you see it before getting pissed off.

Why wait? I will *hate* the play, and I will *hate* the fact that I've been dragged there, and I'll resent the fact that we'll have to talk about it afterward.

We could drop you off at the new *Transformers* movie. Bea looked at her pulsing phone. Rog and Pen were outside, picking them up.

They're here, she said.

A WOMAN TOOK THE STAGE and acknowledged that the land they were on once belonged to First Nations; she cited the Mississaugas and Huron-Wendat and a few others. This was how every event started now, a guilty recognition that we destroyed their way of life. And now we're destroying our own way of life.

The play was a bit disjointed. The set stark, the lighting harsh. At the intermission Roger ran into a former student in the lineup at the bar, a woman who looked to be in her thirties, wearing torn jeans and an elegant top, a sense of self-possession, the kind of woman who would have had an affair with her professor when she was twenty. Bea watched the encounter, saw the woman assess Roger, trying to parse this shaggy mess with the man she had slept with fifteen years ago, if she had in fact slept with him.

The play went on too long. Everything did these days. The standing ovation was spotty and awkward, a few people popping up, most sitting, then a few of those who were standing sat down just as a few of the sitters finally stood. Sang sat defiantly, not clapping, checking his phone.

They all went back to Bea's. She'd arranged a charcuterie plate—some pedigreed cheeses, a strip of truffle running through, covered in ash, created by monks; pecans, pears, rosemary crackers, figs, soppressata, wild boar and apricot pâté. The six of them sat in the candlelight, drinking wine, dissecting the play. A lot of energy went into dissecting things these days; taking apart movies, books, couples, dinners, lives, family. All the simple parts laid out like the workings of a watch.

A tad unfathomable, Roger said.

That doesn't make it profound, Sang said. He was terse, brittle. He'd been twitchy throughout the play.

I'm not sure about those stark sets, Katherine said. They're a bit oppressive.

You can't have fights onstage anymore, Philip said. Film has killed them. All that choreography and those quick edits and fight scenes like violent ballet. Onstage it's so clunky and fake-looking. Like slow motion.

Maybe it's actually more real-looking, Bea said. That's what we no longer recognize: reality.

The reality is, Sang said, if you're going to charge eighty dollars a ticket, you have to deliver something that resonates.

We're talking about it two hours later, Bea said. That's resonance.

I *fucking* hated it, Sang said with some force.

There's your headline, Roger said, getting up heavily to go outside and smoke. His appetite was getting more Falstaffian by the day. He and Pen were zero-sum; as he ate more, she ate less. At some point he'd be Orson Welles and she would disappear.

The candlelight was thick and yellow. Bea was fatigued. Their faces had that Renaissance glow.

Bea looked at Philip's wine-smeared face and guiltily remembered reading part of his sixteen-page manuscript on his un-password-protected computer, his biography of Wittgenstein. Very little of it had made sense. She'd taken a philosophy course at university, but anything she had learned was lost or garbled, too abstract to hold on to. She remembered typing into his manuscript:

> Ludwig called his buddy René Descartes. "Hey, do you feel like a cheeseburger?" he asked.
>
> "I *do* feel like a cheeseburger," Descartes said philosophically. "Perhaps I *am* one."
>
> "You might be overthinking it, Dude," Wittgenstein replied with an Aryan shrug.

SHE HAD LINGERED OVER THE Save button then pressed it, wondering if she should wipe her fingerprints off. It was an awful thing to do. Bea wondered if he'd even noticed. When was the last time he'd looked at the manuscript. Philip could be an intellectual tyrant at times, so maybe it served him right. This is what she told herself now. And he'd gotten grant money for this, quite a bit. He'd gone to Austria to do research, had spent time at Cambridge. All for sixteen pages.

The five of them sat there with their wine and their secrets as Roger stood outside smoking. The charcuterie plate had been a thing of beauty. It was ravaged now, scraps strewn on the wooden platter, as if animals had torn something apart.

THE LOCK GAVE UP EASILY. She'd seen them both on the street—Dennis and Leslie. Younger, mid-thirties, meticulously put together. There was something about them, a human version of a Potemkin Village.

She'd followed them into the bank, stood behind them in the longish line, listened to their conversation. They'd wanted to be overheard, happy for the audience.

I have to get the manager's signature for this. She said this imitating the teller, a little girl voice.

Bea followed them back to their house at a discreet distance, a two-storey semi-detached with a struggling garden. She went around to the lane and looked at it from the back. Small yard, high fence. No obvious alarm, no sign.

She'd returned the next morning to see them get into a white BMW SUV, drive away, maybe both working downtown.

Forty-two seconds for the Weiser, a new record. Their furniture was unremarkable. No children. The main floor was neutral, no hint of personality, a few generic prints on the wall. The living room felt unused; the magazines on the coffee table might have been arranged.

Bea went to the basement, smelling mould at the top of the stairs. Half the houses around here were built over underground rivers. It was a mess down there. An old couch with a blanket on it, mismatched throw pillows. Piles of things: tools, magazines, paperbacks, stuffed animals, a stack of towels that might have been hijacked from a health club. A massive TV took up one wall. A chipped coffee table had a few dishes on it. This was the other version of themselves, what they'd meant to leave behind in the suburb they had come from, the chaos and second-hand furniture and peanut butter and jelly sandwiches and macramé they'd grown up with. They'd come to the city to reinvent themselves and only gotten as far as the main floor. Down here they ate the food that gave them comfort, watched the shows that made them laugh, wore their baggy sweats.

Bea went upstairs, to the second floor. It was closer to the basement than the first floor, clothes strewn, furniture they'd brought with them. There was a credit card bill on the dresser and Bea looked at it—$49,584.32. She scanned the list of what they'd bought last month. That TV, it looked like. A local restaurant showed up eleven times, groceries, a cash advance of $3,500.

In the medicine cabinet, there were two medicine bottles. She looked at the label. Most of it was in Spanish. It was Nembutal. She opened them. Both bottles were full. She went back to the credit card statement. There was an entry for Vida Termino. End of life. She googled it on her phone. *Vida Termino: order Nembutal online for Euthanasia for Veterinary Purposes*. Where was their pet? Was this a suicide pact? They would live well for as long as they could, drive the BMW until they couldn't make the payments, live here until they couldn't manage the mortgage. Their lives were finite, free from worry. It would become a movement, have a name, maybe Vida Termino. A new definition of life for a new world.

Bea sat for a moment then googled a suicide hotline number and called it.

Hello, the voice said, how can I help you?

Well, it's not me you can help, Bea said.

Who needs help?

It's . . . Bea picked up the credit card statement and read, Dennis Wallace. He's planning on killing himself.

Is he there with you?

No. I'm…

You're a friend?

Yes.

Why do you think Dennis is in danger of taking his life?

There's a bottle of Nembutal in his medicine cabinet. I think Dennis and his wife are planning on taking it.

Have you noticed any change in their behaviour lately?

They both seem depressed. Weight loss. A kind of twitch-iness.

Do they use drugs?

Bea thought about this. Yes, she said, I'm afraid quite a bit.

The woman on the other end probed for information and Bea constructed a history that built on their debt and included trauma, unemployment, drug use, a previous history of sui-cide attempts.

How much convincing do you need? Bea finally asked.

We just need to deploy our limited resources where they are most needed, the woman said.

They are needed here, Bea said, and gave her the address.

What exactly is your relationship with Dennis and his wife?

I'm all that is standing between them and oblivion, Bea said. That's my relationship.

Mmm, well, I think it would be best if Dennis or his wife called.

That's probably not going to happen.

Why not?

Because they'll both be dead.

Bea spent another ten minutes trying to mobilize whatever suicide prevention resources were available, which turned out to be almost none, then finally hung up. She went upstairs and took both bottles of Nembutal and put them in her purse. She looked through kitchen drawers and found some paper and a pen and wrote a list:

Sell your car
Downsize
Consolidate your debt
Live live live

She added the number for the suicide hotline. Is this enough? she wondered. A leaden doubt sat in her head. She put the list on the refrigerator, using the magnetic bumblebee. A siren sounded, an emergency somewhere. She quietly left.

gridlock

THE TRAFFIC HAD A PERSONALITY, a malevolence. Bea sat in her car, fiddling with the radio. There was a station that dealt with traffic, explained where problems were (too late for that), what they were (overturned semi-trailer? six-car pileup? road closure?). She couldn't remember the call numbers. It was midday, safely between rush hours, and she was stopped dead on the 401 highway. Twelve lanes in the unseasonably hot October sun, not moving.

She rarely ventured to the outer suburbs but had gone to get plumbing fixtures for the gallery bathroom at a deep discount. A Philippe Starck brushed nickel faucet at 70 percent off. She couldn't find the traffic station and finally gave up. After ten minutes, Bea turned off her engine.

She got out of her car and tried to see what the problem was. There might be twenty thousand people stopped. Why were both directions stopped? The air was hot and exhaust-laden. Hundreds of people milled.

Bea asked a woman if she'd heard anything on the radio.

Apparently a truck turned over, the woman said, blocking the lanes. She was in her twenties, wearing a tank top with

Tweety Bird on it. Like we need this, she said.

Hazardous materials, a man said authoritatively. He was standing beside an Audi. Some kind of spill. Need haz-mat people to come in for the cleanup. I'm picking up my god-damn kid.

Twenty minutes went by. The sun was punishing. Most of the cars were turned off, but some people had their engines running, sitting inside with the AC on. The people outside were on their phones, searching for information. Bea found references to the traffic jam but no definitive cause. The air was poisonous.

What is this, China? the Audi man said to no one in particular. Fuck's sake.

The frustration level ramped up, everyone imagining what they would be doing if they weren't stuck in traffic, the peaceful yoga class, the pleasant lunch. Heat rose from the asphalt. Bea sat in her car with all the windows open. There was no breeze and she was perspiring freely.

Her phone was at 12 percent. She wondered why more people hadn't managed to get off at an exit. You'd think the snarl would gradually bleed out onto the exit ramps and people would pick their way through the city streets, grateful just to be moving. But there didn't seem to be any movement. Bea searched for a site that showed an aerial photo of the traffic jam and finally found one (another 2 percent). It was a blurry satellite photo that enlarged imperfectly, black and white, striated with pale lines that bled. It was grey and inconclusive. The sun lit the windshield glass. A few horns still blared uselessly.

Thousands of people were standing on the highway, frozen, like an ambitious art installation. *Modern Life*. Bea looked in an open window at a woman who seemed to be having trouble breathing.

Are you okay? she asked.

The woman held up one hand that might have indicated she was okay.

Do you need anything? Bea asked.

The woman shook her head no, then managed, I get a bit claustrophobic. She was sweating heavily. It ran down her panicked face in rivulets.

Do you want some water? Bea asked.

The woman nodded.

I don't have any in my car, but I'll see if I can find some, Bea said. I'll be back.

Bea asked the people around her if anyone had any water. A medical issue, she added. No one offered any. Maybe they didn't have any water, Bea thought, or maybe water was already a precious commodity and everyone was keeping it for themselves.

She walked east, past thirty cars that didn't have water. It was eerie to venture so far from her car on the highway. The sun bore down. Tempers frayed. People yelled into cellphones and swore. Women with crying children in car seats, men with their shirts off shaking their heads, people sitting on the asphalt, leaning against their cars in the meagre shade. They hoarded water, made makeshift hats against the sun, fashioned out of T-shirts or paper. A few had left their cars and walked off the highway, carrying purses and crying children, guiding elderly parents, refugees. Do you stay or go? Bea tried to calculate the risk/reward scenario for both. Ten thousand cars (a random guess) filled with First World problems—divorced dads not picking up kids, Pilates instructors, people heading to affairs, AA meetings, preliminary hearings, a sale on Italian floor tile. It would only take three hours in the sun to become the Third World.

Bea heard a loud thump, metallic. It was up ahead somewhere. She heard a man yell, *Turn off. Your FUCKING CAR!*

Another few thumps.

Now, fucker!

Someone was kicking a car that was running, the owner inside with the AC on, exhaust spewing. There was the sound of glass. People's voices. Bea couldn't see. It wasn't that far up ahead, though.

She heard a pop. A gunshot. It didn't sound real, or at least it didn't sound like gunshots in movies, which was her only reality when it came to guns. There were screams and people ran toward her.

More shots. Bea was knocked to the asphalt by a man trying to run by her. Her glasses disappeared under a van. She got up and ran. Dozens were running now, away from the shots, off the highway. Bea scrambled with them, her vision blurred. She had no coherent thought other than escape.

They kept moving in a ragged herd, not knowing exactly what they were running from. More people joined them. Bea finally stopped, then bent over the scrubby dead grass beside the highway, heaving, breathless. People moved past her. There were screams. Helicopters hovered loudly overhead. Bea stood up, her eyes trying to focus, remembering suddenly that her glasses were gone. Everything was softly awry, blurry figures moving through a dream landscape. Her hands had blood and grit on them from being pushed to the asphalt. Her elbow was sore and she turned it to see a raw scrape.

She kept moving with the exodus, hundreds now. People asked one another what had happened, but no one knew. They ran the way buffalo run from danger, a herd signal; they run not knowing the cause, right into the jaws of a greater danger.

Bea walked to Jane Street. Cars jammed the exit. There was a fight among several men, women yelling. A man jogged by her with a large dog on a leash. Bea looked at her phone. It was the hottest October 12 on record, her weather app said. She phoned Sang but ran out of battery before he picked up.

Jesus. Jesus. She looked up, put her phone away, asked three people if she could borrow theirs. No; another precious commodity. She walked south, down Jane, until she got to a bus stop. She'd take the bus to the subway station. She realized suddenly that she'd left her purse in the car. She stared north, gauged the possibility of going back. She thought she could see a bus coming, but without her glasses she couldn't be sure. After a few minutes a bus suddenly loomed and braked in front of her. The doors opened.

I don't have any money, she said to the driver. My purse is in my car.

My purse is in my car, the driver mimicked in a high voice. He closed the door in her face and lurched away.

Bea stared after the bus, shocked and furious. You shithead bus driver dick. I'll report you—medium build, stupid face, asshole, *asshole,* Jane Street, midday, failing to respond to an emergency. A woman walking by stared at her. Bea knew she sounded like a madwoman. She was a madwoman. She stood for another five minutes as her anger subsided, then decided to walk back to her car and get her purse. It took twenty minutes to get back to the highway and there was already yellow police tape that stretched for a hundred yards. Emergency vehicles filled the shoulder—police, ambulance, fire trucks. Bea heard a chorus of sirens.

Bea approached a young woman in uniform.

My car is in there, Bea said. A Honda. My purse is in the front seat.

Can't cross the line, ma'am, the cop said.

I just need my purse. I…

Investigation, ma'am.

Homicide? Those shots. Someone was murdered?

I can't tell you anything at this point in time.

The woman wasn't actually facing Bea when she talked. She talked to a point about three feet to the left, reciting. Bea was an abstraction.

I was there, Bea said.

The cop stared.

I was there when the shots were fired. I ran, like everyone, and I left my purse in my car. A Honda.

You can make a statement downtown, the cop said.

Bea turned and walked south back down Jane, past doughnut shops and roti stands and shifty electronic stores crowded into strip malls. A dozen emergency vehicles went past. She was thirsty, getting hungry, perspiring heavily. It took forty-five minutes to get to the subway station. To walk home from here would take three hours, she reasoned, and these weren't the ideal shoes.

At the subway station, she hung back, waiting until someone was at the wicket needing something from the only employee in the station, blocking the view. She saw a man use his card on the wheelchair gate, then breezed in right behind him, apologizing softly, her head down, waiting for someone to yell at her to stop, her heart hammering madly.

She walked to the end of the platform and stood there, so relieved she began to cry.

THE EVENING NEWS WAS ALL about the traffic jam, the worst in the country's history. There were still thousands of cars stranded on the 401. Bea watched the footage, hoping to see her car. A man had started shooting, the news anchor said. He'd killed three people in a rage and injured two others. There had been hundreds of other violent incidents. At least six people had been stabbed, one of them fatally, and dozens of fights had occurred. A baby had been born, a dozen pets lost. More than sixty cars set on fire. The highway was still closed. The footage looked like something from a Third World revolution—random fires and abandoned vehicles and scattered clothing.

Bea was on the couch, watching it with Sang, her knees up around her chin. Sang had his arm around her.

A photograph of the shooter appeared on the screen. An unemployed plumber, divorced, father of two.

Jesus, Sang said. You saw this guy.

Not really, it was just up ahead. I was trying to find some water for this woman who was hyperventilating. Bea wondered what had happened to that woman.

The actual cause was labelled a black swan event—an overturned semi-trailer believed to be carrying toxic materials (baby formula, it turned out), several smaller accidents on exit ramps, a westbound car that pulled over and caught on fire.

Her phone rang. Bea looked at it—Pen. Oh my god, Bea, she said. Are you okay? It must have been *devastating*. I mean, did you actually *see* him?

Just a blur, Bea said. He was up ahead. I heard the shots. It was surreal. I know that's what people say, but it's true. Some part of you doesn't actually believe you're there.

So the guy just flipped.

Apparently there was a car beside his that was running. Someone sitting inside with the AC on. But, you know how hot it was and it was probably five degrees hotter on that highway, and the exhaust…

You should see someone, Bea. I can give you the name of my psychologist. She's great. There are specialists for this kind of thing. Crisis counsellors. I don't know any, but she would.

They chatted while the footage on TV replayed. A hastily assembled panel of experts talked about gun control and grief and mental illness and social media. There was a montage gleaned from phones, frantic images of people running, a glimpse of the shooter, someone getting stabbed. A big guy punching someone, his sweaty face twisted with hate. The images filled social media, hasty, frantic footage of urban life. The event was deconstructed then carelessly thrown on the pile of violent, uncomprehending death that filled the world— school shootings, bombings, police choking jaywalkers.

In the next two hours she talked to Katherine and Thomas and her sister, who was worried, though Bea thought she detected a very faint smugness; her city, celebrated for its low crime rate, for its niceness, could no longer feel superior to violent Chicago. But murder rates had shot up everywhere, the heat making everyone itchy. Other numbers came up on her phone, friends, neighbours, but she didn't have the energy to answer and go through it all again.

IN THE COURSE OF THE next few days, thousands of cars were towed, including Bea's. Charges were laid against more than three hundred people. There were far too many towed cars for the municipal compounds and hundreds were diverted to empty lots. There was a hotline you could call and when you gave them your licence number, they told you where your car was. Bea's car was in an old lot in the Portlands, not all that far, thank god.

She went to pick it up, walking across the cracked asphalt, weeds poking through, as high as her knee. Her purse was gone. So were the Philippe Starck brushed nickel faucets. Hundreds of cars had been looted while they sat stranded on the highway. Police had set up sentries, but they weren't enough to patrol a four mile parking lot.

Bea sat in her car. She was part of history. But not even history was part of history anymore. There would be another shooting tomorrow: in Virginia or Texas or a Paris café. The names of shooters and victims lost, the motive undefined or quickly faded, a moment of modern rage, all of these events—thousands of them—woven into a red red tapestry.

most of our suffering is avoidable

BEA WENT ONLINE TO FIND a therapist. Her criteria were that she be a woman, and that she not live in the neighbourhood. She didn't want to be running into her at the grocery store. She found Phyllis Saxon, who had an approval rating of 3.9 out of five, a solid B. Phyllis turned out to be a concerned-looking woman in her sixties who wore leather pants. Her office wasn't far from her mother's place. She could visit her mother afterward.

Do I just start talking? Bea said.

If that's what you'd like to do, Phyllis said pleasantly.

And everything I say is confidential.

It is. Unless you've killed someone. Then it gets a bit murky.

She had a small smile, a therapy joke perhaps.

I haven't killed anyone, Bea said. I saw someone get killed. On the 401.

This wasn't exactly true, but Bea felt some pressure to deliver a more concrete problem.

The shooting?

Bea nodded.

Tell me what happened.

Bea went through the events, how the scene didn't seem real at first, then suddenly it was overwhelming, then it felt like a movie, then something else. She didn't know what she felt now. A grief for the people who were shot. They talked for half the session about survivor's guilt, about PTSD, about acknowledging what had happened.

There's something else, Bea said.

Yes? Phyllis had a gentle, leading voice.

Bea hovered over her confession. I've been breaking into houses, she said.

Breaking into houses.

If Phyllis was surprised, she didn't show it. She would have heard odder confessions than this. They weren't supposed to judge.

You started this after the shooting? Phyllis asked.

No, no. Before.

What do you do when you're inside?

I look around.

Do you take anything?

No, Bea said, which was almost true, one dress. Though the point of therapy was to tell the truth.

Do you know these people?

Sometimes.

What do you feel when you're in someone else's house?

Bea thought: Alive, fearful, singular, but said, It depends on the house.

Bea thought about standing in the house where her brother would have spent his brief life. She didn't want to drag that into their first session.

When did it start?

Several months ago, a friend's house.

What was happening in your life at that time?

My son is away at school, in Montreal, McGill. Sang and I—

Sang?

Sanger. My husband.

How would you describe your relationship?

We don't really talk anymore. I mean we *talk*, but we're sort of going through the motions. We haven't had sex in a while.

What's a while?

Five months.

Or fourteen, she thought. Truth.

Phyllis wrote something.

You think they're connected? Bea asked.

Phyllis looked up with an unreadable therapist expression. Well, it's possible, she said. On a conscious level, the thief wants gain—she wants the power that comes with being inside another person's house, another person's life. But unconsciously, she wants to get caught, she wants loss—loss of freedom, loss of respect. It could be a way of acting out an unresolved inner conflict.

Bea thought this sounded somewhat textbooky.

I think my husband might be having an affair, she said. It felt liberating to say it out loud.

Why do you think that?

I saw him walking in Little Italy. He works at the university, he didn't say anything about being there. And he lied about teaching that night.

Phyllis nodded.

My husband's a professor. It's a cliché to sleep with students, but it's a cliché for a reason.

Phyllis wrote for a solid minute. Bea wondered what those notes looked like.

When you saw him, she said, when you saw—Sanger?—walking in Little Italy, what did you feel at that moment?

I don't know. I wasn't actually sure it was him. You get to a plateau in a relationship and it's not great, but you settle in. Marriage is work, that's what they say. But we haven't been working at it, it's like we both took a thousand sick days.

But it was good at some point.

We have these foundation myths, don't we. Maybe it was never as good as I thought it was. Maybe we just didn't have enough of those moments you need to sustain you through the shitty times.

What kind of moments?

I don't know, romantic weekends, a crisis we weathered together...something that turns you into a couple.

Phyllis nodded. Let's go back to the breaking in, she said. You go inside. Then what do you do?

Bea thought, Examine other people's lives, anthropology.

When you're alone in a house, Bea said, you get a sense of the lives that you don't get if you're at, I don't know, a party maybe. You get a sense of the events that led up to this moment . . . Bea gestured. This house, these kids, these debts.

What are you hoping to find, do you think?

Bea shrugged. I'm not sure.

Do you measure your own life against these lives?

Sometimes I feel like they're there, the people, that I'm watching their lives, not in real time, more like an essence. I don't know, I'm not explaining it very well.

What parts of their lives do you see?

The parts they don't show the world.

THE CONVERSATION CONTINUED UNTIL THE fifty minutes were up. Bea felt relieved that she'd unburdened herself, but also felt relieved that the session was over.

She wasn't in the mood to visit her mother but went out

of a sense of duty. She knocked once then let herself in. Her mother was on the couch, lying down, asleep. The television was on, an ad for some pharmaceutical, a comforting voice reeling off all the possible side effects—suicidal thoughts, diarrhea, nausea, memory loss, unusual urges, billowing fear, festering doubt, unrequited love, searing regret. Bea turned down the volume. She walked over and stared at her mother's vulnerable face. How coherent would her dreams be at this point? She straightened a few things out of habit, sat down wearily, the disorder of her mother's life quickly closing in on her.

As a child, Bea had wanted a life in the suburbs, a desire formed while driving through Don Mills during the week before Christmas when her mother had gotten completely lost looking for a discount store that a neighbour had told her about that sold second-hand private school uniforms— pleated plaid skirts and white blouses. It was dark by four thirty and they glided through the ordered streets and every house, it seemed, had Christmas lights, that festive, colourful geometry—running along the triangle peaks of dormers, traversing the lengthy horizontal planes of the eavestroughs and down the vertical of the two-car garages. And she imagined lives inside those houses that were filled with contentment and nice siblings and normal fathers and not filled with driving in the dark looking for a store in a strip mall that sold second-hand pleated skirts for two dollars.

She got up and kissed her sleeping mother and left.

She drove home and mixed herself a rare martini and sat on the couch and gave her therapy session as much reflection as she dared. Suddenly everyone needed to resolve life, a modern impulse. Bea let the sharp and wonderful martini flow through her, and by the time she was finished, her problems seemed both clearer but more distant, less threatening. Bea thought about mixing a second martini but decided against it, knowing it would replace this semi-therapeutic moment with simple impairment. Though it's only impairment if you're trying to *do* something, she thought—walk, talk, think, chop onions. If you're just sitting, wallowing slightly, it doesn't impair *that*. It may even be an enabling device, a tool. Man the Tool User, she decided as she walked back to the kitchen.

Sang came home late. He was a bit drunk, weaving slightly, surprised to see her up. Bea sat up on the couch. She'd been reading a magazine, deep in the Amazon rainforest with an environmentalist who warned it would go condo in our lifetime. She'd fallen asleep on the couch and woke up when Sang came in.

You're teaching tomorrow morning, Bea said. It was 1 a.m.

At this point I'm on autopilot. Like my students.

She examined him, this alien thing in her living room, fresh from fucking someone else. Things were being taken from her: son, husband, mother, the planet. Had she been that careless?

I'm dead, Sang said, and moved heavily toward the stairs.

Who killed you?

Sang turned around and tried to focus on her. How is that book club going? he asked. It sounded like an accusation.

We don't talk about books anymore. Just drink wine and talk about sex. Skip the middleman.

He nodded uncertainly, a bobblehead. I read that sex is 90 percent mental, he said thickly.

And that figure can climb.

Sang heaved himself toward the stairs with a hint of violence and climbed up to bed.

rosy

THE HOUSE WAS ACROSS THE valley in Cabbagetown, a narrow Victorian, two-storey, the exterior brick sandblasted, a well-intentioned garden. It belonged to a woman who looked to be Bea's age. She'd been working in the garden when Bea walked by, planting something, looking up with a generic smile, the harsh light washing her out, her face shiny, wiping her forehead with the back of her gardening glove, leaving a dirt streak. Bea smiled back and stopped on the next block and wrote the address on her phone. She walked home and the wind blew grit that hit her face like a sandstorm.

THE INTERIOR WAS WELL-KEPT, TIDY. A pair of red Hunter rubber boots in the hallway, a Barbour coat hanging on the hook. There was a coffee-table book about dog breeds on the glass coffee table. Bea went upstairs and looked in the medicine cabinet in the bathroom. There were two prescription bottles, both filled with what Bea thought might be antidepressants, it was impossible to remember all the names now.

There was a book on the bedside table, it looked like a journal, with a padded Liberty print cover. Bea opened it and looked at the neat cursive handwriting.

> Violence, not really clear. A dog, huge, black. Someone shot it and it's lying on the street and no one seems to notice or care. The streets are stylized, uneven. Something vaguely medieval.

It looked to be a dream diary. There were short entries, a few that went on for several pages.

> I'm flying, holding on to something—an animal?, it's dark but not night, like the light before a summer thunderstorm. It's hard to see and we're flying over a landscape that is grey, not anything I recognize (is this a bad sign—that so many of my dreams take place in a landscape that is unrecognizable). There is broken concrete, quite a lot of it. I don't see any signs of life. (why are my dreams so depressing and why are there so few people in them? Is this normal? I know what you're going to say—there is no "normal.")

Bea sat on the bed and flipped the pages. She'd always meant to keep a dream diary. The dreams were so vivid, but they evaporated so quickly; by breakfast she couldn't recall anything, only that she'd had a troubling dream that meant something profound.

> I'm at a party and I think I came with friends but I can't find them and I don't really know anyone. The house is labyrinthine and oddly angled and goes on forever and I pass a lot of people talking, though I can't recall any faces. Then I'm outside, but not consciously. More like in a

movie, a quick cut and I'm outside looking for my car. I walk several blocks, and can't find it (I'm not sure I know what car I'm looking for). Again, it's not really day or night, but a sort of Bladerunner twilight. I can hear music, it's the Beatles—but an odd distorted version of something, maybe "Norwegian Wood," I'd been playing it in my car. I realize my car is buried somewhere nearby and I start digging.

Bea closed the book and put it back on the bedside table and stood up and smoothed the sheets. She went into what would be the woman's study, a lot of books, mostly British novelists. All the Brontës leather-bound, an antique rolltop desk. On the desk there was a Visa bill and Bea picked it up. Evelyn Madding was her name. The rubber boots and Barbour jacket were on the Visa statement. Bea went downstairs and looked at the dog book from the coffee table. There was a pad of paper beside it and she'd written down three different breeds in her neat script: golden retriever (too cliché?), collie (temperamental—why don't you see more of them?), English sheepdog (climate?).

She was planning on becoming a dog owner. She would join those people in the dog park, asking one another what their dog's name was, exchanging cute stories, watching them frolic, talking to them in that baby voice. What else, meet a man/woman? with the same dog, wondering what sex would be like at this point.

Bea stood by the back door for a longish time. Outside, the day was grey, moody. The garden was well tended, fighting the heat, the roses wilted. Bea closed the door and walked through the garden. She stopped by one of the rose bushes and leaned over to inhale them, faint and dying.

the end of childhood

THERE WAS A FLIGHT SALE and Bea found a hotel on Sherbrooke on a travel site that offered a discount. When she'd phoned Thomas to tell him she was coming to Montreal for a few days, he'd sounded both vaguely happy and vaguely resentful, as if she was conducting an inspection. She said she was checking out a Montreal artist, which was true.

She took a cab to the hotel, the traffic ugly and snarled, the highways crumbling as the substandard mobbed-up concrete gave out, the whole city under construction. After checking in, she walked east along Sherbrooke Street then down to Sainte-Catherine, heading to a gallery in the east end. She loved the feel of Montreal, remembered her student years, a city discovered in increments, complicated and feminine.

It was a dusty forty-minute walk to the gallery. The air was hot, the streets grey and buckled. Bea yearned for walking weather, the crisp weather of a real autumn. She walked past restaurants, past a bondage store, discount clothes, a dozen cafés. She remembered sitting in a café in the Plateau, falling in love with an English major in the fading afternoon light, smoking, talking. So much to talk about then, conversations that went for hours, days. She woke up with him the next morning, no longer in love. It wasn't anything obvious, just a grey doubt that occupied space on the small, badly painted table in his cramped apartment as they sipped the coffee he'd made with the stovetop espresso maker. She wasn't sure of his name now, though it had been something grand—Blatchford? Tennyson?—and maybe that had been part of the appeal.

She wondered at the emotions that might have run through Thomas in his first year here. A hopeful romance, a failed romance, a yearning that's a sickness, the drunken, stupid sex at the end of a night of god knows what, the sex regretted before orgasm. Then staggering home in the dark, hopefully free of disease. But there seemed to be less of that now. They weren't as rabid for experience as Bea's gang had been—shrouded in cigarette smoke, judgmental and confident in politics, conflicted in sex, the most liberated women in history.

The gallery was small and sombre, housed in an old commercial building. L'Esprit empoisonné. The Poisoned Mind. The city still held the detritus of a radical left, anarchist bookstores and beards and brick-red jeans. She'd seen the paintings on slides sent by the artist—Jean-Luc Cassel—a series of recognizable children's toys painted in a way that made them human, filled with doubt, facing a crisis: Barbie and Ken, Chatty Cathy, a Cabbage Patch Kid, Tickle Me Elmo. The paintings were large, six feet by four. They were moody, with dark, almost Renaissance backgrounds, and verged on kitsch. They had a surprising impact.

The artist was standing by a table in the centre of the room. She recognized him from the headshot. He was both taller and older than she expected. Mid-fifties, grey hair, orderly, stylish rather than dishevelled. Bea approached and he smiled, his hand extended.

Bonjour, Bea said. *Monsieur Cassel?*

Oui. Bonjour, Beatrice.

C'est magnifique, Bea said, her arm indicating his work.

Merci. And thank you for coming all this way.

My pleasure.

It had only taken two lines to establish the language hierarchy; his English was better than her French. An apolitical adjustment, the simple pragmatism of a bilingual city.

She solemnly paced the room and took in the ten canvases, then they walked to a nearby café and she asked him about his work, where it had come from. She knew from experience that this question could result in anything—hostile silence, two hours of bullshit—but he talked about his work with logic and clarity, unspooling the idea that childhood had ended. It was, he said, a construct of the nineteenth century. He talked about European peasants living in small huts for centuries, everyone illiterate, children exposed to the coupling of their parents ten feet away. Adults didn't know much more than children; they knew a trade and by the age of seven the child might have a pretty good grasp of that trade and then grow into it. There wasn't anything that resembled today's version of childhood, which was essentially an invention. The concept reached an apex in the 1950s, spilling into the 60s, treasured, protected. In the Age of the Internet, he said, we had reverted to the Middle Ages, where everyone has access to the same information; a seven-year-old can watch the same pornography as his sixty-year-old grandfather. Everyone is exposed to everything and childhood has disappeared. So these toys are in mourning, an existential crisis. Jean-Luc gave a Gallic shrug, his hands going up.

They talked for more than two hours.

Perhaps you are free for dinner? he asked, his English perfect though oddly formal in places.

I'd like that, but I'm meeting my son for dinner. He's at McGill.

Jean-Luc smiled. Of course. If you have any time tomorrow.

He took a card out of his wallet that had his email and phone number. This is my studio, he said. His hands and forearms were more like a carpenter's than an artist's. Capable-looking.

That would be nice, Bea said.

They left and stood outside in the afternoon light.

À bientôt, Beatrice, he said, kissing her on both cheeks.

À demain.

BEA WALKED NORTH. TO HER left, Mount Royal thrust up like a benevolent fist, the heart of the city. The magnificent park. There were people playing tennis, a man wearing a V-necked white sweater who looked like he'd stepped out of the 1920s. She sat on a bench and listened to the muted thwack of the balls. It was pleasant, a hint of autumn finally in the air, the most humane season. Couples strolled, middle-aged, assured, armoured against the future. She heard languages she couldn't identify. Other languages held an urgency. The sky was a soft quilt of greys.

She was meeting Thomas at L'Express, a restaurant she had favoured as an undergraduate, prized for its bistro atmosphere. *So authentic,* they had said, the holy grail in all things back then.

A simple pleasure, to sit in the sun in another city and watch its citizens file past. She wondered if Jean-Luc had a partner. Perhaps his wife would have joined them for dinner. He was flirtatious, but the whole city was flirtatious, a currency here rather than a strategy. She finally got up and started walking to the restaurant, past stone facades and iron staircases and graffiti. When she got there, Thomas was inside waiting at a table, a glass of wine in front of him. She could see him through the window, unaware he was being observed. He looked younger than she remembered.

She went in and smiled at the maître d' and pointed to her son. *Mon fils,* she said, a little awkwardly. The man nodded and motioned her in.

Thomas got up slowly and accepted her longish hug. She sat down and stared at him. The last vestige of the boy was still in his face, though perhaps she was the only one who could see it.

He wanted to hear more about the shooting, although they'd talked about it on the phone at length. She went through it again. Each retelling brought her farther away from the reality; it was only a story now.

She told him about Jean-Luc, about his work and his theory of childhood. Thomas nodded, sipped his wine.

We used to come here, she said. It was so exotic for us.

We mostly go to those places on the Plateau, Thomas said, super cheap, bring your own wine.

How is the revolution going?

Thomas stared at her.

Your class, the Revolutionary Politics class.

Yeah, I don't know, I may drop it. The prof is one of those old lefties who probably grew up in a suburb somewhere and acts like he's Che Guevera.

Have you thought about where it's headed?

Where it's *headed?*

Do you want to continue in poli sci, get a law degree, MBA …

I don't know, I don't really have a plan.

Bea wanted to tell him that it's never too early to start, though she'd had this conversation a dozen times, beginning in high school, and didn't want to sound naggy fifteen minutes into the evening.

I feel I'm in some kind of, I don't know, like a lull, he said. Life is full of lulls.

Life was mostly lulls for most people, Bea thought. Occasionally all lull. Her sustaining fear, not entirely irrational, once more rose up within her: that her son would somehow be unable to find a place for himself in the world, that she hadn't properly equipped him for modern life.

They ordered dinner. The light outside was gone, replaced by a soft dusk. Thomas looked vulnerable in the candlelight. Jean-Luc may have been right about the end of childhood. In its place was an extended adolescence that lasted from the age of ten to forty. All those growing pains.

Are you and Dad going to get divorced?

What? Why would you ask that?

Thomas shrugged. You know, basically everyone's parents do.

No, we're not getting a divorce.

Had he been talking to Sang? What had Sang told him?

They talked for an hour, then left and walked down Saint-Denis, the sidewalk filled with people wearing light, flowing scarves, the citrus colours of summer. Students stunned by freedom. They got ice cream cones from a vendor and watched a guy juggle flaming batons. He was dressed as a Harlequin, keeping up a patter about burning love. He was roughly Thomas's age and Bea wondered what his mother thought about this line of work.

They walked the ten blocks to Thomas's apartment, shared, allegedly, with another poli sci major and a physics geek. There were restaurants and cafés on his street and dozens of young people milling. He nodded to a few of them and stopped and kissed a girl on both cheeks, saying a few words in French. He didn't invite Bea up and she didn't press, though she was dying to see the state of his apartment. She gave him a long hug and watched him disappear inside. She was oddly comforted. If he was lost, it was in the way most of us are lost at twenty.

She suddenly realized how much walking she had done that day and flagged a cab. She sank into the seat and watched the city go by, all the lurid life, everyone searching for something they couldn't find during the day.

SHE WOKE UP EARLY, WENT to the small hotel gym, where a few businesspeople were sweating and watching the news, then showered and went out for breakfast. She went to a café in an old bank, the high ceilings and pillars intact, as dark as a nightclub. No one needed light to read anymore; they were all on their computers or their phones. She'd brought a newspaper from the hotel and could barely read the print, hunched into it like an accountant out of Dickens.

After breakfast she hiked up the path on Mount Royal. After an hour her T-shirt was wet with perspiration. She stopped to look back at the view of the city. She could see Ste-Catherine Street. As a student Bea had participated in a Die-In, lying on the warm asphalt with hundreds of others, most of them with bicycles, protesting the murderous qualities of the automobile. Their jeans and T-shirts were stained with red dye and torn in places. On their faces makeup, blood and black eyes and crude gashes. Bea remembered the sense of anticipation and excitement, as if she was going onstage. Which she was, in a sense. And part of the excitement came from not knowing what the performance would bring. As it turned out, it brought a lot of things. One of the car enthusiasts, a chunky man with a cap advertising a brand of motor oil, yelled into the face of a sparsely bearded boy who was lying with his bicycle, his arm around it like a lover. The man finally kicked the boy, swearing in French. You've already killed us, you animals! a dead cyclist yelled.

Fights broke out. More police arrived. Some of the blood was real now and it gave the event drama and heft. It made it scary and something else Bea couldn't quite articulate, a combination of fear and excitement and the concrete belief that what they were doing must matter to provoke this kind of violence.

Afterward a dozen of them went back to someone's apartment and they celebrated their wounds and toasted themselves with convenience store wine, and felt, for those few hours, like genuine revolutionaries, united with brothers and sisters in Guatemala or El Salvador or wherever there was an actual revolution.

In the course of the next several months there were other protests—student tuition, nuclear weapons, whales, injustice in a country none of them had visited. In the course of all this, Bea had brief flings with three different men (and one fumbling, awkward lesbian night with a woman named Tania whose hygiene was a bit feral and Bea was unsure of the rules in this new arena so didn't say anything). With all of them she lay in the unclean student sheets afterward discussing the *power* of art and how it would eventually change the world.

Bea continued walking and when she got to the top of Mount Royal, she took out her cell and called Jean-Luc.

Oui allo.

Bonjour Jean-Luc …

Beatrice.

His slight accent softened her name. She could see the St Lawrence River, a few ships meandering. He invited her to his studio. Why not.

HIS STUDIO WAS AN APARTMENT on Clark, a few walls taken out to create a large room. The kitchen was perfunctory. A hallway led to what Bea assumed was a bedroom, maybe used for storage now. There were canvases stacked against one wall, some of them even larger than the childhood ones. She riffled through, uninvited, out of habit. The three largest canvases against the wall were all paintings of different handguns, the guns themselves five feet long, two of them angled aggressively toward the viewer. They unsettled her; a flashback to the shooting.

Jean-Luc hovered behind her. My gun phase, he said. They were a bit aggressive for this market. Shrugging with his face, a local tic.

How many did you do?

Ten. One sold here. Six were sold by a dealer in Dallas. He laughed.

Why guns?

I used to own them. I belonged to a shooting club when I was young. My father thought the world was coming to an end, nuclear war, famine, dog-eat-dog. He used to drive my brother and me to a shooting club every Saturday morning to improve our chances of survival. On the way we'd get a lecture about how much vodka the Russian president drank and how close the button was to his bed.

Do you still have the guns?

I kept one. A Browning. For its beauty. I buried the rest when I buried my father.

Jean-Luc showed her what he was currently working on. A dozen paintings were on the walls. He was the kind of artist who reinvented himself each time rather than sticking with a signature style. He poured two glasses of wine, an expensive-looking Bordeaux, and handed one to her. There was a small table near the window that looked as if it had been cleared just before Bea arrived; paints were piled up by the wall. They sat there and drank wine and talked, the afternoon light coming in.

It was after six when he asked if she was free for dinner. Jean-Luc suggested they walk, the restaurant wasn't far, it was a nice night. He called the restaurant to make sure they could take them, talking quickly in French. They walked for twenty minutes, the streets starting to fill up, people in small clumps.

The restaurant was small, intimate, almost full. The light dimmed, candles flickered, a bottle of wine disappeared quietly, a silky red that lingered. Jean-Luc asked about her life, her time at McGill, how she got into art, what had driven her toward it, the doomed, joyful pretensions of her undergraduate years. The food was adventurous. He laughed easily. By 10 p.m. it would be hard not to call it a date, which, Bea reasoned, wasn't against the law. People went on dates. Not *date* dates. Just.

They ordered coffee and Armagnac and Bea felt she should pay, that was usually the relationship between artist and gallery owner, but he protested, said dinner was his idea and it was his city. He paid and they left and walked toward the mountain then turned back toward his neighbourhood and the tidal pull of his studio.

HER FLIGHT WAS AT 9 a.m., which doesn't sound early, but she'd had to get back to the hotel, pack, check out, and deal with the insane rush hour traffic to get there at eight. So the morning goodbye had been a bit rushed and sleepy, though lovely. He'd gotten up and started to make her coffee, standing naked in the tiny kitchen. She didn't have time and said she'd get one at the airport and he held her and kissed her and she could feel him harden and they laughed and she bent over and kissed that partly tumescent middle-aged cock.

As she sat waiting for her flight, she went through the evening in a skewed montage. They'd gone back to the studio then kissed and walked together down that hallway. He was patient and adventurous and she was engaged in a way she hadn't been in a while and she used these details as mounting evidence that this wasn't technically cheating since she and Sang weren't having sex anyway. She decided not to take the extra step and suggest that this was in fact *good* for her marriage as it relieved a certain tension and she could be more generous now, but she did emphasize to the jury sitting in her head that Sang was almost certainly having an affair, which made her own, very brief fling morally inert.

So there it was. She sat in that airport glare amid the business travellers, many of whom would be guilty of some kind of indiscretion. Heading home. Back to the life that had driven her to this moment.

SHE WAS SURPRISED TO FIND Sang sitting at the breakfast table. He had a bagel and coffee and the Sunday paper. She put down her suitcase and walked over and gave him a quick, guilty kiss on his jam-tasting lips. Hers a bit more complicated.

How was Montreal? he asked.

I love going back there. They do so many things well.

Like politics.

I had a nice dinner with Thomas. We went to L'Express. For the nostalgia. I don't think they've changed the menu in twenty-five years. You wonder about the chef.

Bea poured herself a coffee and sat down and tore a small piece off Sang's bagel and put it in her mouth.

It settled me, somehow, she said, seeing Thomas up there, in his world. He has friends, he's coping.

Sang nodded, his head tilted slightly as if he wasn't entirely convinced. The morning light stretched across the kitchen. It lit the counter. The stove gleamed. They talked about Thomas. She took a section of the paper and they sat there and read in silence and everything was different.

narrative arc

THE KITCHEN WAS IN MID-RENO, cabinets torn out but nothing in their place. A sheet of cloudy plastic hung from the ceiling, held in place by tape. The second floor was empty, the basement unfinished, crowded with furniture. They had run out of money in mid-reno perhaps, or the contractor had absconded. The living room couch folded out into a bed. Wine bottles near the door. Their lives were lived on this floor.

There was a natural real estate arc: we begin in shitty student apartments, then a larger space, a starter home, a move to something larger to accommodate the growing family, downsizing after the children moved out, moving to a condo, then a modest apartment in an assisted living residence, and finally a small room in long-term care. We start small and end small.

Bea surveyed the squalor. That natural arc, the hopeful narrative from her parents' generation, might be gone. Houses were unaffordable. It would be a flat line, a trail of shitty apartments. Outside, the heat still loomed. The world was now either too much or not enough: rain, sun, heat, food, money, love. It would never find equilibrium.

exploiting weakness

SHE WAITED FOR WILL. IT was lazy mid-afternoon, the café half-full of people staring at laptops. Bea held up her own house key and recited its parts in her head: Head, Collar, Shoulder, Biting Cuts, Profile Contours, Bow, Blade.

Summer was breaking-and-entering season. You could stretch it into the fall, but you didn't want to be fumbling with locks in December with freezing fingers, leaving CSI footprints in the snow. And everyone was at home. They stayed inside and ate popcorn and watched television and emerged in spring, blinking like groundhogs. She was coming to the end of her quasi-criminal career. Its rewards were subtle—a sense of urgency and purpose (sort of), something completely her own. A nice dress.

Electronic locks were the way of the future and they were too abstract for her. So much of the future was discouraging. When she was a child, the future was something they anticipated like Christmas: individual rocket packs, robots doing housework, Dick Tracy watches with tiny TV screens on them. Everything the future was going to bring was welcome. Now every innovation encroached on something—privacy, freedom, employment. And it arrived so quickly. It used to be that a year would go by and the only new things would be the Wonderbra and touch-tone telephones. Now every week brought something overwhelming and suspicious.

Mechanical locks were straightforward; you exploited a weakness, in either the manufacture or the design. But electronic locks were replacing them, and they required not just a new set of tools but a new sensibility, and Bea wasn't prepared for that world. But the future always happens.

Though the future wouldn't look like the future—monorails and jetpacks whizzing by. It would look like the fourteenth century: feral dogs, highwaymen and ragged people warming themselves beside burning trash, lifeless cities, the sun obscured by permanent smog.

Bea took a sip of her cappuccino. Will wasn't coming. She checked her phone again.

She watched people passing by and tried to imagine how they looked to someone who loved them. Perhaps the obese man with the small whales on his shorts (a sense of humour!) was a kind father and decent man and his wife observed his difficult gait and knew that each day he set out into a sea of ridicule and unchecked appetite and she saw quiet courage and a dignity that transcended the physical. A pigeon-toed girl wearing knee-high boots and a leather jacket (a few weeks early for both) walked by a bit self-consciously. In the cheap purse with the skull on it was a copy of Sylvia Plath's poetry, or maybe they carried a different poet now. And some thin boy saw this gawky thing still adjusting to the big city and found her coltish and fascinating and told her she was amazing as they lay in the complex afterglow of that first shared orgasm.

You found something to love inside a person then bent the exterior to meet your minimum needs. Or else you fell in love with the glamorous exterior and rationalized the unappetizing contents. Like opening a beautiful German refrigerator to find the rotting carcass of a schnauzer.

She suddenly felt nauseous. Outside, cyclists zipped by dressed for the apocalypse: helmets, sunglasses, breathing through industrial filters, a spandex army.

october is the new september

BECAUSE OF THE HEAT WAVE inside the Arctic Circle, a piece of ice twice the size of Manhattan had calved off Greenland and was floating idly. Bea tried to not watch the dire forecasts, but couldn't help herself. The Weather Channel had become an obsession. There was a running tally of heat-related deaths in fifty major cities. New York led the pack with 36,320. They didn't include deaths where heat may have been the precipitant, where an insurance adjuster stuck in traffic in a car with faulty air conditioning took the six-iron that he kept under the back seat and hammered on the window of the tinted SUV that had cut him off, killing a soccer mom.

She catalogued the melt rate of glaciers, the number of species lost each year to extinction, the acres of forest lost to wildfires on any given day, the melt rate of Antarctica (twenty-four cubic miles annually), the vanishing bees (who knew they were so crucial), the vanquished songbirds dying in their billions. Smoke had drifted up from out-of-control wildfires burning in Michigan; you could taste it in the air. Beijing's air looked like coal dust. More than 300,000 dead from smog-related illness, and it wasn't even the most polluted city in China, just the one everyone could pronounce. It could rain frogs now and humanity would take it in stride, she thought. *Oh, it's always rained frogs.*

Bea knew it was going to end. She knew our Saviour had thrown in the towel and gone back to His golf game, and knew that mankind deserved to be punished. Certainly Bea deserved it.

OUTSIDE, THE BREEZE WAS WEAK, a hint of something corrupt beneath the smoke. Air had become like wine; they analyzed it, sniffed it, tasted it, applied arcane descriptions (barnyard notes, hint of licorice particulate, traces of oxygen). The sky used to have a limited palette of blues and greys, but today it was the brown of rotten teeth, faint yellow highlights winking dully.

Her fear was that something would happen to her and Sang, and Thomas would be left to fend for himself, his life stretching out like the prairies. Suddenly a fifty-year-old man, the way everyone turns fifty, not sure where their forties vanished to. What else will have vanished by then? Civility, governments, order. The billion people displaced by submerged coastlines walking inland like zombies. Where to put New York and Miami?

And where did art fit into the apocalypse? Masterpieces burned for fuel: Gauguin's *Spirit of the Dead Watching,* Monet's *Impression, Sunrise,* Picasso's blue period. The only art would be survival. There was a way to make fire using snow, Bea knew. You palmed a snowball until it turned to ice then used it as a lens to capture the sun's rays then directed them onto one of Warhol's early works until it caught. Her one survival trick. Though where would you find snow?

Bea lined up for coffee, and faced with the hearty, oversized barista with a lizard tattooed on his throat, she suddenly forgot her regular order.

What can I get started for you? he asked.

Latte?

Bea thought she saw the girl from the Weather Channel, the one who had been lying to her for the last four months. It certainly looked like her, the dirty-blond hair, not as expensively tended as an anchorwoman's hair, her arms not ideal for that sleeveless dress. Her slightly pugnacious face spoke to a childhood of bloody noses and Kraft Dinner. Bea wanted to go up and ask her where she got her meteorology degree, if there was such a thing. What exactly do you have to study to get the forecast wrong every day? Bea wondered if she knew more than she was letting on, if she would suddenly turn to Bea and yell, *You can't handle the truth!*

The First and Third Worlds were beginning to blur. The southern hemisphere had gotten a head start, but we're closing fast. Soon we'd have twelve-year-old soldiers with ancient guns washed away by freak typhoons. What had the weather girl said yesterday, October is the new September, folks. And there she was pouring milk into her coffee as if everything was fine.

Bea got her latte and walked to the gallery and opened it up and turned on the lights. She turned on the air conditioner out of habit then turned it off then turned it back on again. On the radio, Tony Bennett blended with a woman's voice she couldn't place. She took a sip of the coffee and brought out the photo album then emailed Air with a link to "celebrity stomachs that look like bums" to cheer her up.

The morning went by quickly, most of it spent sorting and pasting photographs. On the back of some of the photos her mother had marked the date and who was in them. *The girls, 1973, hippies on Halloween!* Bea had a headband and a plastic guitar and a tie-dyed T-shirt that would have been obscured by the parka.

At a little after twelve she ate the lunch she'd brought, a joyless salad that had flax seeds in it. She thought about closing the gallery for a few minutes and getting a cappuccino but thought it might keep her up this late in the day.

Some of the photographs triggered detailed memories. Sitting on the sled they used on the small hill near their home. She and Ariel on a rink in matching red outfits, pretending they were figure skaters. Others were unfamiliar, shots of neighbours she couldn't place, kids whose names she couldn't recall, alien parks.

She was meticulous about the chronology. If every photograph was in order, then she would be able to see the arc of her parents' lives. Maybe there wasn't an arc. Maybe their son died and after that it was a flat line that ran horizontally until her father died then it dipped down (or went up). Bea imagined an arc anyway; that first black-and-white happiness, then the faces in the photos getting more complicated.

She looked out the window and saw Roger framed there, taking two quick, aggressive drags on his cigarette before opening the door. The smell of smoke wafted in with him. He was wearing a loose, expensive sports jacket and loafers with no socks. He took off his sunglasses and walked over and kissed her on both cheeks.

Bea, how are you?

Fine. This is a surprise. Are you working in the area?

Here? Roger gestured to the neighbourhood with the sweep of one arm. Too low-rent. Just wandering.

He walked up to one of the paintings and stared at it, judging. What would you call this? he asked.

Unsaleable.

They seem a bit 1973.

Roger walked around, taking each one in quickly. He looked like a man who was hiding something. He looked like a man who was hoping for a blow job. He was witty and engaged and had an attractive energy, though it wasn't the right energy for real estate. You needed to look detail oriented for real estate and Roger was definitely big picture.

Bea wondered if Rog actually wanted an affair with her. That was her impression, though she could be wrong. He probably recognized that things weren't brilliant between her and Sang, and Roger was one of those men who loped behind the herd, waiting for the lame to drop back before pouncing. He would never consider that Bea couldn't possibly do that to Pen, even if she was interested. And now she was having an affair, though that was perhaps too grand a word. Jean-Luc had sent a lovely, carefully worded email that gave her a little lift. She hadn't planned on having an affair, hadn't sought it out, but suddenly it was there. How much of the world was suspended in this lazy equation, fidelity simply a function of opportunity.

Have you had lunch? Roger asked.

Bea thought about going for lunch; her salad barely qualified anyway. But she didn't really have the energy for Roger today. And you needed energy for men whose best years were behind them. They needed affirmation and sex and it would never make up for the lost adulation of those young women sitting in his classroom, basking in his advertised brilliance.

Just ate, unfortunately, Bea said. I bring lunch. Have to keep the doors open.

In case there's a run on derivative, overpriced art.

I live in hope.

They chatted for a few minutes, caught up, and Roger left, reaching for his cigarettes before he was out the door. Bea wondered if he would visit another woman, ask her to lunch. Maybe there was a list of women he half pursued. Bea wondered where she ranked on that list. He pursued women the way people put in a dozen low-ball bids on houses, probing to see who was desperate to sell.

SHE DROVE TO THE GROCERY store on the lakeshore and parked and picked up a basket and wandered among the sparse produce. There were empty shelves. Crops had failed. The vegetables were puckered, the fruit shrunken and spotted.

She took out her phone and pressed Air's number. It was always easier to talk to her sister while doing something. When all her attention went to Ariel, she could quickly get annoyed, but if she was watching television with the sound off, or cooking, or shopping, it gave her a welcome distraction. She could examine red peppers or stare at the cheese display while Ariel went on about something.

Hi.

Hi.

So how did your lunch with Levi go? Bea asked.

Well, the thing is, you sit there and stare at him and he's mumbling something vaguely conciliatory and doing that clicking thing with his teeth and he picks at his food like a six-year-old, moving things he doesn't like to one side, and I had this urge to stick my fork in his eye.

Well, you know, they say murderous thoughts are the foundation for any healthy marriage.

Bea picked up a nine-dollar cauliflower and weighed it in her hand. It had a few dark spots, the leaves were limp.

But then I looked around the restaurant and it's like every guy there probably has his own set of annoying traits. So, do you stick with the annoying asshole you know or do you take a chance on a new annoying asshole, because that is all that is out there at this point. Anyone who is even acceptable, like a C-plus kind of guy, he's gone.

Or go asshole-free.

They should change the word "single" to "asshole-free."

Bea looked at the cauliflower. Who liked it enough to pay nine dollars a head? And wouldn't this be local this time of the year? They'd have two growing seasons at the rate they were warming. She lingered over the organic lemons, and finally took two. She picked up some garlic and some grape tomatoes and examined sweet potatoes that looked a bit worn. She looked up to see Dick and Jen Semple sorting through saggy herbs two aisles away. The master thieves. Her heart suddenly pounded. It looked like them. This couldn't be their local store. She walked toward them. Her only peers; she felt an odd collegial pang. These people would understand her, though Bea wasn't sure she understood herself. Bea got closer, stopping to look at blackberries as they picked out some horrendously expensive, allegedly organic blueberries.

She now wished she'd taken a cart. This happened all the time; she didn't want the cumbersome responsibility of pushing an unwieldy cart through the aisles so took a basket but inevitably bought more than the basket could comfortably hold.

We have to ask her, Air said.

What?

We have to ask Mom what happened to our brother.

I don't know, Air. I mean, how badly do we need that information?

We have a right to find out what happened to our own brother.

What if she's managed to bury this, sort of, and we drag it up and it devastates her? Is it worth it then? We have to look at risk /reward here.

Maybe it would be cathartic for her to have someone to grieve with, Ariel said. Maybe deep down she doesn't want to take this to the grave on her own. Maybe she's trying to tell us but doesn't know how.

Bea looked at the wrinkled red peppers. She handled a few and finally picked one. It suddenly occurred to her that Ariel would have phoned their mother, would have tried to get that information, and since she was as subtle as a car accident, she would have asked point-blank and maybe hammered away at her like a prosecutor grilling someone on the witness stand.

You asked her, Bea said. You phoned Mom and asked her what happened to Patrick.

We have a right to know.

Jesus, Air. You bullied her, didn't you?

I didn't *bully* her. I just asked what happened.

And when she didn't say anything coherent, you kept asking her, didn't you?

I asked her, like, *twice*. It isn't a big deal.

And she didn't tell you.

She quoted something, maybe from the Bible, I think.

Bea could hear their conversation in her head, Air badgering their mother, asking the question more than twice, their mother confused, sad, vulnerable.

Did it ever occur to you that her feelings are more important than your fucking curiosity, Air? Did that maybe make some small impression on your self-centred brain once she started crying? Why do I tell you *anything*?

Because you don't have anyone else to tell.

This stung, and Bea was afraid she was going to say something that would result in one of their six-month détente silences. She was following Dick and Jen at a discreet distance.

Air, I have to go. I'm at the grocery store and I see someone I know.

Who? Air clearly didn't believe her.

The Yamamotos.

They're Japanese?

Ish.

Bea pressed End and walked more quickly to catch up with Dick and Jen. They turned down the pasta aisle and she turned after them. There were large empty gaps on the shelves. Supply chain issues and/or panic buying had taken toilet paper, canned beans, pasta, and coffee, everyone preparing for the next weather event: tornado, flood, wildfire.

Jen was wearing a tailored white cotton shirt and those Prada walking shoes. Bea wondered what their lives had been like since the break-in. Had they been scared straight? She had a sudden irrational impulse to introduce herself. What had they done about the break-in? What had that conversation been like?

Someone knows.

A thief knows.

Still.

What are they going to do? Go to the police? Think about it.

They could come back.

Why? All they took was the dress. If they wanted anything else, they would have taken it then. The locks are changed. We have an alarm. We're safe.

We're never going to be safe.

That's what you wanted, baby. Give up the safe life.

Bea picked up a box of black quinoa. She'd make seared salmon with maple syrup and mint on a bed of quinoa, a former perfect food.

She waited until Dick and Jen were in line then stood behind them. He looked like a retired model, a lot of steel-grey hair, lines around his eyes in that Marlboro Man way, tanned. They possessed a physical logic; they looked like they belonged together. What kind of pact had they made? What had they convinced themselves of—that they were different from other people, that they were smarter? They didn't look smarter. They looked like people who would be obsessed with surfaces; he would need a Porsche and she would need a show home in order to impress the world. Yet they drove a crappy car and lived in a modest semi-detached house. Their wealth was subtle and invisible to the outside world; those clothes, the paintings, the thousands in cookware—it was only for themselves. They were more complicated than she gave them credit for. Was this the perfect union? A handsome couple who needed nothing from the outside world, not its approval certainly, not even its envy. To be free of humanity's gaze, that need for approval we carry around like a bag of rocks.

They were childless, anchored by their pact, their profession. In the end, a more profound connection perhaps. She wanted to hear them talk to one another, wanted to gauge the tenor of that conversation. To hear them say something revelatory or, better, something banal.

But they didn't speak to one another, each lost in thought as they placed their groceries on the conveyor. The mystery couple. He paid with cash, peeling off three fifties.

Her phone buzzed and she checked the text. It was Thomas. *Start the revolution without me.*

autumn

BEA DROVE THROUGH UGLY TRAFFIC, on her way to pick up her mother. The late October air had finally cooled a bit. It would be winter soon, and more difficult to push the wheelchair. Though maybe there won't be any snow. Maybe there would never be any snow. She remembered a winter when the sidewalks were icy and there were gale-force winds. On Yonge Street, city workers had strung yellow nylon nautical rope along the sidewalk, attached to poles, hundreds of feet. People pulled themselves along on the rope to keep their footing on the ice as the winds buffeted them, heads down, one foot in front of the other. She couldn't remember why they were out in that weather. Their father at the front, their mother behind them, and she and Ariel in the middle. She might have been six or seven. The winds howling so that they couldn't hear what their father was yelling. A block from the most famous intersection in the country and they looked like a family that was lost in the wilderness after their plane crashed.

She picked up her mother and they drove in silence past quiet houses, past public tennis courts that had four old men playing doubles, moving with the jerky, laboured movements of arthritis. They weren't much younger than her mother. Bea envied them. They only had to stay healthy and keep occupied, the two pillars of their existence. Their responsibilities long behind them, all their parenting done. Hit the ball, complain about your hip, go home, pour a stiff drink, remember your meds. Maybe this is our prime.

They drove out to the beach. Bea had planned on taking her on the boardwalk though wondered if she had the energy. She liked the colour here in fall, the pale sand, the lake turning light grey, the faded sky.

Her mother was looking straight ahead, muttering something, a speech that was gathering momentum. Not for the faint of heart, she said emphatically. Not for all the tea in China.

Bea glanced at her, tried to find some trail to follow. Sometimes her outbursts related, vaguely, to real events, some kind of abstraction of her history. But increasingly Bea couldn't find a thread.

Bea parked and took out the wheelchair and transferred her mother then pushed her down to the boardwalk. There was a couple being married under the gazebo, a small, solemn crowd listening to the modern vows *I promise to remember that you are human* . . . People cycled along the path. Dogs everywhere. A busker sang a Hank Williams song.

Bea sat on a bench, her mother parked beside her. They stared out to the horizonless lake, sky and water joined in a pale blur.

What happened? Bea said softly, wondering if she was no better than her sister.

Her mother stared at the lake.

What happened to Patrick James?

Her mother nodded slightly. She looked as though she was gathering something, the pieces of a story she'd carried inside for decades. A minute later she said, Our baby. I knew, I knew.

They both looked toward the lake. Rochester lurked beyond it. There were people sailing, the colourful sails static from this distance, fixed in one place. It must have been crib death, inexplicable and heartbreaking. She would have come to wake him in the morning, that tiny, lifeless form. The devastation was unimaginable. She would have picked him up and held him and wept and wept.

Bea sat on the bench and cried for quite a while. Her mother's face was too bleak to look at. She dabbed her eyes and stared at the endless lake. She wondered if her father had somehow blamed her mother. The baby's welfare was the mother's job, especially then. As if somehow she had allowed this to happen. Maybe her father never really forgave her.

Both of them carrying that sorrow. Her father sitting in his study, reconstructing a world that still had his son in it. The family he'd had wasn't enough to fill that hole.

They sat for an hour in the pale sun. The air was cooling, the water dark. The featureless horizon, the sailboats had all moved on.

a great laugh

IT WAS THURSDAY NIGHT AND Sang left to teach his imaginary class. Bea watched through the window for less than a minute, then put on a light jacket, grabbed her hat and sunglasses, and left. It was walking weather, a slight breeze. It was five and the sun was low. She stayed a block behind Sang. They went south then west for a pleasant twenty minutes. When Sang stopped, Bea stopped, turned in another direction as if that would disguise her. They went past the lurid themes of Chinatown, into the remnants of Little Portugal, now filled with students and young families. She observed the yards, the people. A couple walked toward her, pushing a stroller that held all the survival gear you needed for a walk: soother, toy, formula, diapers, extra clothes. This fifteen-pound thing taking up every inch of their world. They turned south, then onto Queen, walking past stores that sold vinyl and second-hand clothes and Australian footwear. A toothless woman sat cross-legged on the sidewalk in front of a hat, her head moving back and forth like Stevie Wonder at his piano, humming. The restaurants were minimalist or retro with ironic names and pierced staff.

Bea saw her.

A woman sitting at a table at a tiny outdoor patio, waving. Sang waved back. He approached and leaned down and kissed her. There were heaters on the patio.

Bea stopped. There was a small restaurant beside her—Nine Alarm. It had a garage door facade that was open and she went in and took a seat where she could lean out and see them.

The waiter came up to her, and she ordered a glass of red wine. She could leave those citrusy whites behind until next spring and embrace a troubled red.

You aren't going to be too cold here? he said, though it wasn't cold. We can close it.

No, I prefer it open, thank you.

She had felt Sang's affair, like a cold coming on that you're not sure you'll actually get. But here was the evidence and she was hit with a lurching stab of nausea. There was a stunned minute—like those movies where a bomb goes off then that violent silence for thirty seconds, the café blown up, detritus floating down onto the street in slow motion, a waiter's tray thrumming on the pavement like a dropped dime. Her limbs felt rubbery and unreliable, her vision blurred. She took deep yoga breaths, looking up at the hammered tin ceiling then down at her hands spread out on the wooden table. Unarticulated, Sang's affair was tolerable, but now the manic pheromones danced inside, spreading the information like *samizdat*—handed first to the lungs (shortness of breath), then the solar plexus (a well-timed punch), and finally the heart (that dead weight).

She observed the woman's face, her listening face. She wasn't young, mid-forties. She had dark hair, probably not the original colour. Slim, her legs crossed, a pair of heels chosen for this occasion. If she walked here, she must live nearby.

Bea examined the woman examining Sang, her face breaking out suddenly into a hearty laugh. Bea couldn't hear it, but it was a big laugh, her head going back, her eyes almost closing, her hand going to his forearm in a reflex. Sang's face had the creased, happy expression of someone repeating a punchline.

Bea felt as if she was watching a home movie of the early days of their own relationship, arriving in flickering black and white. The laughing, the leaning in, tasting each other's wine, the proximity. Sang would go down on her. There would be that newness—her skin, the taste of her cunt, her history, the greatest hits of their childhoods exchanged in a rhythmic litany. Sang picked up her hand and examined it like one of those people on the antique shows, turning it over, assessing its worth.

Was he telling her *it's complicated?* Perhaps it wasn't that complicated. He was no longer in love with his wife, he was in love with this woman, a professor of something, history or feminist theory. He'd leave his wife. Leave me.

The waiter came over and Bea ordered the first thing from the chalkboard menu on the wall—a braised lamb shank ravioli with caramelized onions, though she didn't have any appetite.

Was Sang in love? Maybe still circling around that word, more likely it would spill out just after he came. Bea had said it to four or five men in her life, not all of them truthfully. In twelfth grade she'd said it to Ron Bentall after he'd whispered it in her ear while they were necking in his father's Buick. Bea felt compelled to respond in kind though she wasn't in love, wasn't even caught up in the moment. The car had one of those pine tree–shaped air fresheners hanging from the rearview mirror and there was an antiseptic smell that mingled with Ron's unfortunate cologne that he'd applied like a crop duster. He groped her, hands squeezing experimentally.

Sang's gaze swerved and for a minute Bea thought he might

have seen her. But she was in shadow and partly obscured by the wall. He turned to face the woman, telling her something. Maybe he was telling her he was in love.

Bea had told the man she was seeing before Sang that she loved him. They only lasted a few weeks after that. Perhaps the weight of that declaration had crushed them. When he moved out, suddenly and after an argument that escalated quickly and spun out of control, a crescendo of slammed doors, she started driving by his place in the evenings. It became a habit. She would drive around in the evenings then turn onto his street as if by accident then sometimes park a few buildings down and look at the lit window, wondering if she'd see him. Or see a woman perhaps. For months she was sick. *Sick with love.* A phrase she repeated as if she was diagnosing herself. She ate little, drank a lot of coffee, smoked too many cigarettes, slept poorly, got up and obsessed, watched a lot of late night television, though it was only animated wallpaper, a companion for her thoughts. Who was he with? As if that made a difference. It took months for the ache to subside, though it didn't entirely disappear. Something remained, part of the geological imprint left by the Anthropocene.

Her dinner came, prompting a fresh wave of nausea. Bea picked up her fork and put it down, picked up her wine and took a sip. Love. Was it gone with Sang? Love was like cocaine: the first few lines were the best, then diminishing returns set in, and finally, a dull, grinding habit that presented a hole every morning that could no longer be filled. Though she'd only done cocaine once. But a girl she knew from university—Beth?—had gone down that road. Bea bumped into her after a ten-year gap and they had a coffee and Beth outlined her downward spiral in a concise, practised speech, then got up to leave, saying she was late for her NA meeting.

It wasn't supposed to be that way. Love was supposed to deepen as you waded through life. Perhaps it was her generation, one that needed instant gratification, everyone believing they deserved a happiness that came in the shape of an uplifting movie.

Bea looked at the woman across the street. She was talking now, explaining something. She peeked out to see Sang's interested face. He nodded sombrely, and Bea felt another sharp pang. How much, she wondered, was simply territorial?

She sipped her wine. There were bold, bruised clouds in the dark sky, a threatening chiaroscuro. This was the time of day husbands and wives returned, retailing their day, editing, disguising.

The waiter came by and hovered. He was in his mid-thirties, perhaps a bit old for this.

Is everything all right? he asked.

Is it ever?

Your dinner...

It's fine. I'm afraid I don't have much of an appetite.

Should I clear this?

Bea nodded.

Would you like anything else?

Just a coffee please. A latte. And the bill.

He nodded and left and Bea wondered if he would eat her untouched dinner. During her brief, wobbly tenure as a waitress, they all used to do it. They'd laugh and quickly wolf down someone's uneaten french fries. They were eighteen. But the thought of a thirty-six-year-old man eating her dinner depressed her.

The waiter returned with her coffee and took away the unfinished red wine. She was glad it was red wine season. The whites had become thin and unsatisfying. They went through you but didn't leave much of an impression. She took a sip of her coffee, took money out of her purse and left it on the table, and looked up—they were gone.

Bea quickly scanned the street. They were walking east on Queen, then turned north. Bea got up and followed, half jogging. She stayed back. They only walked half a block then turned to go into a house. Bea jogged behind and stood on the other side of the street. She wasn't sure if it was 83 or 85 they'd gone into. She stood beside a tree for a moment. A light went on upstairs in 85. The blind was drawn, but it had a translucent quality, registering silhouettes, two figures moving, one disappearing behind the other then re-emerging. She wondered if she'd see them fuck, like shadow puppets. The house was two storeys, uneventful, untended. The lights downstairs weren't on, which suggested that the house was divided into two flats and the woman lived upstairs. Bea took out her phone and wrote down the address.

witness

THE FOLLOWING THURSDAY, BEA LEFT before Sang. The mistress; was that the right word? She walked past her house, not really looking at it. She was hoping they were meeting at a restaurant, but Sang could be meeting her here. Bea walked the length of the street, glancing back every few seconds. She stood behind the line of cars where she could see the woman's house and took out her phone and scrolled through emails.

Ten minutes went by. Bea wondered how long it had been going on. And if this was the first. She'd read an article about why people cheat. It was less to find a new lover than to find a new self. Or get in touch with an earlier version of ourselves, more adventurous, less burdened.

Did she feel more adventurous? She'd flown to Montreal for the day on Monday, catching a 9 a.m. flight and returning on the 7 p.m. flight. A long lunch with wine, a lovely afternoon in bed. Free of guilt this time, though vaguely marred by doubt. Jean-Luc was charming and thoughtful, though he was also a fifty-four-year-old artist who wanted exposure in another city and Bea was a way to get that. She didn't really know anything about Jean-Luc that hadn't come from him.

He had sparked something, a version of herself that had been whittled over the years. We grow and retreat at roughly the same rate, she thought. She enjoyed her time with Jean-Luc and enjoyed the idea of it, the knowledge she carried inside. Though romance got more complicated as you got older, motives more difficult to divine—love or financial security or the simple human fear of being alone. Bea had never been to his apartment. Maybe there was a long-suffering wife there. Or maybe there wasn't an apartment and he was living in his studio like the bohemian he hadn't wanted to be.

She walked south to Queen Street then turned around. A couple walked toward her, both dressed in black, in a cloud of smoke and laughter.

A squirrel darted onto the street then stopped and convulsed, leaping in the air and collapsing onto the pavement. It looked like a marionette, possessed. This macabre dance lasted a full minute then it sped erratically into a yard.

The woman suddenly appeared on the street. Bea thought it was her, anyway. She was heading north and Bea followed up the street quickly. Would she know what Bea looked like? She might. Maybe she'd gone online to see who the aggrieved wife was. Bea was well back, with a baseball cap on and the sunglasses, even though it was dusk. She could see her from the back, half a block away, an athletic walk.

They might be having a quick dinner in Little Italy before coming back to fuck. Bea budgeted twenty minutes, just to be safe, and set the alarm on her phone. She walked briskly to the house. The porch offered a little cover. The street was heavily treed, which helped. The front door wasn't locked. Inside were two mailboxes and two locked doors, one for the main-floor flat, the one on the left leading upstairs to the woman's flat. The lock was a pedestrian Schlage. She inserted the pick, probed, a subtle pressure, felt the pins softly yield. Less than a minute.

Bea moved quietly up the stairs. The flat was a bit jumbled, mismatched furniture and homely crochet and a few framed posters. Bea picked up some mail in a wicker basket. Angie Arany. AA. Divorced maybe, and they'd sold the house, split the equity, but it wasn't enough to get back into this insane housing market. No sign of any kids. Bea moved through the flat quickly. There was a thick coil-bound manual on the coffee table. An instructional guide for those working in Human Resources. Bea had assumed she was a prof. An IKEA bookshelf stood imperfectly against the wall. Several self-help books, some bestsellers that were soon to become major motion pictures. So it was mostly the sex.

She opened the top drawer of the small desk. There were credit card receipts. Bea scanned one—a monthly yoga membership and a monthly gym membership. She'd bought a pair of shoes at Winners for $89.99. There were two passports, one Canadian, one Hungarian. Perhaps she'd left a husband in Budapest, a controlling, abusive man. Or she wanted a different life and he was too timid to follow. Was Angie in love with Sang? Bea wandered, picked up things, put them down, bent down to look at photos, judging. Maybe she wasn't in love; it was simple comfort, something to cling to, someone who was happy to see her. That was enough.

This was a life reduced, Bea decided, a setback. It was how most lives proceeded—options vanished, sometimes suddenly (sickness, accident, getting fired), sometimes slowly (love seeping away, age creeping, friends drifting). There was a collection of figurines set up on the windowsill, fifteen or so circus figures—a sad clown, an elephant, a master of ceremonies. From childhood maybe, or inherited from a grandmother.

They suggested a vulnerability, something an adolescent girl would have in her room, something to look at and rearrange while she thought about a boy she liked who didn't like her.

She didn't feel any animosity for this woman. Sang wasn't being stolen from her like women did in country and western songs. Bea felt like an insurance adjuster viewing the scene of an accident, trying to assess the damage. She felt a sense of vertigo.

She looked through the HR manual, paging idly through the chapter titled "Retention and Motivation," then on to "Successful Employee Communication." She tore out five pages and folded them into abstract origami forms, sort-of dogs, which she placed on the small table that had her computer. Parts of words were visible: Cont, Motiv, dia, ation.

Bea went into the bedroom, reluctantly, like someone identifying a body at the morgue, lifting the sheet and nodding, *Yes, that's him*. The room was small and neat. The bed sat there like exhibit A. Should she imagine all the Hungarian sex that happened right here? What did Sang feel? An earlier version of himself. The pleasures of teaching gone now, his marriage a bit stale, his son away. Don't we all deserve some joy in our lives? This was the standard rationale.

How would you behave if you knew the world was ending? But it was ending. Roger was right. They'd missed the window to set things right.

The curtains were closed and Bea walked over and pulled them aside. The window looked onto the neighbour's window five feet away. A woman was standing in her bay window, staring at Bea. They could have touched if the windows were open and they leaned out. Bea stopped breathing. Her phone alarm went off, startling her. She closed the curtain and quickly raced down the stairs, out the door, and walked briskly toward Queen Street, away from the house with the witness. She took off her hat and stuffed it into a garbage bin near the alley, walked as quickly as possible without running until she got to Queen Street, then merged into the pedestrian traffic, anonymous among the tattooed masses.

we'll be fine

BEA SAT IN THE CAFE for forty-five minutes, thinking about her husband and his time with Angie, imagining a world where their marriage is over, imagining another world where their marriage survives. And what would that poisoned landscape look like? The two of them silent and resentful, marking the days like prisoners. Or would she be one of those women in magazines who talk about how it made their relationship stronger? She tinkered with these narratives, added details, conversations, struggled to find a version she could live with.

She was supposed to be meeting Will, happy for the distraction. She sent two emails, worried that something must have happened to him. There was the light clatter of dishes and Leonard Cohen's basso melancholy that still had the power to melt her. The light came in the large windows. People hugged and laughed and drank their coffees.

She left and got into her car, and drove two blocks then pulled over and picked up her phone and emailed Murray. The traffic was bunched and hostile and hemmed her in. She waited two minutes for a response then phoned him.

Murray answered and she reintroduced herself.

Oh yeah, Murray said. You used to come. You brought wine. She asked about Will.

I'm afraid I have some bad news. And there is a lesson here for all of us. I wish we'd talked about this before. We *should* have. It was the elephant in the room and I blame myself.

Bea felt a sudden gust of precognition. She could see Will standing in someone's house, crane-like, that useless height, harmless, as the police came through the door.

He broke in, she said. He broke into someone's house.

He's young, Murray said. I blame myself.

Oh god.

He's in *jail*.

She could see Murray at the other end, his natural slump, face like a pastry, his fussy home.

A crazy thing to do, he said. Crazy.

Bea hung up and pulled into the aggressive traffic. At first she thought she'd drive to the jail, but she didn't know where it was or how many there were and there was probably a proto-col, at least there was in the movies; there were visiting hours. She had let him down. She should have been more parental, should have shaken him and made him promise. But she had made him promise.

SHE DROVE HOME, WENT INSIDE, checked her phone. There was a text from Thomas. *Thinking of quitting*. She immediately called him. He didn't pick up and she left a long voice mail that essentially said, *Don't*. She sent a text telling him not to do anything until they'd spoken. Then she called Sang.

Thomas is thinking of quitting school, she said.

Jesus.

You have to talk to him.

I have a class in five, let's talk about this tonight.

Bea was silent, but he took this for condemnation.

Of course, it's my fucking fault, Sang said.

At the moment, everything was his fault.

Bea wondered if Thomas would move back home. Another chance to be a mother. Though now the mother of a surly man careening around the house, moving from the refrigerator to the internet like a migrating bird. She called him twice more, leaving a long message the second time. Then she spent an hour on the phone trying to find out where Will was being held. There were more prisons than you would think. She tried not to think of prison movies.

WILL LOOKED SO YOUNG. HE was wearing his own clothes. Bea wasn't sure what she'd expected—an orange jumpsuit, talking on a germ-ridden phone separated by safety glass. Instead, they sat in a loud, depressing space at a round table surrounded by faded plastic chairs. Will had a bandage wrapped around his head and one side had been shaved. One eye was black and his face was puffy and drained. One hand had a bandage on it, two fingers in steel splints.

There were other tables and other people talking. It looked more like a refugee camp, people in ill-fitting clothes who'd done something desperate. Conversations echoed through the room. The lighting was harsh and gave everyone's skin a greenish pallor, as if they'd all caught the same disease. And she supposed they had. A handful of guards stood against the walls.

Oh Will, I'm so sorry, she said. Bea didn't know if she should take his hand or not, if it was allowed.

His head was hanging down, shaking slightly. I wasn't even going to *take* anything, he said. His eyes were red. Bea wondered if it was from the injuries or he'd been crying or it was just sleeplessness from being in here.

Will, I feel like it's my fault. When you told me you'd gone into a house, I should have been harder on you. I knew you would try it again, I knew you'd been bitten and you'd go back, and I should have said, over and over, Will, don't do it. It doesn't make sense, it isn't worth the risk.

I'm not a criminal, he said. A whisper.

I know you're not.

But no one's going to understand that.

He was on the verge of tears.

We'll make them understand, Will. I'll come to the hearing, I'll tell them about the lock club. You got carried away. That it was about the locks, not about taking people's things.

He wanted to kill me, Will said. He started sobbing. He had a bat and he kept hitting me and I was screaming. But he wouldn't stop.

A frightened man facing a tall stranger in his house, the primitive impulse to survive, to protect, hammering at this thing the way you kill a rat you found in the basement, the ancient fear.

Will put his head in his hands. The irony of Will being locked up occurred to Bea. She wondered if he could get out if he wanted to. You would think they had good locks here. Bea noticed that one leg was pushed out straight.

Your leg, she said.

I need to get an operation on my knee. He wouldn't stop hitting me. Will was sobbing, thick, heaving gusts.

Oh Will.

She started to cry. Faced with her tears Will tried to compose himself, looked around the room, wiped his face with his sleeve, calmed himself. I feel like my life is over, he said. That whatever happens now, it's just going to be this, like, long, sad ending.

Don't think like that, Will. She was emphatic. It's not over. Nothing is over at your age, believe me. In a year, this will be a tiny blip. This isn't the kind of thing people like you go to jail for.

I don't even know who "people like me" are. I don't know why I did it.

Bea understood him so completely. She wanted to tell him this, tell him she understood and why, but it would leave her too vulnerable and she would regret it. You didn't take anything.

I thought he left. I was sure.

He started to cry again and Bea moved closer and held him. She put her hand on his shaggy, sobbing head and pulled him close, sobbing herself. A guard already moving toward them to break it up.

We'll be fine, Will, she said. We'll be fine.

breathing lessons

PENELOPE WAS MEETING HER AT the restaurant, a new place, one word, which Bea couldn't quite remember. Epiphany? Shame? She knew the street, though. Bea drove slowly until she saw the small sign—Burnt Offering. Two words. She parked and got out.

Pen was already there, sitting at a small wooden table, looking at her phone. There were ten tables painted different colours, mismatched chairs, a slightly daycare-ish vibe. The only other diners were two other women.

Hi Pen, sorry I'm late.

I think I'm early. I'm always early.

The waitress approached, a woman with wild hair held almost vertically by a wide tie-dyed bandana. She was vamping to the music, her twenty-year-old ass swaying, not quite singing along, her lips barely moving. She started to move toward them, half dancing.

Hi, she said. Welcome to Burnt Offering. Can I get you something to drink while you look at the menu?

Water is fine, Pen said.

Bea nodded. Same.

The waitress pointed to a small blackboard. The specials, she said. It's, like, pretty straightforward, except we're out of numbers two, five, and six. The great cheese/cod/whatever shortage. She moved away, picking up a rhythm as she moved. Behind them, Bea could hear the two women talking about the worst sunburns they'd had, lobster versus third degree, waiting for the melanoma to arrive like a dinner guest who couldn't find parking.

Are you seeing someone? Pen asked.

It took a few seconds to realize she meant was Bea seeing a therapist. As opposed to seeing a lover.

I saw a therapist, Bea said. I don't know how much good it's done. It feels like it happened ten years ago. It's weird. I don't know if going through it all is doing me good or just dragging it out.

There was a shooting in the suburbs, Pen said, apparently a new breed of terrorist. They don't want anything, they're not against anything. No politics, no religion, just the blank thing the suburbs are producing, an empty vessel that can be filled by a video game or a horror movie or a whim or a bad date.

She had gone to Phyllis for three sessions then felt they'd hit a wall, that their relationship was becoming like the stale marriage that was one of the underlying reasons for her visits.

You should probably stick with it, Pen said. Sometimes it takes a while to process things.

Bea nodded. She was wary of the language of therapy.

This probably isn't going to come as a surprise, Pen said, but Roger and I are splitting up.

Yet it was a surprise. No matter how obvious the problems in a marriage, there was still a large, dark territory between a bad marriage and splitting up. A territory Bea was about to explore.

They ordered and their lunch arrived quickly, and in the pleasant light of the struggling restaurant Bea listened to Pen matter-of-factly deconstruct her decision. She wasn't tearful or emotional. She'd passed that phase. Perhaps if there had been kids, she said, shrugging. She was moving back west, had been offered a good administrative job at UBC. They were going to sell their house, Roger was going to sell it, taking the commission.

You're not angry, Bea said, an observation rather than a question.

No. I let it go on too long. Everyone does, don't they? You know, I read this article about how our choices in mates are biological, how we instinctively move toward someone who gives us some kind of evolutionary equilibrium. I don't know that I believe it, but it was probably true in my case. What better choice for an introvert. And Rog needed an anchor for his messy life. Something to return to. I feel like I'm dissolving a corporation and I feel sad that I don't feel sadder.

Pen's phone buzzed and she pulled it out and examined it. Bea looked around. A woman had come in, she was sitting by herself, a few years older than Bea, drinking a glass of wine, reading a novel, the ghost of Christmas future.

Outside, the autumn light was brittle and focused. People walked by briskly with dogs or children, taking advantage. Bea wanted the soft ruin of autumn. She'd gone to yoga that morning and still felt the faint afterglow. But it wore off, that calm, and the world crept back in with its random fears. She watched a woman about to cross the road with her four-year-old, bent down to his eye level, pointing in both directions. The boy had a backpack in the shape of a happy bear. Bea remembered teaching Thomas to look both ways, then finally having him cross the street himself, standing back and observing, the street suddenly looking endless, like sending him out into the desert to find his own food.

What was the best time in your marriage? Bea asked. The best years.

Pen stared over Bea's shoulder, squinting slightly, assessing the two decades she and Roger had been together. We went to Italy, she said. We'd been together maybe a year. It was off-season, not that many tourists, the weather was like this, kind of autumn. We walked everywhere, ate these huge lunches then had a nap, made love, got up. It's what formed us, sort of. And I thought that was enough. I had my purse stolen in Rome, two guys on a scooter swooped by and one of the guys grabbed it and pulled me off balance as he yanked it away. Roger ran after them, but they were gone. We went to the police station and reported it and they gave us this form, it was six pages long. We had to fill it out. The last question was, "Who do you suspect?" Roger wrote down Pavarotti.

Bea smiled. I guess we all start out with a narrative.

They chatted in the lovely light, had coffee. Outside, they stood on the sidewalk and people stepped around them. A car lurched into an empty parking spot. A cyclist yelled a death threat to a passing car. Leaves rattled in the breeze.

So you'll have to come out west and visit, Pen said. We'll go skiing. It'll be fun.

Bea nodded.

I mean, we'll see each other before I go, Pen said, and hugged Bea.

Of course, we'll have another nice lunch.

That would be great.

They hugged again and Bea walked to her car. There was a poster taped to a pole, someone offering breathing lessons. Even basic biology a challenge now.

On the way home Bea stopped at the grocery store and wandered a bit, unsure of what she felt like for dinner. She decided, finally, on a roast chicken. She hadn't made one in ages. Simple, nostalgic. She bought fresh rosemary and garlic and potatoes. She picked up Granny Smith apples and brown sugar for a pie. Comfort food.

She checked her phone—a cryptic text from Thomas about university, one from Katherine, and one from her therapist counselling her not to quit therapy. These short, misspelled notes were her link to the world.

AT HOME SHE TURNED ON the radio and put away the groceries. She wondered how she would feel Pen's absence, the social fabric slowly unravelling.

But you take a piece out of the puzzle and the whole landscape changes. Pen's split from Roger was like one of those controlled demolitions, the building collapsing on itself, the dust rising and settling daintily on the rubble, no real casualties. But that absence would affect them all.

She laid out everything she needed for the pie. Took out the large wooden cutting board they rarely used anymore after reading something about bacteria hiding in the wood, staying alive for weeks, every kitchen an Ebola outbreak. She mixed flour and butter and sugar and salt in the food processor and gave it two quick blasts, then added cold water and gave it another pulse. She spread the dough on the board and kneaded it lightly. She sprinkled a little flour, rolled it, covered the pie pan, and gently pushed it into shape, then cut off the excess with scissors. She cut the apples and mixed them with brown sugar and cinnamon and nutmeg and covered it with dough and made four elegant slits, using a Nigella accent *four quick slashes, not random, a purpose to everything* and put it in the oven.

She texted Thomas: *call me.* She poured a glass of wine, fretted. That was why he'd wanted to talk. He was flailing in school, didn't see the point. She'd missed the signals. This was second-year disease. The first year is simply an adventure, to choose your own courses, to be in another city. Second year was a reckoning.

She remembered going to his Christmas pageant when he was eight, though it wasn't called that, the word "Christmas" already a casualty. The gym was overheated. Parents came in late, tired from work and traffic, fighting sleep, filming their talent-free children bravely work through a song in three different keys, guided by a patient teacher who mouthed the words and conducted. It was raw and lovely and uplifting.

Her phone rang.

Hi, she said.

Hi.

It was Thomas.

Tell me you haven't already quit.

I haven't already quit. This was said in a flat monotone.

Look, Thomas—

I don't want the speech about starting what you finish, Mom . . .

That's not the speech I'm going to give you. What I'm going to tell you is that the twenty-year-old version of you doesn't know what the thirty-year-old version will want. Or the forty-year-old version. I was filled with certainties at your age. Most people are. But we change, Thomas. All of us. We grow and we carry every decision we ever made within us. And every regret. I don't want you to have regrets, Thomas. You will, everyone does. But the old saying that the person who dies with the most money wins isn't true. It's the person who dies with the fewest regrets who wins. I don't know what you're going to do with your life and neither do you, but I know this: you will regret quitting university. Not next week or even next year, but you will wake up in the night five years from now, ten years, and you will feel a searing regret that will leave a mark.

She went on for a while and Thomas didn't interrupt. It took restraint to not trot out all the things she regretted—not sticking with the piano, losing her French, not taking a doctorate, not living in Florence for a year. But she needed to focus on Thomas. In the end, he promised to stick out the year and reassess during the summer.

She pressed End and sat back, sort of relieved, wondering if he'd have a different view tomorrow morning and quit anyway.

The door opened and Sang came in, fresh from teaching or fucking. He poured a glass of wine.

Is that an apple pie? he asked.

Yep.

When was the last time you made a pie?

Bea shrugged.

This is the best part of pie, Sang said. Right now. Seriously. Walking in, you smell that baking pie smell. It's Pavlovian, a Western comfort. It's better than actually eating it.

She told him that she'd just spoken with Thomas. Sang had talked to him too, it turned out, had given his own carefully considered speech. So they'd done what they could, they'd been parents.

Pen and Rog are splitting up, Bea said.

Seriously? Though I guess you can't say it's a surprise.

It's a surprise to me. I wonder how Roger will manage.

Heavily self-medicated.

They sort of worked for a while, though, the whole opposites-attract thing, Bea said.

You complete me. Sang said this in another voice, slightly mocking.

They did, in their way.

I guess it depends on your definition of completion.

Marriage is like one of those exams that are designed so you can't complete it, Bea said. A test of something other than knowledge. Bea took a sip of her wine. Apparently Roger was having affairs, she said. She threw this out as casually as possible.

Roger always had affairs, Sang said. It was part of his DNA. Not lately, though not from lack of trying, I would guess.

You knew about his affairs?

Not the specifics, I just know Roger.

Why, I wonder.

Why did he have affairs?

I mean why so many.

A pathology. And he's one of those guys who's immune to rejection, he just keeps asking until someone says yes. It's what got him fired. Part of it, anyway.

A student?

He didn't understand that you can't even ask anymore, that it constitutes abuse. Roger's problem was that he lost perspective. And he lost track of history.

Though no students for Sang. A line he didn't cross. At least not that Bea knew of. And for that he held on to this righteousness.

Poor Pen, Bea said. She's moving back west. I wonder how much we'll see of Roger.

Less of him, certainly. Will we have to set him up with someone?

Who? God, I couldn't do that to anyone.

Maybe after living on his own for a while, he'll just want a normal relationship, someone to come home to.

He wants to fuck me, Bea said, surprising herself.

Seriously?

You don't think anyone would want to fuck me?

I don't mean it like—

He wants to fuck everyone. I'm not special. But he trails after me like a dog in heat. One kind word and he'd be down on me like white on rice.

Sang stared at her.

That's all it takes for a lot of people, Bea said. A kind word and they're off to the races, fucking someone they hadn't given a thought to.

They sat with this thought and sipped their wine for a few minutes.

What's for dinner? Sang finally asked.

Apple pie and red wine.

Outside, a few leaves had turned. A handful had fallen in the garden. Three squirrels moved with a sense of urgency. It was almost dark. Her mother made an apple pie at Christmas every year, convinced it was part of some tradition. Bea remembered the Christmas when their neighbours the Catellis had a loud argument. Bea could hear it in her room. She looked out her window and the sliding door at the back of the Catellis' house opened and their Christmas tree came flying out. It had all the ornaments on it, the tinsel and lights. Then Mr Catelli appeared and heaved the tree off the deck into their yard. It landed soundlessly in the snow. He went back in and came out with something. Bea watched him walk up to the tree and spray it. It was the lighter fluid he used to start their barbecue. Mrs Catelli emerged from the house, standing on the deck, her head shaking, crying, *For God's sake, no*. Mr Catelli, his eyes glazed, using his lighter to set the tree on fire. It went up quickly, the needles already dry. Mrs Catelli stood there, her hands on her face. Her husband standing in the snow, lit by the flames like Mephistopheles, his eyes wide, filled with madness. Bea remembered the pop of those small bulbs as they exploded.

home is where

THEY HAD TO START SOMEWHERE. The Talk. It was like a chess game, there were standard openings then a million variations. Sang sat there, impassive, swirling his wine, staring at it not staring at it.

They'd almost had sex a few nights ago, after deconstructing Roger and Pen. Bea wondered what it would have been like, not gentle and conciliatory, something vengeful maybe, bearing down on her husband like a winter storm. It might have helped, she thought. It would have given this moment something visceral to anchor it, proof that there was something still there even if neither of them was sure what that something was.

It had built slowly, through the day, like a prairie thunderstorm. You see those clouds a hundred miles away.

Tell me about your book club, Sang said, looking up, a hard stare. On the offensive from the start, the King's gambit.

You thought it was an affair, she said.

It wasn't a book club.

No.

I saw you in a café. With the tall guy.

You *followed me?*

He shook his head no. The tall guy you told me about, he seemed made up. Then I saw you in that café. The one on Broadview.

Will was real. But it wasn't an affair. Were you relieved to think I was having one too?

Sang stared at his wine again.

Who is she? Bea asked. What does she do?

Sang looked up. No one you know, he said. Someone I met, that's all. What were you doing all those evenings?

Bea wondered this herself. There weren't that many. I was in a lock-picking club, she said.

This clearly wasn't one of the scenarios that Sang had mulled over in his head, tinkering with the details, thinking of her and Will in their incongruous May/September mode.

Who joins a lock-picking club? I've never even heard of this.

There are a lot of things you haven't heard of, Sang.

They were sitting in the living room, having a drink before dinner. There wouldn't be an actual dinner. There might never be another dinner. The light was fading. A fragment of the day hovering. She got up and closed the blinds.

What is the *point* of picking locks?

Escape.

What were the others that appeared on lock-picking sites— diversion, empowerment, skill building, fellowship, a few more. There were really just the two questions: Are you in love? When did it start? Sang had been seeing someone when they first started dating, someone he'd been sort of living with for more than a year, a serious thing. Then he and Bea met at a party. They were in the backyard, dozens of people going in and out, smoking in the autumn air. It was fresh outside, the perfect temperature. They'd both graduated three years earlier, Sang with his PhD,

Bea with her master's, still struggling, both of them. Someone in the neighbourhood was burning leaves, an oddly comforting smell. They got caught up in one of those conversations that are really about the two of you, a reason to keep talking, to get closer, the first touch (his hand touching hers as he lit their cigarettes). They were in the shadows, against the fence, all the signals, the pheromones zipping back and forth like a firefight. They left the party and walked to a bar and drank wine then went back to the apartment she shared with a stubborn, angry girl who loudly broke up with her lumbering boyfriend every week then had what sounded like short, brutish make-up sex in the living room. In her apartment she and Sang had started on the couch and finished in the bedroom, a bit furtive and drunken, driven by passion, though both perhaps a bit relieved when it was done, lying there with the next step hovering over them. *I sort of have a girlfriend.* That's what he'd said as they smoked and stared at the wall together. And she had asked if he was sort of in love with her and he turned to Bea and shook his head. No.

Are you in love? Bea asked.

Sang took a long breath in, as if this was the first time he'd given it any thought.

When was the last time we were in love? he said.

This was yet another thing that annoyed her, that everything seemed to deflect off him, never addressing anything head-on, always directing her to a related link. For the last few years he had managed to stay on the sidelines of their relationship. They had once gone to a basketball game together and on the bench beside the line of elongated players were several middle-aged white men in suits. Bea asked who they were and Sang said they were assistant coaches. They didn't pace or yell like the Black head coach. They sat as a group then got up during the time outs and milled around then sat down again.

It looked like an avant-garde dance, something about race or alienation. And Sang was one of those, an assistant coach wandering the sidelines, not really a part of the game.

Was he just caught up in the intrigue and sex? That's what Bea was caught up in. Just to be caught up in something. When they were first caught up in each other, they'd gone to New York, before Thomas was born. They'd booked a hotel, back when you couldn't see what you were getting into, when you just called and hoped for the best. It was in Hell's Kitchen (she thought), still hell then, a once-grand building fallen to seed. The lobby was empty, a vast concrete floor. In the centre was a large wire cage over a desk with the room's only bright light. It looked like something out of a science fiction movie. The guy at the desk was huge, dishevelled, smoking a cigarette, a Brooklyn accent, right out of central casting. They would have looked elsewhere, but they'd taken the bus from Toronto to save money and it was late, almost midnight, and they were exhausted, and they took the key from him through the small slot, not knowing what the hell to expect.

But the room was huge, two bedrooms with locking doors. It had been an apartment at some point. They undressed, lay down, toyed with the prospect of sex, feeling obliged since the whole idea had been a romantic weekend. Then they heard the main door open. Someone came in. *Hello.* It was a trill, a woman. She poked her head in through their open door. *Hi there, I'm Becca. Actually Rebecca.* She was from Australia, a student, blond. So that's why the rooms were so cheap, Sang said. Becca nodded and left for her own bedroom.

They spent the next morning looking for another hotel. It was a warm day and they dragged their suitcases around with them like hicks from the farm belt. Every hotel was full. A dentist convention was in town, a girl at one hotel told them, tens of thousands of them wandering the streets. Apparently, they have the highest suicide rates, she said. They spent the whole day looking until they stumbled onto the Algonquin. It was right there, and they shrugged and thought, why not? There was a room available, a cancellation, or maybe a dental suicide. It was more than they could afford, but it will be a piece of history, Sang said. You can be Dorothy Parker. They drank martinis in the bar, had a romantic dinner and insistent sex. The next day they'd walked around sort of aimlessly, and stumbled onto a photo exhibit at a small gallery where a photographer a century earlier had taken corpses from the morgue in Mexico City and dressed them up in formal clothes and taken pictures of them. He'd created families, different groupings. The effect was eerie. You started to overlook the decomposed faces and gunshot wounds and skeletal grins and started to see just another family in a photographer's studio. They spent two hours in there. If we don't know death, Sang said, quoting someone, how can we know life.

These were the moments that a marriage was made of. The miscalculated vacations, the quotidian terrors of raising a child, birthdays, sickness, death, pets, tears, silent breakfasts, sex amortized over a quarter century.

Unwanted tears formed. Bea would have taken her deep yoga breaths; instead, she took a sip of her wine. She could feel that pricking sensation in her face. She started to cry. She heard her phone vibrate and reached into her purse and took it out, grateful for the interruption. A text from Thomas. *Taking Intro to British Novel. Frying pan, fire.*

Here he was, a boy losing his family in real time. How horribly modern.

She thought about Sang's question. When were we last in love? There wasn't a moment when you fell out of love. Maybe there wasn't one when you fell in love either. But falling out was more protracted, subtler, the slow decay of radioactive material, cooling quietly, that toxic landscape. They wouldn't fall out of love at the same time. When was the last time they'd said I love you? Probably after sex more than a year ago, a reflex.

Bea wiped her eyes with a tissue. The room had darkened slightly and she got up and turned on a light near the bookcase. Sang looked a bit thinner, she thought. He was a monochrome man, a palette of greys—skin, hair—giving him an almost transparent quality. There were times when she felt she was married to a hologram. Now he sat there, a shimmering image of him projected onto the saggy couch, his heart elsewhere.

Sang reached over and emptied the wine bottle into his glass.

Have you thought this through? Bea said abruptly.

Sang looked up.

You deal in history, she said. You look back. You're less adept with the future. You won't tell me, so I'll guess. It's not a student—you're too old for that. A colleague? Possibly. Though there aren't a lot of female history profs, except that feminist history woman you said you can't stand. Though perhaps that's sexy. I think it's an outsider. Maybe someone doing mid-level admin work, someone who would be impressed by a professor.

Sang took a sip of his wine. There was only a bit left in his glass. Bea could tell he was mentally gauging if he could get through this without opening another bottle.

She's younger but not young, Bea said. Forty-eight? Ish? So, divorced maybe. Living in a flat somewhere. They had to sell the house, split the equity, if there was any. Not enough to get back in the housing market.

Sang got up heavily and went into the kitchen and brought out the only really good bottle of red they had, a Bordeaux he'd bought after being seduced by a wine column, almost eighty dollars, four times what they usually spent. He opened it and poured six ounces into his glass and took a healthy sip.

She's fit. Yoga instructor fit. The sex was a revelation. She doesn't mind a little mess.

For Christ's sake, Bea.

You want history, Sang. Here is your history: You're going to go to New York for a romantic weekend, walk in the park, hold hands, go back to the hotel you booked with an online discount, fuck your brains out. Then you come back to Toronto, to her cluttered flat, to her taste in cloying movies—

What the fuck do you know—

You can't have *our* friends over for a dinner party. Her place is too small, and she doesn't quite fit in, does she? Anyway, our friends are all falling apart. So it's her friends. A few admin people. You'll be the star. So there's that. Then you're going to wake up six months from now and realize that her bookshelf should have been a clue, and you're bored shitless but the sex is still good…

Sang looked a bit surprised. The first real reaction from him.

I don't need to—

And she still basks in your alleged brilliance. Then one day she doesn't. A year from now, two maybe, you'll notice you're in bed reading, not in bed getting a blow job, then a decade that disappears like a Vegas magic act, then retirement, a small party to acknowledge your increasingly distracted contribution to the dead, then a cancer scare, yours, hers, you're older, more brittle, walking with a hitch—

I'm not going to sit here and listen—

She's still fit, but you're shrunken and confused and staring at the dust floating in the sunlit air of the Events Room at the care facility. She'd like to visit every week, but, you know, *life,* and they seem to be taking good care of you—

Shut up! Sang sat up straight in his chair, spilling some of his wine. Just shut the fuck up, Bea.

They sat in that silence for a long moment.

Maybe the circus figurines should have been a deal breaker, Sang, Bea said quietly. Sad clown.

The effect was like one of those slow-motion bullets you see in movies, travelling slowly, inevitable, exploding on impact. He was mentally putting it together, dumbstruck now, his mouth open. *You were in there!* he yelled. *You broke in!* Jesus, what fucking *right*...It's a *crime,* you could go to *jail.*

It isn't a crime, Sang. Just a hobby.

Sang was doing a mental tally of all that Bea would know, a complex algorithm that he struggled with. The air was leaden, the room suddenly small. The radio was on, the music too soft to identify. She stared at her husband, his face smeared by alcohol, doubt lurking. A man who was used to having his cake and fucking it too.

When she was six, she and Air climbed a tree that got them onto their garage roof. They each had an umbrella. They opened the umbrellas and jumped off, Mary Poppins–style, landing much harder than either was prepared for. Bea fell awkwardly and felt the sharp pain. Her arm was broken. She had to go to the hospital and have it set and put in a cast, Air envious of the attention. The cast came off a month later and Bea looked at her arm, the pale, wrinkly skin, still a part of her but alien-looking and slightly shrunken, and she wondered if this was what divorce looked like.

They battled back and forth like scorpions in a bottle for another thirty minutes, then Sang got up unsteadily and left, slamming the door theatrically. There was something to the finality of a slammed door. The sheer volume surprised Bea. For a moment there was a livid silence, then the soft jazz quietly broke through. There was a change in air pressure. In that moment, she was simply numb. Everything else still lurked offstage—anger, relief, fear, regret—all waiting for their close-up.

BEA WOKE UP IN AN unfamiliar void. She glanced at the empty space beside her on the bed then stared at the ceiling, replaying the events of last night. Sang yelling, shaking with anger. But it wasn't just anger. There was something else there—fear. It was in his voice, his eyes. He hadn't contemplated this version of the future; she'd been right about that. Maybe he felt his marriage was tolerable as long as he was having the affair. How would the affair go when it started to resemble a marriage? she wondered. And now he would be waking up beside his Hungarian mistress, suddenly promoted to partner, and he might be wondering the same thing.

They had argued support and lack thereof, sex and lack thereof. Parenting, money, chores. The Greatest Hits of every marriage. They were knee-deep in *Who's Afraid of Virginia Woolf?* territory, and the brutal escalation surprised them both. Did this scene lurk in every marriage, waiting for a trigger? She remembered pouring the rest of the expensive Bordeaux into the sink, an appropriate and irrational gesture.

She wondered if she should call Sang, tell him she would be out of the house between 2 and 5 p.m. and that would be a good time to swing by and pick up his clothes and whatever else he couldn't live without. A text would be better. They were at a delicate moment. Bea imagined them inching back toward one another over the next several months and simultaneously imagined them never seeing one another again, maybe nodding to one another in a grocery store two years from now.

They couldn't afford an angry divorce, one driven by the need to inflict pain, one that would benefit both of their lawyers. They would need to tell Thomas, though what would they say? Sang might have called him already, getting his version in first.

It occurred to Bea that she might have to break into houses to make a living.

out of the woods

HER FATHER HAD WORKED FOR the city, in the transportation department. When Bea was a girl, she'd asked their mother what he did, and she said James was the one who kept the city running. See all this, her mother had said, pointing to the traffic, to the streetcar lumbering along College, pedestrians bunching at the intersections, he keeps all of this moving, sweetheart. And Bea had imagined this literally, saw the city shuddering to a stop, the subway train below screeching on the tracks, all the cars locking up their brakes, two million people waiting for James Billings to get back from his coffee break and get things moving again. He retired at the age of sixty-eight, then died of a heart attack four years later. He'd been by himself, at home, reading a biography of Winston Churchill. Her mother came home and found him slumped on the couch, lifeless.

Bea wished she'd known the man in the photograph, the one holding the baby. It was odd that she was thinking about her father while sitting in the hospital waiting room. The girl from Galileo had called Bea and said very quickly, very calmly, as they would be trained to, I'm afraid Dorothy has collapsed. We called an ambulance and they're taking her to St Joseph's.

Bea pressed for details, but there weren't many. She was found lying on the floor during a routine check. Dialed 911 immediately. May God be with her.

She called Air, who said she'd catch the first plane in the morning.

At the hospital, a sympathetic nurse said they were doing everything they could. *Your mother is stable but not out of the woods.* The image of her mother in her wheelchair, struggling with the soft forest floor, grateful for the patches of sunlight coming through the trees. She would never find her way out of the woods.

Bea remembered her mother backing their new car into the garage, scraping the paint alongside the door jamb, her father blowing up like a character from one of those cartoons where the wife was always doing something ditzy. *Do you know how much this is going to cost? Do you? You have NO idea what it's going to cost.* Her mother putting on lipstick, holding up the tiny mirror with a shaky hand, saying, *Oh for God's sake, James, let's not make a federal case out of it.*

There were only a few people in the waiting room—it was 4 a.m. Bea took off her shoes and lay down on the worn couch. It was too short to stretch out, so she tucked her legs up and put her purse under her head. The first dream to arrive, forgotten upon waking, was a flock of starlings forming kaleidoscopic patterns, a murmuring, that soaring communal joy.

WHEN SHE WOKE, THERE WERE a dozen people in the waiting room. Bea sat up. She was stiff and her back and legs were sore. It was 6:47. A family of what Bea thought might be Syrian refugees huddled in one corner. A tired-looking man and his wife and their two children. He was wearing a sports jacket that was much too large, donated by someone who felt they were helping the crisis.

There was a coffee shop in the lobby and she wondered if it was open. She got up and put on her shoes and walked to the washroom and looked at her face in the mirror in that antiseptic light. The lines around her mouth, so faint, almost non-existent in her own mirror, were dangerously pronounced. As if she hadn't been vigilant and age had crept up on her while she slept. The café in the lobby was open, but there was a surprisingly long line for what she suspected was not very good coffee. A lot of the people were in green gowns—orderlies, nurses, a few pallid patients. There was a café down the street and she decided to see if it was open. Outside the hospital, a man was holding an IV stand, smoking a cigarette. A security guard approached him and Bea observed that pantomime, the guard, a small East Asian man, pointing to a sign, the man using his arm to gauge the distance from the door. Soon they'd have to drive to the municipal dump to have a cigarette. The man was in a thin hospital gown that waved in the breeze, his white stick legs suddenly exposed. You didn't want to get too far from the hospital in that outfit, to lose your frame of reference.

The café was just opening and a middle-aged woman walked around turning on lights, turning on the espresso machine, checking things.

First customer of the day, she said to Bea cheerily. She had dark rings under her eyes, her hair done up but stray hairs fallen out, making it look as if it was the end of her day.

Bea ordered an Americano and a very healthy-looking muffin and walked back to the hospital. The sky held a few clouds, the sun just starting to rise. People walking to the subway briskly, their day already unfolding in their heads. A school bus was stopped and mothers stood in their pyjamas and coats, waving, relieved. Bea sat in the waiting room and ate her muffin and drank her coffee. The Syrians were gone.

After twenty minutes the nurse came into the waiting room and approached Bea. Her face was tired and sympathetic.

You can go in now. Dr Ebert is there.

How is she?

Dr Ebert can give you a full update.

They walked in and Ebert was standing there, a compact man who looked to be in his twenties. He had close-cropped hair and brown eyes. He appeared to be so new to this that he was still working on the right expression.

Her mother took up so little room in the hospital bed, her face turned to one side, bruised-looking. The lines joining on her cheek, one thin arm on the blanket, the multicoloured veins, her small hand in a weak fist. *She isn't going to make it.* It wouldn't matter if she survived this, Bea thought, there just wasn't enough left.

Your mother had a stroke, Ebert said. She's stabilized now, but because of her age and her condition, the prognosis isn't good, I'm afraid. She may not have the resources to recover. He looked at Bea. We are hoping for the best outcome, but your mother has suffered a serious blow.

What would be the best outcome at this point? Bea asked.

Well, Ebert started, then fell silent. They stared at her mother, incredibly frail. Ebert murmured something then excused himself and the nurse trailed after him. Bea pulled a chair close to the bed and sat down. Her mother's hair was flattened and thin, like the rest of her. Where had she gotten the strength to do anything? She had given them advice on men, *you need to be the strong one,* on work, *a good job brings respect,* on their neighbour Mrs Catelli, whose breasts had let her down*, they didn't get her what she'd hoped for—let that be a lesson to you.* Both she and Air looking at their flat chests, relieved they wouldn't attract a combustible alcoholic like Mr Catelli. She had taught them to cook, though she was a listless cook herself, the three of them in the kitchen, their mother reading the directions from the back of the box as Bea and Ariel tried to make shepherd's pie using instant potatoes. Their father coming home and looking at the mess on his plate, *This is what I break my back for?*

Bea's phone buzzed. Her sister.

Hi.

How is she?

Bea looked over at their mother. Oh Air, she just looks so small, like there's nothing left.

So what was it?

A stroke. The doctor beat around the bush, but he isn't hopeful. It's hard to believe she's going to recover.

I've got a four thirty flight, the earliest I could get, so I should be there like eight thirty, nine. I'll see you there, okay?

Bea put away her phone.

She remembered when her mother decided that both Bea and Air needed to have a hobby. She'd read somewhere that children with hobbies got into better universities and took both of them to one of those hobby stores and made them pick out a hobby and neither of them had the slightest interest in anything in the store. Air had a bit of a tantrum. Their mother finally bought Bea a stamp collecting kit—a book to keep them in, a small package of worthless stamps to get started, and a pamphlet that showed how much fun it could be once you got started and how much money the collection would be worth when you were grown up—up to $100,000! Air got a rock collecting kit (You are now a rockhound!) that came with a magnifying glass and a piece of limestone with part of a fossil in it. She threw both of them at a squirrel in the garden.

It was an era of relentless comparison—who had a newer car, whose child was doing better in school, who went to Florida at Christmas, who had the best TV. All that had gratefully disappeared. Bea had no idea what kind of car anyone drove. No one cared about TV. People talked about their children's flaws, up to a point.

Bea leaned in to her mother. Remember that policeman who pulled you over for changing lanes twelve times? she said. You told him, well, it's not like marriage, you don't have to choose one and stick with it. We were on our way to a movie and we were late. Then we were even later after he gave you a ticket for speeding, and when we got there, we went into two more movies without paying because you said it would even out the ticket and life was all about balance. We saw half of something, then snuck into *Annie Hall*. What was the last one we went to? We didn't even want to see it, a war movie that went on forever.

Her mother was immobile, her breathing so shallow it hardly registered.

She had looked so happy in that photo, in the backyard of the Shaw place, holding that baby. Her first miracle.

When Bea had mono and stayed home, her mother brought her soup and flat ginger ale and said she should read a book a day, but Bea was too exhausted to read and they watched soap operas together on that saggy couch, sinking down with the blankets pulled up to their chins. Her mother seemed almost as tired as she was and they watched those beautiful women on the screen, always plotting something.

Bea was crying now and she caressed her mother's face, cold as a stone, then held her hand and told her she loved her and fell asleep in the chair. She dreamed of getting off a train in one of those opulent European stations, someone waiting for her in the sepia glow, off to drink coffee and smoke cigarettes and be in love. When she woke up, she knew her mother was gone. She checked her pulse and couldn't feel anything. She kissed her forehead and kissed her hand. She started to cry again and stayed for a while, holding her hand, pressing her head against her mother's.

OUTSIDE, IT WAS AFTERNOON, BRIGHT, an autumn evanescence. The first week of November. Some of the leaves were still green, though a maple tree was denuded entirely, a carpet of red around it like a crime scene. She walked up the street. She hadn't told anyone in the hospital. Maybe Ariel would arrive in time to sit with her, before their mother was taken away, processed for the grave. She took out her phone and walked toward the park and hit Ariel's name.

Hi, Ariel said, I'm in the airport.

She's gone, Air. Just now.

Oh Bea. She began to sob, triggering Bea, and they cried into their phones for a few minutes.

She's still there, Bea said. At the hospital. If you're here in three hours, maybe...

I'm boarding in, like, ten.

Okay, I'll see you there.

Bea walked to the park. The tenor of the park changed with the seasons. In the summer it was filled with joggers and children and large families having elaborate picnics that went on for hours, tables and barbecues and blankets, occasionally tents. Three generations just grateful for the weather and each other. But in the fall the groups were smaller, couples walking, people on their own. The mood was more contemplative, the stillness of a George Stubbs painting.

Bea called Thomas to tell him his grandmother was gone. She was both surprised and comforted by his sobbing. They talked for ten minutes and Bea said she would arrange for Thomas to come back for the service.

She dialed Sang. He didn't pick up and she left a message: Mom died, just now. She had a stroke. I thought you should know.

He'd picked up some of his clothes though not all of them. It had been two weeks and they hadn't spoken. They were no longer the same people.

Sang called three minutes later.

I'm so sorry, Bea.

She was asleep, Bea said, a mercy. She just didn't wake up.

Sang's affirming sound at the other end, followed by silence. You were good to her, Bea, he finally said. You brought her comfort these last years. Joy even. That's something.

Yes, she said. I suppose it is.

They chatted for a few minutes, a bit stiffly, but there was some kind of solace there. Someone who had known her mother for decades, who knew her at her best. This would be something Sang couldn't replicate with Angie; all that history. We carry it with us, every marriage, with its fights and burdens and quiet moments all adding up to life. And when you shed that, you're unburdened, but you stare into a void.

The leaves of the poplar trees were a soft yellow. A couple walked down the path in front of Bea, each holding the hand of a toddler who dangled between them like a marionette. Sang recalled the time her mother made Thanksgiving dinner for everyone. She had bought some contraption to deep-fry the turkey, a vat filled with boiling oil that she put in the backyard. It exploded, sending hot oil and turkey parts into the air, settling on the grass. They had to put out small fires with a wet towel. The neighbour called the fire department and there were four emergency vehicles parked in front of the house. They ended up ordering pizza. They both laughed at the memory, then Sang said he had a class.

Let me know if I can help with any of the arrangements, he said.

Bea hung up. She hoped Air would get here before they took their mother away. She remembered when their parents had rented a cottage on Lake Huron for a weekend in late October, cheap because it was off-season, a bungalow that had holes in the screens and smelled like someone else's life. In the morning they'd gotten up earlier than their parents and gone down to the water. They'd been told not to go in unsupervised, though the water was freezing and no one wanted to swim, but their mother had gotten on one knee to look in their eyes and make them promise. *Say the words, say I promise.* They walked along the shore, a long beach littered with twigs and stones and damp leaves. It was calm in the morning, the sun just up.

They walked for half an hour, past small cottages set well back from the lake, aware of its menace. Most of the cottages were empty. Ahead of them, partly in the water, was what looked like a seal. A black shape slumped on the sand. They approached cautiously and when they got closer, they saw it was a man. His face was a colour Bea had never seen before, white though with shades of something like lavender. He had black hair that was matted with sand. He was wearing a black coat, a uniform almost. There was writing on it, though neither of them understood it. Cyrillic script, it turned out. His eyes were open. He was both sad and monstrous and she and Air were frightened as they leaned closer.

Should we touch him? Bea whispered.

Air shook her head. Their mother had told them not to touch dead birds. This would be worse. Ariel got a stick and pressed it slowly against the heavy fabric of his chest. She gently pressed it against his face and there was no response.

287

A dead guy, Bea said, still whispering.

Someone killed him, Air said authoritatively, a Nancy Drew veteran. This was no accident.

They'd stayed there for a while, conjuring up different scenarios: he was a spy who'd been discovered and thrown overboard; he was someone famous; a man who knew too much.

They went back and brought their parents with the breathlessness that all discoverers have. Their mother called the police and when they came, they all went back again and stood around the corpse and Bea felt proprietorial. The police presence convinced Air that she was right; it had been foul play (a drowned Russian sailor, it turned out). And on the walk back to the cottage their mother had talked to them about the fragility of life and the indifference of nature. Years later, when they were both home from university and sharing a bottle of wine and catching each other up on their classes and their romances, Air had turned to Bea and said, Remember the day we discovered death.

the current version

SHE IMAGINED THE RELIEF OF autumn, the cool notes in the breeze, almost cold, the comfort of decay. You just let go— the leaves turned and died and fell and people talked of winter. The darkness creeping up on us all.

She examined the familiar Schlage with satin nickel finish and a latitude keyed lever. She knelt and opened her kit on the patio stones and selected the pick and lever she needed. Her watch said 11:23. She felt for the pins, reluctant, standoffish at first. With her right hand she applied a subtle rotational pressure with the lever. The first pin gave and she probed deeper. It took less than a minute. She gathered her tools, put them in her purse, opened the door softly, and stepped in.

The main floor was dark, the shades all drawn. The only light was the clock on the stove. The room was still, she could hear her heartbeat. She examined the bookshelf, the familiar titles. Evidence, she supposed, all of it. The books and furniture, the framed photographs of their vacation on Georgian Bay, moody black and whites that made it look like the ocean. The house itself. Standing in the living room, she could see the four-year-old Thomas's sudden angry tears when Bea put the vacuum against his stomach and the loose fabric of his Spiderman T-shirt was sucked in. She thought he'd be delighted, but he was frightened and the look of betrayal on his face was still vivid.

Sang upstairs sleeping, his desires doled out by his subconscious in confusing dreams. In the morning he would half remember them and hope they didn't mean anything.

Things went wrong, it was the central law of the universe. You had to be vigilant. She had certainly learned vigilance. Forgiveness was something else.

Her grandmother hadn't been able to forgive. Not her husband for dying, not the Germans for starting the war, not this country for its prosperity, and not her children, who bore witness to it all. Her father had never been able to forgive. But Bea's mother had embraced the life that was left to her. Perhaps forgiveness is something you have to learn, like a new language. Awkward sounds committed to memory, then one day you wake up speaking like a native. You don't choose love, but you choose forgiveness. What was the alternative? The days passing in useless regret until the heart delivers its last sour beat.

Bea saw everything that the house contained, a snapshot of their lives. There was the year of dinner parties, every week plates of exotic cheeses and Bosc pears and berries. Sang's lips purple with wine, all those cigarettes, the candlelight making everyone look like the Medicis. Empty bottles lined up in the flickering candlelight, everyone laughing about something. Summer nights on the patio, Thomas asleep in that little basket, she and Sang planning it all. The society they'd created, friends swept away in the centrifugal force of time, drifting into new relationships, away from one another. Holding one another in the dark, when faith was weakest. And every version was the current version.

Bea went upstairs and undressed and slid into bed and put her arm around her husband. She remembered the October they'd seen the monarch butterflies flying south, millions of them caught in a fierce headwind, suspended, and Bea was afraid they'd exhaust themselves and fall like black-and-orange rain. They stood there, holding hands, faces upturned. The sky was filled, a dark cloud. Then the wind shifted and they all flew home.

acknowledgements

I DON'T IN FACT KNOW any middle-aged women who break into houses, but Beatrice Billings is informed by countless conversations with women friends over the years. I am grateful for their friendship and their insights.

My thanks to Dan Wells at Biblioasis, for his belief in this book and his astute edit. Thanks to the early readers: Ellen Vanstone, Denise Clarke, my sister Alison Gillmor, and, as always, my steadfast agent, Jackie Kaiser. I would also like to thank the Ontario Arts Council and Toronto Arts Council for their generous support. And finally, thank you to my wife Grazyna Krupa, for her ongoing and unwavering support.